HAUNTING DANIELLE - BOOK 19

THE GHOST
OF CHRISTMAS SECRETS

HAUNTING DANIELLE

HAUNTING DANIELLE - BOOK 19

THE GHOST
OF CHRISTMAS SECRETS

USA TODAY BESTSELLING AUTHOR
BOBBI HOLMES

The Ghost of Christmas Secrets
(Haunting Danielle, Book 19)
A Novel
By Bobbi Holmes
Cover Design: Elizabeth Mackey

ISBN: 9781731463715

Dedicated to all those kind strangers who generously answer my questions--like the National Packard Museum, Dave Bayowski of Mahoning Auto in Ohio, and the kind folks from the City of Astoria.

ONE

She was early. Slowing down in front of the house, Zara Leighton read the numbers on the mailbox just before fog engulfed it, the house, and her battered Volkswagen Beetle. Had she arrived ten minutes later, she would have never seen the mailbox, much less been able to read the house numbers. Confident she was at the correct location, Zara pulled over to the curb she could no longer see and parked her car.

When turning onto the unfamiliar street a few minutes earlier, it had reminded her of a scene from one of the horror movies she had watched as a kid on Mrs. Crocket's old black-and-white television set. Gray washed the neighborhood of stately old houses, its land-scape and skyline devoid of color as a massive fog cloud rolled in, concealing all in its path.

Turning off her ignition, she glanced at her watch. He wasn't expecting her for another fifteen minutes. Being too early was often as bad as being late, she thought. Looking toward the house, all she could see was a dense gray mist. If he happened to look out his window, he would never see her sitting in her car in front of his house. Instead of going up now, she decided to wait a few minutes and show up on time instead of early.

Zara leaned back in the seat for a moment and smiled. If she could convince him to give her the information she needed, she would be one step closer to crossing off what she considered the most important goal on her bucket list.

After unbuckling her seatbelt, she reached over to the passenger seat, picked up her purse, set it on her lap, and opened it. She pulled out a small notepad and began flipping through its pages, reviewing her notes. It would have been easier on her if he had simply verified the information she had requested when she had met him at his office several days earlier, instead of insisting she meet him at his house this afternoon. Although, she understood his desire for discretion—after all, Chris Glandon was his nephew, and considering their turbulent relationship, he wouldn't want to be caught handing out personal information on the man, not if he wanted to get back in his nephew's good graces.

Still holding the notepad, she glanced toward the house. All she could see was a misty gray wall. A chill went up her spine. She shivered in response. It must be the fog, she thought, knowing she would have to drive through it in order to return home. It couldn't be trepidation over meeting with a virtual stranger at his house. After all, Loyd Glandon was hardly a threatening character, more a benign senior citizen.

"DO you think she's going to make it in this weather?" Wearing gray slacks and a tweed jacket over a white dress shirt, Simon stood akimbo, gazing out the front window, his back to Loyd.

"Would you get away from there!" Loyd leaned forward in his chair, attempting to swat his brother with his cane. His manner of dress was similar to Simon's, yet instead of a tweed jacket, he wore a red cardigan sweater. "She'll see you. I told her I'd be alone!"

"Have you even looked outside?" Simon asked. "There's no way she's going to find the house."

"I'm sure she has one of those GPS gizmos on her phone. Now move away from that blasted window!"

Aside from stature, the two brothers could have passed as twins in their younger days. Just two years apart, with Loyd being the oldest, they resembled their father, with the same blue-gray eyes and strawberry blond hair. Most of that hair had since fallen out, with the remaining wisps now snowy white. Loyd was slighter and a good six inches shorter than his brother Simon. Both brothers were

2

widowers, and neither had had children. Simon's wife had died first, and then Loyd lost his wife two years later. That had been twenty years earlier. Since then, the two brothers had lived together.

There had been a much younger third brother. He had looked like their mother's side of the family, with jet black hair and deep brown eyes. But he was dead now. While he might not have looked like his two older brothers, he had been no more prolific than they had been. He and his wife only had one child, and they had adopted him.

The doorbell rang.

"That's her!" Using his cane more for show than function, Loyd stood.

"I'll be in the kitchen," Simon said while his brother ambled to the entrance hall.

WHEN LOYD OPENED the door several minutes later, he found Zara Leighton standing on his front porch, behind her a backdrop of dense fog, giving her a surreal—almost ethereal quality.

He had never cared for tall women—he saw them as some sort of perverse measuring stick, reminding him of his own height deficit. His late wife had been a little over five feet tall, which had been the first thing that had attracted him to her. Leighton was a few inches shy of six feet, an Amazon of a woman in his mind. But she was thin—thin enough to be a model. She didn't seem to have many curves, but she had a pretty face and enormous blue eyes. However, her hair was far too short in his estimation.

Loyd greeted Zara and ushered her inside. He led her to his living room and to two matching wingback chairs. They faced a leather sofa. Sitting between the two chairs was a small mahogany table, and on it sat two glasses of iced tea, each sitting on a coaster.

"I thought you might be thirsty after your long drive." Loyd motioned to the beverages sitting on the table as he took one of the wingback chairs.

"That was very thoughtful, thank you." Zara set her purse by her feet as she sat down.

"I hope you understand why I didn't want to discuss this at my office." Loyd picked up the glass closest to him and took a sip.

"Certainly. Does this mean you can give me the information?" she asked hopefully.

"I have many regrets in regards to my nephew, Chris," Loyd began. "At the time, we were sincerely trying to do what we felt was best for him. He was young. For most of his life he was sheltered. Probably too sheltered. He has no idea how many people out there are ready to take advantage of someone like him. But I know now, we went about it the wrong way, and it is something I deeply regret. I won't do anything that will hurt him."

"I don't intend to hurt him," she promised.

"How do you know it's really him?" he asked.

"It has to be him. I told you what I found," she reminded him.

"Who have you discussed this with?" Loyd asked.

"I don't really feel this is anyone's business. I haven't talked to anyone about it. Anyone but you."

"You have to understand, if people discover this connection between you and my nephew, you'll find yourself as vulnerable as he has been. Why do you think he takes such measures to avoid publicity? It's not just Chris I'm concerned with, it's you."

"I appreciate your concern, but I have to do this."

Loyd took another sip of his tea and then said, "I do understand your desire to contact him. But I don't want to see Chris exploited."

She shook her head emphatically. "I don't want anything from Chris. And I haven't told anyone about him, I promise."

He started to take another sip of tea but then paused and nodded to the untouched glass on the table. "You really should try the tea. I brew it myself—sweetened with berries I grow in my garden. It's my late wife's recipe."

Zara smiled at Loyd and reluctantly picked up the tea and took a drink. She paused a moment and then took another sip. "Oh my, this is really very good. I'm not much of a tea drinker, but this has a most unusual flavor. Fruity."

Loyd smiled at Zara and leaned back in his chair, his half-full glass of tea in his right hand. "Take another drink and tell me if you can guess what kind of berries I use. There are two different kinds. No one has ever been able to guess."

Zara took another sip and then said, "One has to be strawberry."

Loyd shook his head. "No. Everyone guesses strawberry. But I didn't use a single one."

4

Zara smiled weakly and said, "That surprises me. It tastes like strawberries. The tea is very delicious, but...are you going to help me?"

"I've given it a great deal of thought, and yes, I would like to help you."

Zara smiled broadly. "Oh, thank you!"

Loyd held up his right palm for a moment. "But you have to understand, it's not just my call."

She frowned.

"I've discussed this with my brother," Loyd explained. "He's willing to hear you out—as I have—and if he agrees, then yes, we will help you."

"Is he here?" Zara looked around anxiously.

Loyd glanced at his watch. "He's supposed to be here any minute. While we wait, why don't you just sit back, relax, enjoy your tea. I'm sure by the time you finish your drink, he should be here."

Zara flashed Loyd a smile and then took another sip of tea. He asked her again to guess what berries he had used, encouraging her to drink more. Before she knew it, she had consumed the entire glass. Just as she was setting the empty glass back on its coaster, she began to sway. "I feel funny," she muttered, closing her eyes.

Silently, Loyd reached over and took the glass from her hand before she dropped it to the floor.

"What's wrong with me?" Zara moaned, her eyes still closed. "Everything is spinning...what was in that tea?"

Before Loyd had a chance to tell her, Zara lurched forward and fell to the floor face-first.

He hadn't expected her to fall out of the chair. Staring down at the lifeless body, he considered taking her pulse, but there was no way he could get down on the floor with his bad knees. He picked up the cane leaning against his chair and used it to jab Zara's unconscious body several times. When she didn't move, he called for his brother.

"Is she dead?" Simon asked several minutes later as he stood over the body.

"I told you, she would have to drink five glasses of that stuff to actually kill her."

"What did you find out?" Simon asked.

Loyd snatched Zara's purse from the floor and started rummaging through it. "She claims she didn't tell anyone. But we need to figure out what we're going to do in case someone else shows up." He fished a set of keys from the purse and tossed them to his brother.

"What's this for?" Simon asked, looking at the key ring now in his right hand.

"You need to move her car into the garage before the fog lifts and someone sees it."

TWO

B eing dead wasn't so bad. Although, Marie Nichols had to admit being alive had been better. She had been born to loving and doting parents who'd had the good sense to invest in beach property. When their estate eventually passed to Marie, it had secured her financial future.

As a young woman she had fallen in love and married. Unfortunately, as the years wore on and her blinders eventually came off, she saw her husband for who he really was—a putz. However, it wasn't an unhappy marriage, and it had produced one child. Regrettably, he turned out to be a putz like his father.

Her son's marriage produced two sons. The eldest, Adam, had given her life purpose and had enriched her golden years. She realized Adam wasn't perfect. In fact, since moving over to the other side, she began noticing he had a number of bad habits. It was one reason she was reluctant to move on to the other side. Adam wasn't fully evolved yet, and she needed to stick around and make sure he got to where he needed to be. One place he needed to be was married.

Adam wasn't the only reason Marie was reluctant to move over to the other side. There was Danielle Boatman, her surrogate granddaughter. Marie wanted to find out how it was going to work out between Danielle and Walt. While she assumed moving over to the other side wouldn't prevent her from learning how it had all turned out, she didn't imagine there was any way she could intervene on the other side if necessary. One thing Marie especially enjoyed about death was how she could instill herself into the living's life and make a difference. Just look at her grandson Adam. He was no longer visiting those shameful websites.

Today was the day Walt's cast was coming off, and Marie couldn't help but wonder how the dynamics might change between Walt and Danielle when he was no longer depending on her as much as he had since the accident. It wasn't just the broken leg—most men wouldn't let something like that interfere with their lives—but Walt was just getting used to having a life again, and the broken leg had slowed down the adjustment process.

After checking in on Adam, Marie headed to Marlow House.

AT FIVE FEET five inches tall, Danielle Boatman had been wanting to lose fifteen pounds for as long as she could recall. She had never been terribly committed to the goal, considering she enjoyed baking, sampling her confections, and she found it impossible to resist Old Salts Bakery's cinnamon rolls. But that morning, as she stood on the bathroom scale, she was perplexed to find she had lost five pounds—without even trying. If her jeans hadn't been loose, she might have suspected the scale was broken.

Later that afternoon, as she stood on the front patio of Marlow House, watching the furniture van drive away, she looked down at her jeans, once again noting the change in their fit. Grabbing hold of one seam, she gave it a tug and frowned.

"You've lost weight," Marie announced when she appeared the next moment.

Letting go of the seam, Danielle looked up at Marie and smiled. The once elderly woman—now a ghost—wore a bright floral sundress and straw hat. Had she been flesh and blood, Danielle imagined a warm sweater and slacks might have been more appropriate considering the chilly May weather.

"Afternoon, Marie. Yes, I have. Five pounds. I just can't figure out how I did it."

"Obviously the normal way. You ate less."

Danielle shrugged. "I didn't mean to."

"It's probably because of Walt."

"Walt?" Danielle rolled her eyes. "If I'm going to try to lose weight, it'll be for my health—for myself, not for a man. Not even for Walt. Anyway, he's always telling me I'm perfect just the way I am."

Marie laughed. "That's not what I meant. Ever since Walt moved back over to your side, he's developed quite the sweet tooth. Who knows, maybe he always had one. Every time I've been over here and you start eating anything sweet, Walt tends to finish it off before you have a chance to."

Danielle considered Marie's suggestion for a moment and then laughed. "Oh my gosh, you're right! That brat has been poaching my share of the cinnamon rolls."

Marie smiled. "The van that just left, was that the furniture for the attic?"

Danielle nodded. "Yes. Everything's set up. Walt can't wait to see it, but I convinced him it was a bad idea to go up two flights of stairs with a cast on. The last thing he wants to do is fall and break something else, especially since he's getting the cast off today. Would you like to see the attic?"

"That's why I'm here. And to tell you my grandson will be here in a minute. He wants to see the attic too."

DANIELLE STOOD at the open doorway of Marlow House's attic, surveying the stunning transformation. Bill Jones had packed up his tools the day before, and this morning Joanne had given the space a thorough cleaning, just in time for the furniture delivery.

Adam Nichols had arrived a few minutes after his grandmother, yet he had no idea her spirit trailed after him. Chris Johnson had arrived a few minutes later, and now the two men walked together in the attic, admiring Jones's work while Danielle and Marie stood silently by the doorway and listened.

"I have to say, I wasn't sure he could pull it off." Chris opened the door leading into the new attic bathroom. "I can't believe he finished all this in less than a month."

"I knew he could," Adam said. "But I had to talk him into it. Bill wasn't thrilled to be working up here alone, but he hired a couple of guys to help him. This attic tends to creep him out." Adam shivered at the memory and then added, "Sort of creeps me out too, but it seems different now. Maybe the remodel got rid of all the old ghosts." He laughed nervously and glanced around.

"Hmm...should I take offense?" Marie asked Danielle with a chuckle. Danielle flashed Marie a smile.

"Maybe," Chris muttered under his breath as he entered the bathroom.

Adam turned to Danielle and asked, "So you're really going to rent this to Marlow?"

"I have to rent it to someone. After all, that's what I do—I rent rooms."

"You're a B and B, not a boardinghouse," Adam reminded her. "At least, that's what you're always telling me."

Danielle shrugged. "Maybe I like the idea of a real Marlow living under the roof. And considering I have the portraits back in the library—well, at least the reproductions—it might be fun for the guests to get to meet the Marlow who looks exactly like the man who used to live here, the man in the portrait."

Marie lovingly watched her grandson. "I find it sweet how concerned Adam is for your welfare."

Danielle resisted the temptation to roll her eyes.

Adam glanced briefly to the ceiling by the window, where, according to legend, his great-grandfather had found the original Walt Marlow hanging from the rafters after being murdered. Back then the general consensus was that the man had committed suicide. Adam shivered at the thought and then looked at Danielle and shook his head. "I just can't get over the fact he is staying. I thought by now he'd be ready to move on. Isn't he getting his cast off today?"

Danielle glanced at her watch and then looked to Adam. "Yes, and I'm taking him. I'll have to leave in a few minutes."

Chris stepped out of the bathroom and said, "Looks great, Danielle. Walt's going to love it up here."

"If you guys don't mind, could you lock up for me? I really need to leave, or Walt's going to be late for his appointment."

"No problem." Chris flashed her a smile.

"Thanks. See you guys later." Danielle turned and dashed from the room.

"I just remembered, I have to leave too. I promised Eva I'd meet her this afternoon at the theater," Marie said right before vanishing.

Adam stood quietly for a moment, listening to Danielle's steps as

THE GHOST OF CHRISTMAS SECRETS

she made her way down the attic stairs. He turned to Chris and shook his head.

Chris frowned. "What?"

"I don't get you. What happened with you and Danielle?"

Chris shrugged. "Nothing happened..."

"I guess not. Not if Marlow is moving in here, and you don't seem to have a problem with it."

Chris wandered over to the window and looked out at the street below. "Danielle and I are good friends. I just don't think we were meant to be—well, you know."

Adam shrugged and walked to Chris's side. "No. I really don't. And frankly I can't believe you're okay with Marlow staying here. It's only been—what—eight weeks since the accident? Eight weeks ago he was engaged to another woman and taking off to Europe. Now he's moving into Danielle's attic."

"I'm okay with it—honest. Anyway, I have other things on my mind right now." Chris turned from the window and faced Adam. "I was hoping to talk to Danielle about it, but I forgot she was taking Walt to the doctor this afternoon." He leaned back against the windowsill.

"You can talk to me. I'm a good listener." Adam paused a moment and then chuckled. "Actually that's not true. I've always been a crappy listener, but I'm working on it."

"Because of Melony?" Chris teased.

"Something like that." Adam grinned. "Go ahead, I need the practice anyway."

Chris let out a sigh and then said, "I got a letter from my uncle Loyd."

Adam arched his brows. "Is that one of the uncles who tried to take your inheritance?"

Chris nodded. "I only have two uncles—my father's older brothers, Loyd and Simon. Dad was the youngest. There was a huge age gap between him and my uncles. They were old enough to be his father."

"So what did he want? Money?" Adam asked.

"Claimed he didn't. Said he wanted to apologize for what happened after my parents died. He insisted both he and Uncle Simon regretted what they had done."

"I bet," Adam snorted. "Not too bright pissing off your billionaire nephew."

"They claim this isn't about money. Insisted they aren't asking for anything. It's not like they need any money. They each inherited a few million from their parents, and both of them have been frugal all their lives. I'm sure they still have the money their parents gave them and more."

"But not billions like you inherited?" Adam asked.

Chris shook his head. "All the sons inherited the same amount. I'll just say Dad was better with money than my uncles."

"No kidding," Adam muttered. "So is that why they tried to contest your parents' will, because they were jealous their younger brother did better with his inheritance?"

"I used to think so."

"Used to?" Adam frowned.

"According to my uncle's letter, the reason they contested my parents' will was that they were worried I'd end up giving it all away." Chris chuckled. "Which I have been trying to do. Uncle Loyd insisted what they really wanted was to control the inheritance so I wouldn't end up broke. Claimed they were ultimately doing it for me, but things spiraled out of control."

"So what does he want, just to apologize?"

"That's what he said. Told me he and his brother don't want— or need—a penny of my money. They just want me back in their lives. They don't have any children. I think they're just getting old and realize how alone they are."

"How did they even find you?"

"No secret my foundation headquarters is located here. They sent a letter to the office."

"So what are you going to do?"

Chris shrugged. "I don't know. That's what I wanted to talk to Danielle about. What do you think I should do?"

Adam considered the question a minute. "You know, I never thought I'd say this, but you and I have a lot more in common than I realized."

"What do you mean?"

Adam shrugged. "Just thinking of the money I inherited from my grandmother and how my parents and brother were barely included in the will."

THREE

The date had been arranged two weeks earlier. It had been Walt's idea. After having his cast removed, he would take Danielle out to dinner at Pearl Cove to celebrate. No one else was invited—not even Lily and Ian. When they returned home from the doctor's office, Danielle immediately took Walt upstairs to see his new room. Marlow House now had three master suites, and the one in the attic was the most impressive.

Joanne had offered to move Walt's wardrobe and other belongings up to his room after she had finished cleaning earlier that day. Walt had objected, telling her he didn't want her carrying his things up two flights of stairs, insisting he would do it later, after his cast was removed. Joanne thought the gesture considerate. After all, she was a hired employee of Marlow House, and he could have reasonably expected her to move his things up to the attic. What Joanne didn't realize was that Walt planned to levitate his belongings up to the attic when he and Danielle were alone in the house. Of course, even if he hadn't been able to levitate items, he still would not have felt right having Joanne do it for him.

Since the new bed and furniture hadn't yet arrived when Joanne had cleaned the room, she hadn't been able to put the linens and blanket on Walt's new king-sized bed. Instead, she had left a neat pile of folded linens in his closet. Danielle watched in amusement as the linens and blanket floated from the closet, and the bed appeared to make itself. After that, Danielle left for her room to take a shower and get ready for dinner while Walt stayed in his room and did the same.

———

DANIELLE SAT PRIMLY in the parlor, waiting for Walt to join her so they could leave for the restaurant. Her cat, Max, napped on a nearby chair. She had chosen a pale blue dress for the occasion—it reminded her of spring. She had added leggings under its skirt, because while it might technically be spring, it still felt like winter to her, especially in the evenings.

Restless, she fidgeted with the handbag on her lap while looking toward the hall, waiting for Walt to walk through the doorway any minute. "Dang," Danielle said aloud, "I don't think I was this nervous when I went on my first date in high school. Get a grip, Danielle!"

Her outburst woke Max, who lifted his head and looked her way, letting out a lazy yawn and then a meow.

She looked to the cat. "Sorry, Max, did I wake you?"

He blinked in response. She knew he didn't understand what she was saying. Of course, had it been Walt who was talking to him, Max would know exactly what Walt was saying.

"I don't know why I'm so nervous, Max. I mean, we're just going out for dinner. Heavens, this is Walt; why should I be nervous?"

Max stared at her with unblinking eyes. Danielle had the oddest sensation that the cat understood what she was saying—and he didn't believe her for a moment.

Danielle groaned. "I know exactly why I feel nervous." Max blinked and then resumed his nap. "Walt and I are alone in the house..." She paused a moment and added, "Not counting you, of course." If offended, Max didn't show it. He kept sleeping.

Danielle closed her eyes and took a deep calming breath.

When Walt had been a spirit, he had frequently joined Danielle in her bed, where the two would chat for hours. After she fell asleep, he would often take her for a dream hop. But then Walt rejoined the living world and moved into the downstairs bedroom of Marlow House, and Danielle began to miss their nightly chats. One evening, after the terrifying encounter with

Beverly Klein, Danielle had slipped downstairs and crawled into Walt's bed.

In some odd way Walt's cast had served as a bundling board. Their nightly encounters were almost as platonic as they had been when he had been a spirit—yet not quite. There had been kisses—some rather passionate kisses, even more so than the ones they had shared in a few dream hops when he had been a spirit. Danielle blushed at the thought.

She hadn't visited Walt every night—only when there were no guests in the house. Of course, all that could change now that he was moving into the attic bedroom, and there was a secret staircase leading from her room to his. If either one of them wanted to visit the other one in his or her bedroom, it would now be possible to do without any of the guests—or Joanne—ever having to know. Although, it wasn't as if it was anyone's business. They were adults. They had both been married before. And the truth was, Danielle had long ago accepted the fact she was in love with Walt Marlow. She had realized that when he was still a ghost—which had been utterly futile at the time. She loved him in a way she had never loved her husband Lucas.

Her train of thought was broken when a voice asked, "Ready to go?"

Danielle opened her eyes and looked to the parlor doorway. The moment her eyes set on Walt, it felt as if a hand had reached in and roughly grabbed hold of her heart and refused to let go. It squeezed; and she found it difficult to catch her breath.

No longer encumbered by the cast, he stood casually by the doorway, smiling in her direction. Before Walt had come home from the hospital two months earlier, Danielle had purchased some clothes for him to wear. The pants had been selected to accommo-date the cast. However, last week she had driven Walt to Portland, where they had gone clothes shopping. Instead of Danielle picking out his wardrobe, Walt had made the selections, and Danielle had to admit, he didn't need a woman to dress him—he was fully capable of doing that himself, and he did it well.

Her breath caught in her throat as she took in this new Walt. She hadn't realized how much she appreciated looking at a hand-some well-dressed man, with his tailored slacks, silk shirt—and for some reason his new jacket stirred the memory of how Walt looked shirtless. She swallowed nervously and then licked her suddenly parched lips. In that moment she no longer faulted Walt for the times he had made comments to her about wearing a dress. If she enjoyed the sight of a well-dressed man, then why fault Walt for enjoying the sight of a well-dressed woman? Although, she suspected she would not be experiencing this physical reaction with just any well-dressed man.

"You look lovely this evening," he told her as he stepped farther into the room.

"So do you," she said, her voice faltering a bit.

He frowned. "Are you alright?" He sounded sincerely concerned.

She stared into his vivid blue eyes and thought, *I don't think I'll ever be alright again.* Instead she stood up and said, "Yes, I'm ready to go."

THEY SAT at a small secluded window booth on the west side of the restaurant with a view of the ocean. Outside, the moon cast a golden glow over the water's surface. In the background, music played, obscuring any other voices or sounds beyond their table, giving them a sense of intimacy. The server had just brought them each a glass of wine. Danielle looked down at the table as she absently fiddled with the stem of her wineglass while Walt sipped his drink, his intense gaze focused on her.

"Is everything alright?" he asked after a moment of silence.

Danielle looked up and smiled softly. "I was just thinking about the symbolism of your cast."

Walt's smile widened. He set his glass on the table and asked, "Symbolism of my cast? What do you mean?"

"In some ways the cast was a link—between Clint's life, when he broke his leg—and you, when his body became yours. You kept telling me you were certain the leg was no longer broken, like in some way Clint's body morphed into what had once been yours—but there was still the cast, a reminder of where the transformation had begun. It wasn't just limiting your movement; it was tying you to Clint's old life. But now it's gone and you're free to move forward —to resume your life fully. Does that make sense?"

Walt picked up his wineglass, took a sip and then said, "In a way. It does feel as if today is officially my beginning...on many different levels. Which reminds me, I haven't told you yet about what Ian told me."

"Ian? Told you about what?"

"When you were showing the attic to Chris and Adam, Ian stopped by to talk to me."

"And?"

"He liked the manuscript. In fact, he asked me if it would be okay if he sent it to his agent."

"You're kidding me? I thought it was great, but that's amazing!"

The manuscript in question was actually a novel of historical fiction Walt had written over the last three weeks. The idea had come to him after he had finished sorting through the historical documents Beverly Klein had given Danielle weeks earlier. Since his story was set in the 1920s, in coastal Oregon, involving prohibition and bootlegging, it didn't require any research—Walt knew that era, location, and subject matter intimately. The story itself was based on true events from Walt's first life, woven together to create an intriguing mystery rich in accurate historical detail. Ian had been surprised Walt managed to finish the first draft in such a short time.

"Not sure what this means—if it will turn into anything. But it's a good feeling knowing Ian liked my manuscript—liked it enough to want to send it to his agent."

"I'm very proud of you." Danielle reached across the table and took hold of his left hand, giving it a gentle squeeze.

Walt placed his right hand over Danielle's and gave it a pat and then said, "Which brings me to the real reason I wanted to bring you here tonight."

"I thought it was to celebrate getting your cast off?"

"Like you said, Danielle, the cast was symbolic—holding me back from fully pursuing what I want in this new life—and what I want is you."

The imaginary hand that had been squeezing her heart earlier tightened its grip. Speechless, Danielle stared at Walt.

"Will you marry me?" he asked.

She leaned forward and placed her free hand over Walt's right hand, clutching it possessively. "You want to get married?"

"Of course I want to get married. I'm in love with you. The only reason I'm here right now—that I've accepted this second chance of life—is that the one thing I wanted more than anything is a life with you—with you as my wife."

"I love you, Walt." Their hands pressed together tighter.

"Then will you marry me? Tonight?"

Without thought Danielle leaned back, her hands slipping from Walt's hold. "Tonight? I can't marry you tonight."

"Tomorrow, then?"

Danielle shook her head. "Walt, we can't get married right now. It's too soon."

"Too soon? You don't know yet if you want to marry me?"

She reached back over the table and grabbed his hands, holding them tightly.

"Of course I want to marry you. I love you. You're my best friend." She paused a moment and then added with a smile, "But don't tell Lily." Briefly squeezing his hands, she added, "But think about it. While I normally don't care what other people think, this is different. Aside from a handful of our closest friends, everyone thinks you lost your fiancée just two months ago. As far as anyone knows, I barely know you, and they think you have amnesia. It would make us both look ridiculous. We need to give it more time to put more distance between you and Clint."

Pulling his hands from hers, he sat back in the booth and crossed his arms over his chest. "How long?"

Danielle shrugged. "I don't know…a year maybe?"

"A year! I can't spend the next year spooning with the woman I love!"

"Who says we just have to spoon?" Danielle smiled mischievously. "And we do have that convenient hidden staircase."

Walt shook his head stubbornly. "No. The first time we make love, I want you to be my wife."

"You're serious, aren't you?" she asked quietly.

"Yes."

Danielle considered their dilemma a moment and then said, "I have an idea."

"Does it involve exchanging vows?" he asked.

"Let's elope," she suggested.

"Elope?" he said in surprise.

"Sure." Danielle grinned. "We can elope—and then later, when our relationship no longer appears so odd to the outside world, we can get married again with all our friends there. And I think I would like a real wedding—something like Lily had at Marlow House. Maybe the chief will walk me down the aisle."

"Elope?" Walt repeated, now seriously considering the suggestion.

"Yes. But I don't want to tell anyone—not even Lily."

"Why is that?" Walt asked.

Danielle smiled softly, her gaze intently studying Walt's features. "I don't know…I think it sounds…well…sorta romantic. And frankly, I like the idea of you and I having this time alone—just the two of us getting to know each other—as husband and wife—without anyone intruding."

"When?" he asked.

"You wanted to get married tonight—so—tonight." Danielle grinned happily as Walt pulled her around to his side of the booth to seal the engagement with a kiss. While their intention was to keep their relationship secret until sufficient time had passed, in that moment they forgot, giving no consideration to who might be watching.

FOUR

J ust as the kiss ended, Danielle looked into Walt's blue eyes and said, "Oh crap."

His arms still around her, Walt arched his brow, the corner of his lips turning up in a crooked smile. "Is that a commentary on my kiss?"

Danielle let out a sigh and moved out of his embrace, returning to her original seat. "We can't get married after dinner. We don't have a marriage license, and there's no way we can get one tonight."

"Then we get one in the morning," Walt suggested.

"And we probably shouldn't have just done that." Danielle glanced around nervously.

"Embarrassed to be seen with me?" Walt teased.

"Oh, right." Danielle rolled her eyes. "You know what I mean. Kissing in a public place might not be the smartest thing to do if we want to keep our relationship under wraps for the moment."

Before they could finish their discussion, the waitress arrived with two bowls of clam chowder. As she served the soup, Danielle pulled her cellphone out of her purse and began surfing for information on Oregon wedding licenses.

Just as the server left the table, Danielle—her eyes still on her phone's screen—said, "I don't believe this."

"I take you to a nice restaurant, propose, and you start playing with your phone? What is it with your generation and cellphones?" Walt asked as he picked up his soup spoon.

Danielle lowered the phone for a moment and looked across the table at Walt. "I was trying to find where we could get a marriage license."

"And?" Walt leaned over his bowl and gingerly tasted a spoonful of the hot soup.

Danielle set her phone on the table. "We have to go to the county office in Astoria."

"That's not a long drive. What's the problem?" Walt asked.

"There's a three-day waiting period," Danielle grumbled and then tasted her clam chowder.

"Three days?" Walt looked up at her.

"Yes, three days. Tomorrow's Thursday and the county office will be open. According to the website, they issue licenses from nine to four. Then we have to wait three days, but I'm not sure if that would mean we could get married on Sunday or Monday. It depends when the waiting period begins. Neither day is ideal. I don't want to get married on Sunday, because our guests for the weekend will still be here. And Monday isn't ideal; it's Memorial Day. But we might be able to get someone to marry us on Monday."

"What about in Washington?" Walt suggested. "We don't have to get married in Oregon."

Setting her spoon down, she picked up the phone again and searched for information on Washington marriage licenses. After a moment, she shook her head and set the phone back on the table. "They have a three-day waiting period too."

"I've waited over ninety years; I suppose I can wait five more days—as long as we don't have to wait a year," Walt said before eating more clam chowder.

Danielle smiled at him. "It hasn't been almost ninety years—it hasn't even been two years since we met."

Walt looked up, his eyes meeting hers. In a quiet voice he said, "That doesn't mean I haven't been waiting over ninety years for you."

"WHAT ARE YOU STARING AT?" Susan Mitchell's husband asked

her. The two sat at an inside table at Pearl Cove, some distance from Walt and Danielle's booth.

Susan, who had been peering over the top of her menu, quickly put it on the table and looked to her husband. "I think that's Danielle Boatman and Walt Marlow."

Menu in hand, Mr. Mitchell glanced over to where his wife indicated. "Oh, I think it is. Do you want to go over and say hi?"

Susan quickly shook her head and picked up her menu again, opening it. "No!"

"I thought you liked the Boatman woman?" he asked.

"Awkward," Susan said in a singsong voice while glancing through her entrée choices.

"Awkward, why?"

Susan lowered the menu and peered at her husband. "They were kissing. Right there in the booth, for everyone to see."

"There's hardly anyone in here, and I think we're the only ones that have a view to their booth. But you said they were kissing?" He frowned and glanced over to Walt and Danielle a moment. "Isn't he the one with amnesia?"

"Yes, and his fiancée was killed just two months ago."

Her husband shrugged and looked back to the menu. "Well, if he has amnesia, he probably doesn't remember her. What's wrong with him and Boatman kissing? They're both adults, single. And considering he's staying at Marlow House, not surprising something like this might develop."

"But he's using her," Susan whispered.

"Using her, how?" He frowned.

"He opened a bank account from me, but he didn't have any of his own money to deposit, so Danielle loaned him five thousand dollars. She said he was waiting for a refund from the airlines."

"That was generous of her. But I suppose she can afford it."

"I know she can afford it—and obviously so does he. When he brought in the refund check from the airline, it wasn't enough to cover what Danielle had given him, but he never paid her back anyway. And then he deposited a large check from Danielle. He said she had purchased those reproductions he'd commissioned. According to him, that check was to pay for the paintings."

"They obviously have some arrangement worked out between them," he suggested.

"He's seducing her! Taking advantage of her."

"You don't know that."

"You didn't see how they were kissing; I did!" Susan snapped.

"It's none of our business."

"Danielle Boatman is my friend—and she is a client of the bank. I don't want to see this guy clean out her bank accounts. How do we even know if he has amnesia?"

"Susan—"

"And why doesn't he have any of his own money? We know he and his fiancée were going to Europe after they left Marlow House. If he doesn't have any cash, what were they planning to spend there? Like I said, the only deposits he's made into his bank account have come from Danielle and the airline refund. It's just not right."

Her husband let out a sigh and glanced briefly to Walt and Danielle's table and then back to his wife. "Maybe he intended to use credit cards, or perhaps his fiancée was planning to pay the expenses in Europe."

"Now he expects Danielle to pay his way?"

He shrugged. "Maybe Marlow doesn't have any of his own money. Maybe that's why he's really staying at Marlow House."

"Isn't that what I was just saying?" She frowned.

AFTER DINNER AND DESSERT, Walt ordered them each a brandy.

As Danielle sipped her drink, she said, "I never do this."

"Do what?" Walt asked.

"Have an after-dinner drink. It's all very…sophisticated," she said in a haughty voice followed by a giggle.

His eyes on Danielle, he smiled. Lifting his glass in salute, he said, "This is a celebration."

"So it is." She grinned, her gaze never leaving his as they each sipped their brandy.

"I want to get you an engagement and a wedding ring—but it all seems very awkward, since it's your money, even what's in my bank account."

Danielle shook her head. "A good share of my money was yours. And even if that wasn't the case, you have the money from the ticket refund and the sale of the portraits."

"Which is technically Clint's money," Walt reminded her. "I'm actually destitute." He sounded more amused than distraught.

"It is an unusual situation."

Walt chuckled. "The understatement of the century."

"Anyway, there's no reason to buy rings now, it's not like I can wear them—I can't even wear an engagement ring or people would start asking questions."

Walt set his glass on the table and reached over, taking hold of Danielle's right hand, gently massaging her index finger with his thumb. Looking at her hand, he asked, "What happened to that ring you used to wear?"

"My aquamarine one? It's in my jewelry box. I just haven't worn it much lately. Why?" She looked from the hand he held to his face.

"Aquamarine is your birthstone, isn't it?"

"Yes."

Still holding her hand, his thumb caressing her index finger, he said, "I remember noticing your hands when we first met—they're so graceful—feminine. I remember the ring. We were in the kitchen, when you told me I was dead." He smiled and released her hand.

"Well, someone had to tell you," she teased.

"You know what I'd like us to do?" Walt asked.

"What?"

"We need to find a jeweler, one who can take some of those gold coins and make them into a wedding band. It can be your wedding ring for our secret marriage, and later, when we say our vows again, I'll buy you a wedding set—whatever you want. You can wear the gold band on your right hand, and if anyone asks, you can tell them the truth—that it's made from some of the gold coins."

The gold coins Walt referred to were once owned by him and his business partner, Jack. Jack, who had been staying in the house Ian and Lily now owned, across the street from Marlow House, had hidden the coins under some floorboards in a closet. After they were discovered, the courts decided the coins legally belonged to Danielle Boatman. Walt's estate had been left to the mother of Danielle's great-aunt Brianna. After the mother died, it went to Brianna. Brianna left her estate to Danielle, which included what had come from the Marlow Estate—which, decades later, included the gold coins hidden under a neighbor's floorboards.

"I think I like that idea," Danielle told him. "I just have to find someone who can do it."

24

FIVE

I t sounded like a horn, somewhere beyond the surf or perhaps a distance down the shoreline. Zara stood at the end of Frederickport Pier, speculating on where it was coming from. Her guess would be a lighthouse. Overhead, the bright moon painted light on the water's surface, and nearby a fisherman cast out his line.

This was where Loyd had said she would find him. Of course, he had refused to be any more specific than that. Considering what had happened at his house, she didn't imagine he was going to tell her more; he wasn't ready. But she wasn't giving up. If she couldn't find what she needed on her own, she would return to his house and demand he give her the information. Of course he would ignore her, but she would find some way to make him listen.

If Loyd refused to break his stubborn silence, there was always his brother, Simon. It was obvious Simon was in as deep as Loyd, considering his complicity in the drugging of her tea. If they refused to help, then she would find some way to use what they had done to her as leverage.

Turning from the end of the pier, Zara headed toward the diner she had seen when first arriving. It was late, but its lights were still on, so she was fairly confident it was open. She didn't feel it would be wise to start asking the locals if they knew Chris Glandon. From what she had seen, Frederickport was a small town, and small towns often protected their own from outsiders. Instead she would hang out at some of the local establishments, and perhaps if she was lucky, she might hear something that would point her in the right direction.

She was about ten feet from the diner's entrance when she noticed a woman coming her way. Zara paused for a moment, standing in the shadows, watching where the woman was headed— to the diner or the end of the pier. With the lighting, she couldn't make out the woman's face, but her figure's silhouette reminded Zara of a Playboy Bunny. The woman turned to her left and headed to the entrance of Pier Café. Zara waited a minute before continuing on to the restaurant.

Ten minutes later Zara sat alone in a booth, a cup of coffee sitting on the table before her. It was only half full. In the next booth over was the woman who had entered the café a few minutes before her. The woman sat alone, looking through a menu. Zara watched as a waitress with streaks of blue and purple in her blond hair walked up to the woman's booth to take her order.

CARLA STEPPED up to the table, menu pad in hand. She eyed the woman and then asked, "Hey, aren't you the new hostess over at Pearl Cove?"

The woman closed her menu and looked up. "Yeah. Did I wait on you there?"

Carla shrugged. "I haven't been to Pearl Cove in ages. Too freaking pricy for me. But I've seen you around town. Someone mentioned you were working there. I used to hostess at Pearl Cove."

The woman arched her brows. "Really? Hey, could you join me for a cup of coffee? Since I moved here, I haven't had a chance to meet anyone aside from who comes in the restaurant, and it's usually couples."

"I know what you mean. Sure, I would love to join you. I'm due for a break anyway. You want me to put an order in for you first?"

"My name's Mindi, Mindi Scholes," the woman said after Carla joined her a few minutes later. Neither one was aware Zara, in the next booth, was hanging on their every word.

"I'm Carla. Carla Vann."

"Nice to meet you, Carla. So how come you're over here and aren't working at Pearl Cove?"

Carla opened a packet of sugar and dumped it in her cup of coffee. "I was working here first and thought I'd get a side job and pick up some extra cash. But my schedule is always changing here—days—nights." Carla opened another sugar packet. "It was just too freaking hard working both places. And frankly, I make more here waitressing."

"You married?" Mindi asked.

Carla shook her head, took a sip of coffee, and then said, "No. You?"

"No." Mindi sighed. "What's with the guys in this town?"

"Tell me about it," Carla groaned.

"A few of our regular customers are hot, but they always bring a date—or wife—with them."

Carla fiddled with the rim of her coffee cup as she talked. "A while back I hooked up with a guy who wasn't anything special to look at, but at least he would take me to decent restaurants. But he was married, so I shoulda known there was no future there."

"What happened?"

Carla nodded toward the west side of the restaurant. "Fell off the pier. Drowned."

Mindi gasped. "How did that happen?"

"Basically, his wife poisoned him. He had some reaction to food she gave him, and he fell off the pier and drowned. That happened a while back, but they just arrested her. A real nutcase. I'm just glad she didn't come after me!"

"No kidding! Well, fortunately, some of the hot guys that've come in to the restaurant don't seem to be married. I just haven't figured out how to get them to leave their dates at home."

Carla leaned back a moment in the booth and eyed Mindi up and down. "Honey, with a figure like yours, I don't think you'd have a problem."

Mindi grinned. "Thanks, you're sweet."

Carla leaned forward, setting her elbows on the table, and said, "So tell me. Who are some of these hot guys; maybe I know them."

"I think the yummiest is this guy named Chris Johnson." Mindi practically swooned when she said his name.

"Oh, I know Chris! He…umm…works over at the Glandon Foundation."

"Yeah, that's what I heard. What is that anyway?"

Carla shrugged. "I guess they give money away."

"Give money away? Hey, I could use some!" Mindi laughed.

Carla giggled. "Yeah, you and me both. It's some sort of charity thing."

"Chris is super hot. But who's the weirdo he hangs out with? Reminds me of a snotty version of Abby. You know, the character on *NCIS*."

"Ahh…that would be Heather Donovan. In fact, both of them live on this street."

"What's the deal with those two?"

"I think Heather just works for him. I know he used to date Danielle Boatman, but they're not dating anymore."

"Danielle Boatman, she was in the restaurant tonight. I knew it was her, she's been in a few times, but the reservation was under Walt Marlow's name. He's been in a couple of times too. Now, he's another cutie. I wouldn't mind his attention."

"Both Chris and Walt are single. I'll admit I've tried to get Chris's attention, with no luck. And Walt—his fiancée was killed in a car accident about two months ago."

"I don't think Walt Marlow is single anymore."

"Why do you say that?" Carla asked.

"Like I told you, he was in the restaurant tonight with Danielle Boatman."

Carla shrugged. "That doesn't mean anything. Danielle owns Marlow House, it's a bed and breakfast. It's just down the street, that big ol' Victorian. He's a guest staying there, which is why they were probably out to dinner together."

"Does Danielle Boatman kiss all her guests?" Mindi snickered.

Carla gasped. "Are you saying you saw them kissing?"

Mindi nodded. "Right there in their booth. I was about to suggest they get a room."

MAX GREETED Walt and Danielle at the kitchen door. He weaved in and out between Danielle's feet until she picked him up.

"He's jealous," Walt told her.

"Jealous?" Still holding the cat in her arms, she looked down at his white-tipped ears. He began to purr.

"Because you spent the evening out with me."

"Are you going to tell him we're getting married?" Danielle asked.

Walt looked to the cat in her arms and frowned. "I thought you wanted to keep it a secret."

"Not from the animals, they won't tell anyone."

Walt arched his brow at Danielle. "Really? The minute Marie shows up, Max will blab to her. And you think Marie is going to keep quiet? She'll tell Eva, and you know who Eva will tell?"

"Chris?" Danielle asked.

Walt nodded.

She let out a sigh and set Max on the kitchen floor. "You're right. Let's not tell the cat—or any of them."

"It would probably be prudent." Walt glanced at the kitchen clock. "It's getting late. If we're going to get up early and head to Astoria in the morning, we should probably call it a night."

Danielle looked up mischievously at Walt. "We're all alone in the house," she whispered.

"Max might disagree with you."

"I can take care of Max. I'll lock him in Lily's old room." She grinned.

Walt pulled Danielle into his arms and kissed her nose before saying, "That won't be necessary. I'm sleeping in my new bed tonight—and you're sleeping in your room."

Danielle frowned. "I am?"

Walt nodded. "For the next five nights, no spooning...no midnight chats in either of our beds."

"Why not?"

Walt grinned. "Because the next time we share a bed, it will be on our wedding night."

"I'm okay with waiting until our wedding night, but that doesn't mean we can't do what we've been doing."

Walt let out a sigh and pulled her a little closer. "I don't have a cast on anymore. Not that it wouldn't have been possible with a cast —but seriously, if we're going to wait until our wedding night, I think we need to sleep in our own beds—alone—until then."

Danielle moved out of Walt's arms and then took his hand and started pulling him toward the door leading to the hallway. "Okay, Walt, let's get to bed so Monday will get here sooner."

Walt chuckled and walked with Danielle, hand in hand, toward the staircase.

"When Monday does get here, where do you want to spend our wedding night?" Walt asked.

Danielle stopped a moment and looked up at him. "I don't really want to go anywhere. I'd just like to come back here. Is that alright?"

Walt nodded. "I'd like that. Which room? The attic or your bedroom?"

"Gee, why not both?" Danielle said with a giggle before starting up the stairs.

SIX

The stand mixer sat on the center of the kitchen table, its wire whip moving the chocolate cake batter round and round in the enormous stainless steel bowl. Sitting on the table next to the mixer was a large bag filled with gold coins. Danielle sat at the table and watched the batter for a moment before dipping her hand into the bag and pulling out a handful of coins. She dumped them into the bowl and watched as they went round and round with the batter until it turned bright gold.

Just as she grabbed another handful of coins, she heard a beeping sound. She paused a moment. It beeped again. Persistent and irritating, another beep.

Danielle reluctantly opened her eyes and yawned. Another beep came from the alarm clock on her nightstand. Half awake, she reached over and swatted the top of the clock. It stopped beeping.

Rubbing the sleep from her eyes with the back of her hand, she looked up to the ceiling and wondered if Walt was awake yet. It was in that moment she remembered he had proposed the previous night. She smiled at the thought and tugged her blankets up and under her chin, holding them tightly.

"I can't believe I'm not telling Lily," she said aloud, yet didn't for a moment consider changing her mind. For some inexplicable reason, she felt she and Walt needed this time alone—this time together to explore their relationship without being scrutinized by those closest to them.

Before heading downstairs, Danielle quickly dressed for the day, selecting jeans and a pullover sweater. As she zipped up the jeans, she thought about how Walt often referred to them as farm pants. She laughed at the thought but didn't consider wearing something else. *I love Walt,* she thought, *but I'm not giving up my jeans.*

She found him downstairs sitting at the kitchen table, with a cup of coffee and a cinnamon roll. He was already dressed for the day.

"Good morning," Walt greeted her as she walked into the kitchen.

"Morning! I could smell the coffee when I was coming down the stairs. So glad I taught you how to use that coffee maker." Danielle headed toward the counter to pour herself a cup. Before she reached it, the glass coffee pot floated up from where it sat and poured coffee into an empty mug sitting on the counter. Danielle stopped in her tracks and stared at it a moment and then looked over at Walt.

"Here, let me pour you a cup," Walt said with a chuckle as he remained seated. He leisurely pulled off a hunk of cinnamon roll and popped it in his mouth.

Danielle laughed and said, "That is both sweet and lazy of you." She watched as the pot floated back to the coffee maker.

"You might want to do your own cream," Walt suggested. "Not sure about my aim; I might overfill the cup."

"You crack me up," she said under her breath as she added cream to her coffee.

Walt watched Danielle walk to the table. "How did you sleep last night?"

"I slept okay. My alarm clock woke me up in the middle of a dream. I was baking our wedding cake." Danielle took a seat at the table and then reached over and snatched a portion of Walt's cinnamon roll.

"What flavor?"

"Chocolate and gold." Danielle took a sip of her coffee.

"Gold?" Walt frowned.

Danielle shrugged. "It was weird. But it did make me think of something when I was getting dressed this morning. Maybe Aaron Michaels could make the gold rings—or at least, he might know who can."

"I don't seem to recall who that is."

"He's a jeweler in Astoria. We could stop at the bank before we leave today. I can take out some of the gold coins, and after we get the marriage license, we can stop over at his store and talk to him. If he can make the rings, then we can just leave the gold coins with him."

"Rings?" Walt asked.

Danielle took a sip of her coffee and then said, "I think we should have two wedding bands made—one for me and one for you."

"You don't think people will find that odd, us wearing matching rings?"

"You don't have to actually wear yours—maybe keep it in your pocket. Or on your key ring. But if I have a wedding band, you should have one too."

"Alright—of course, I don't actually have a key ring to put it on," he reminded her.

"You need one. Every grown man has a key ring. Anyway, I need to give you a key to the house and a key to the car."

"I don't think it would be a good thing if people see me driving your car."

Danielle shrugged. "Okay, then we buy you your own car."

"One thing at a time," he told her.

ZARA GLANCED down the driveway and spied a vehicle backing up, coming in her direction. She stepped into the bushes along the sidewalk, out of sight, and watched as it pulled onto the street and then drove away. There was a man and woman in the vehicle; the woman was driving. After the car disappeared from sight, she stepped back on the sidewalk and walked about fifteen feet, until she was standing in front of the house. If she wasn't mistaken, this was Marlow House, the bed and breakfast the two women in the café had been discussing last night.

When researching Chris Glandon online, she had come across an article about a murder at Marlow House, where one of the guests, a Chris Glandon, was initially implicated as a possible suspect. She was fairly certain it was the same Chris Glandon she was looking for, because after that incident, the Glandon Foundation opened its office in Frederickport. But then he disappeared again, leaving the foundation under the management of someone named Chris Johnson. If she wasn't mistaken, that was the man whom the women were discussing in the restaurant last night.

"Are you lost?" a woman's voice asked.

Zara turned toward the voice. It was a woman wearing a dark blue jogging suit, her black hair pulled up on the top of her head and twisted into two knots, and a terrycloth headband wrapped around her forehead to catch her sweat. She was slightly out of breath and just stepping up onto the sidewalk as if she had come from across the street.

"Umm...no. Just doing a little sightseeing. This is a really cool house. Is it yours?" Zara nodded toward Marlow House.

The woman looked up to the house in question and back to Zara. "No. That's actually the first house ever built in Frederickport. It's a bed and breakfast now, Marlow House."

"It's impressive. Well, I'd better get going. I parked my car down at the pier, and I have some friends waiting for me," Zara lied.

SUSAN MITCHELL WATCHED as Danielle Boatman entered the bank on Thursday morning. She was with Walt Marlow. Susan wondered briefly if Walt was here to deposit more of Danielle's money into his account. A few minutes later she discovered the real reason Danielle was at the bank—to get into one of her safe deposit boxes.

"That's the one with the gold coins," Susan said as she led Danielle back into the vaults, leaving Walt sitting alone at her desk.

"Yes, it is." Danielle trailed behind Susan.

"Does this mean you've found another buyer for the coins?"

"I'm not really in a hurry to sell them anymore."

When they reached the safe deposit box, Danielle handed Susan her key. After Susan opened the box, Danielle said, "I don't need to take this in the room alone. Let me just take a few out, and you can put it back."

Susan watched as Danielle quickly removed one coin at a time. She would inspect each coin before returning it to the safe deposit box or dropping it in her purse. It only took her a couple of minutes. Susan resisted the temptation to ask Danielle what she was going to do with the coins.

"I ALWAYS GET the feeling I make her uncomfortable," Walt told Danielle after they returned to the car.

"You mean Susan?" Danielle climbed into the driver's side of the vehicle and slammed her door shut.

"Yes." Sitting in the passenger seat, Walt fastened his seatbelt. "I think she was dying to know what I was going to do with the coins."

"You didn't tell her?"

Danielle shook her head. "No. But I did what you suggested. I only took coins that were well worn."

Walt's cellphone began to ring. "I'm getting a phone call," he said with surprise.

"Well, answer it." Danielle started the car.

Walt looked at his ringing phone and said, "It's Ian. I must say, it's convenient knowing who's calling before answering it."

"It's going to go to voicemail if you don't answer it soon," Danielle warned.

Walt accidentally hit speakerphone after answering the call and then said, "Hello, Ian."

"Hi, Walt. Where are you? I went over to your house, and no one was there," Ian asked.

Danielle glanced briefly to Walt. She could clearly hear Ian's side of the conversation.

"Danielle and I are on our way to Astoria," Walt told him.

"What are you going there for?" Ian asked.

Walt looked over to Danielle, who sat in the driver's seat, steering the car down the road. "We're going to see a jeweler."

Danielle glanced briefly over to Walt again and arched her brows inquisitively, but didn't comment.

Before Ian could ask why they were seeing a jeweler, Walt said, "Danielle wanted to see about making some of the gold coins into a ring for her—using a few of the well-worn ones."

"I don't know much about coin collecting, but are you sure she couldn't get more for the coins, even the worn ones, by selling them instead of melting them down?"

"I told her that, but you know Danielle, when she gets an idea, there's no talking her out of it."

Danielle furrowed her brows and flashed Walt a frown. He resisted the temptation to laugh.

"So what did you need?" Walt asked.

"I just got off the phone with my agent. He loved your manuscript."

"Didn't you just send it to him?" Walt asked.

"Yes, yesterday, after I talked to you. I emailed it to him. He told me he stayed up all night reading it. He couldn't put it down. I have to say I'm a little jealous; I haven't heard him this excited in a long time."

Danielle's frown turned to a smile. She listened intently to Ian's every word.

"What does this mean, exactly?" Walt asked.

"He wants to talk to you. I think you have an agent—if you want one," Ian told him.

When Walt got off the phone, Danielle said, "I think that is amazing about the agent—but what was that all about, *it was Danielle's idea, you know how once she gets an idea, blah, blah, blah…*"

"I did it for you," Walt told her with a grin.

"For me?"

"You were the one who wanted to keep this a secret for a while —even from Lily. If Lily and Ian think it was my idea for you to make a gold band from what was once my gold coins, you don't think they might figure it out?"

Danielle considered his suggestion for a moment and then let out a sigh. "I suppose you're right."

"Of course I am," he said smugly.

Unable to suppress a smile, Danielle said, "I'd tell you not to get so full of yourself, but dang, you got yourself an agent! Jon Altar's agent! Woo-hoo!"

SEVEN

C hris pulled up to Marlow House just as Danielle and Walt returned from Astoria on Thursday afternoon. He had come from his office, which was why he drove instead of walked. With his pit bull, Hunny, by his side, he sprinted up the side driveway, meeting Walt and Danielle just as they were about to walk into the back door leading to the kitchen.

Upon seeing Walt, Hunny began squirming from head to tail, lowering her head as her bottom wiggled uncontrollably. She made whimpering sounds. Walt immediately squatted down and welcomed the young dog, roughly scratching along her neck and accepting wet kisses while calming her with his mentally conveyed words.

Chris looked down at the pair and shook his head. Hunny was now sitting, the image of a well-behaved dog. "I don't get the attraction. Frankly, I question Hunny's judgment."

"You're just jealous that she listens to me," Walt returned. He stood up, leaving Hunny sitting quietly by his side.

"I'm going to start calling you Dr. Dolittle," Chris said.

Danielle walked into the kitchen and chuckled, leaving the two men and dog to follow her into the house.

"I'm familiar with the books, but I only read the first one," Walt noted.

"Books? It's a movie," Chris told him.

"You're both right," Danielle said as she tossed her purse on the kitchen counter. "I remember reading the Doctor Dolittle books when I was a little girl."

"After the first one came out, I bought it for a friend's child," Walt explained. "I remember reading it to her."

"I shouldn't be surprised it was a book first," Chris said as he took a seat at the table.

"Making yourself at home?" Walt sat down at the table with Chris.

"Where have you two been? I stopped by earlier," Chris asked.

"We drove over to Astoria for the morning," Danielle explained.

"Shouldn't you be at work?" Walt asked.

Ignoring Walt's question, Chris asked, "Danielle, I wanted to talk to you about something."

She joined them at the table while Hunny curled up on the floor by Chris's feet.

"Do you want me to leave so you can talk to her alone?" Walt asked.

"Yes to the first question, no to the second," Chris said.

Walt frowned. "I only asked you one question."

Chris laughed and then said, "No, it's okay, Walt. You don't need to leave."

Walt stood up.

"No, you really don't need to leave. I was just kidding," Chris said.

"I'm not leaving, but I thought we could all use something to drink. Iced tea?" Walt asked. "Beer?"

"Too early for beer?" Chris asked.

"It's almost noon," Walt said, walking to the refrigerator.

"Tea for me, Walt. Thanks." Danielle then looked at Chris and asked, "What did you want to talk to me about?"

"I got a letter from one of my uncles yesterday."

"The uncles who contested your parents' will?" Walt asked as he handed Chris a beer.

"Yes. I only have two. They're the ones who contested the will. I was going to bring the letter with me so Danielle could read it, but I forgot it at the office. Basically it was an apology and claimed they never intended to contest the will so they could keep my inheritance, but they were worried about me and wanted to protect me."

Walt handed Danielle a glass of iced tea and asked Chris, "And you believe that?"

Chris shrugged and said, "I should have brought the letter with me. It made me start questioning things. That's why I stopped over yesterday." Chris looked at Danielle and said, "I wanted to talk to you about the letter."

Walt joined them at the table with a can of beer.

"In what respect?" Danielle asked.

"It doesn't matter now, since I called them." Chris took a swig of his beer.

"So how did that go?" Danielle asked. "Did you accept their apology?"

Chris shook his head. "I said it made me question things—but forget what they put me through? I'm not there yet. Not sure I'll ever be."

"So why did you call them?" Walt asked.

Chris shrugged. "I figured they probably knew where I was, which they did. I just didn't want them showing up unexpectedly. So I figured I would talk to them."

"What did they say?" Danielle asked.

"They wanted to see me. Offered to come here. So I lied. I told them I wouldn't be here. Told them I would be traveling abroad for the foundation and wouldn't be back until Christmas."

"Does that mean they're coming for Christmas?" Danielle asked.

Chris looked at Danielle and shook his head. "I didn't even consider they would come then. I figured Christmas is, what, seven months away? But nope, I tell a lie that I think is going to let me avoid them only to realize I practically agreed to see them."

"Before you told your lie, you should have consulted Danielle. That's her field of expertise," Walt said before taking a drink of beer.

Danielle scowled at Walt and swatted his forearm, causing him to spill some of this beer. "Oh, stop, you brat. Any lies I told were to get out of some mess you probably started!"

Walt glanced down at the beer on the table and asked Chris, "Did you see that? She assaulted me!"

Danielle rolled her eyes and turned her attention back to Chris. "You could always tell them you don't want to see them."

Walt grabbed a napkin off the table and wiped up the spilt beer. "She does have a point."

"I know I could, but I'm afraid they would just show up anyway. And if they do, I would like some control. So…well…that's why I wanted to warn you…"

Walt and Danielle exchanged glances and then looked at Chris.

"They're going to be calling you to make reservations," Chris said. "I lied and told them you were closed today and wouldn't be open until tomorrow. I wanted a chance to warn you they were calling."

"What do you want me to tell them? That we're full and can't take their reservation?"

Chris cringed. "I know you weren't planning to take guests this Christmas. But if they can't stay here, well, they'll just stay somewhere else. Frankly, I'd just like the moral support if I have to deal with them."

"I suspect you would also like a second opinion in regards to their sincerity when they show up," Walt suggested.

Chris nodded. "Pretty much."

POLICE CHIEF MACDONALD was just getting off the phone when Officer Brian Henderson knocked on his office door. MacDonald looked up to the doorway and motioned him in.

"Did you hear about Ben Smith?" Brian asked when he entered the office.

"Hear what?" MacDonald asked.

"He died in his sleep last night. I'm pretty sure it was a heart attack. His wife woke up this morning and found him dead next to her in bed."

"Sorry to hear that. But when it's my time to check out, that's how I'd like to go."

When Brian left the office a few minutes later, the chief picked up his phone and called Danielle.

"Hey, Chief, what's up?" Danielle asked when she answered the call.

"Not sure you heard yet, but Ben Smith died."

"Died? What happened?"

"Probably a heart attack. When his wife woke up this morning, she found him."

"Is there going to be an autopsy?" she asked.

"I doubt it. He was in his eighties, and he had a bad heart."

"I'm really sorry to hear that. Ben was really nice to me when I moved here. I really liked him. I think that's one of the reasons it bothered me so much after I found out what he and the others were trying to hide from me."

"Did he ever apologize?" the chief asked.

"Sort of. But it was awkward. Actually, the last time I saw him—and the first time I had seen him since I found out what he and the others were up to—was when we picked up the portraits from the museum after I bought them from Walt."

"To be honest, I was surprised you picked them up. I figured you would leave them there until the exhibit with the originals opened."

"I probably would have, had I not been so annoyed at the time. But they never really wanted the reproductions; it was just a ruse so they could get to the papers Beverly had given me. I didn't see the point in prolonging the charade. Anyway, Ben was there; he seemed embarrassed. Told me he was sorry for everything and never meant to hurt me."

"You never told me that," the chief said.

"Well, we haven't had much time to talk in the last few weeks. It has been a bit hectic for all of us," Danielle reminded him.

"So what did you tell him?"

"I didn't say much. I was sort of cool. But I did tell him I appreciated the apology. I suppose if things were different, I might regret not being more forgiving."

"What do you mean?" the chief asked.

"It's possible I might see Ben before he moves on," she reminded him.

AS MUCH AS Lily Bartley loved teaching, she was counting the days until summer vacation. Being back in the classroom had kicked her butt this year, reminding her she was not a hundred percent back to her old self in spite of the fact it had been almost two years since her coma.

When she got home, she was greeted by Sadie, her husband's golden retriever. Although, even before she and Ian had exchanged vows, she had considered Sadie as much hers as his. Before looking for Ian, she took a detour to the kitchen and filled a bowl with double fudge ice cream. Bowl of ice cream and spoon in hand, she found Ian in his office sitting at his desk, Sadie trailing behind her.

While eating her ice cream, she shared her day with Ian and then listened to what his agent had said about Walt's book. He then told her about Walt and Danielle's trip to Astoria to see the jeweler.

Sitting on the small sofa in Ian's office, Lily wrinkled her nose and said, "Really? She's having a ring made?"

"That's what Walt said."

Lily ate a spoonful of ice cream and silently considered what Ian had just told her. Finally, she said, "That is so unlike Dani. She doesn't even wear jewelry. Aside from her birthstone ring, but I haven't seen that for ages."

"She wears jewelry. She wears earrings."

Lily rolled her eyes. Before taking another bite of ice cream, she said, "Pierced earrings don't count unless you change them every day. Dani always wears the same pair."

Ian shrugged in response.

"Seriously, though, she's really going to have a ring made from the gold?"

"That's what Walt told me."

Lily shook her head. "Now, that sounds like something I might do. But Dani? Any idea what kind of ring she's going to have made?"

"Walt didn't say. Just that they were going to a jeweler in Astoria to see if he could do it."

"I bet that's Aaron Michaels. Remember, he's the one they had look at the Missing Thorndike."

"They didn't say which jeweler."

"Oh, I know what she should do!" Lily said excitedly.

"What?"

"If she's having a ring made from Walt's gold coins, I think she should get the emerald back from the museum. She only loaned it to them, and considering that BS they pulled, she's not obligated to leave it there. An emerald from the original Missing Thorndike would be really cool in a ring."

"That reminds me, Ben Smith died this morning. They say it was a heart attack, died in his sleep."

"Wow…no kidding? I know he was old, but that surprises me; he was always so active."

EIGHT

I t wasn't quite noon on Monday. Danielle stood with Walt by the front swing, watching the last guests from the weekend drive away. Inside Marlow House, Joanne was busy changing the linens on the beds.

Danielle leaned against Walt's shoulder, staring ahead blankly, looking like someone had just taken her Christmas puppy.

Wrapping his arm around her shoulder, he gave her a reassuring squeeze. "We could drive to Astoria after the funeral."

"I don't want to get married the same day we go to a funeral," she grumbled.

"Then I suppose we'll just have to get married tomorrow."

"I feel like a horrible person," she confessed.

Walt pulled her closer to his side. "Why is that?"

"Poor Ben died, and all I'm thinking is how this was supposed to be our wedding day."

He pulled her even tighter to his side, kissed the top of her head, and whispered, "Yes, love. You are a horrible person."

Danielle chuckled in spite of herself and said, "I love you, Walt."

"I love you too." He glanced around. "I suppose we shouldn't be standing out here like this. Joanne could come out any minute, and anyone could drive by."

Danielle let out a sigh and stepped away from Walt, his arm

dropping to his side. She looked up to him and asked, "Tell me again why we have to keep all this a secret for now."

He smiled down at her and said, "I could remind you it was your idea, but the more I think about it, I believe you were right."

She arched her brow. "I was right about something?"

"You normally are, but please don't let it go to your head."

"So you think it's best we keep it a secret for a while?" she asked.

He nodded. "Yes. Marriages are hard enough without looking for problems. I'd say giving your friends—like Adam and Melony, for example—or even semi-friends, like Joe and Kelly—reasons to question our relationship and start worrying about my motives will just bring unnecessary stress into our lives. Let them get used to me a little longer—and used to seeing us becoming friends."

"There's one perk; according to Aaron, he'll have the rings finished by tomorrow afternoon. So we won't have to make two trips over there," Danielle said.

"Unless you take Lily's suggestion and have him add the emerald."

"I don't think that emerald would look right on a gold band. I'm not even sure he could add it to the ring without some serious redesigning."

Walt nodded. "True."

THE BEACH DRIVE BUNCH—WALT, Danielle, Ian, Lily, Chris and Heather—drove together to Ben Smith's funeral later that afternoon, taking Danielle's Ford Flex. Lily and Heather squeezed into the far back seat, while Ian and Chris sat in the middle seat. Danielle and Walt's friends had no idea this was supposed to be their wedding day. After the funeral, they planned to go out to dinner together.

The service was being held at Pastor Chad's church, which made it doubly odd for Danielle, considering all that had gone on. Just as she started to pull into a space in the church parking lot, everyone in her car—except for Ian and Lily—let out a scream.

"What is it?" Lily asked, frantically looking around.

What Lily and Ian didn't see was the elderly woman standing in the middle of the hood of the car, looking in at them through the windshield.

"Marie," Danielle grumbled, "did you have to do that?"

Marie stuck her head through the windshield and grinned. "Sorry, dear, did I scare you?"

"Is Marie here?" Lily asked.

"I hate when ghosts do that," Heather grumbled from the back seat.

A moment later Marie stood outside the car and watched as the six people exited the vehicle.

"I'm sorry, dear," Marie said. "Have you seen Ben yet?"

"No, have you?" Danielle asked, shutting the car door behind her.

"No. But I can't imagine he's moved on already. He was always such a nosy busybody," Marie said. "I'm sure he wants to see who came to his funeral. Although, I can't imagine why his wife decided to have it on Memorial Day."

"I wondered the same thing," Heather agreed.

Fifteen minutes later they were seated in the church, with Marie sitting at the end of the row and Danielle next to her. It was agreed that if anyone came to take Marie's seat, Danielle would say it was already taken.

At the front of the church was the open casket. Disjointed bits of conversation blended with a background of organ music while family and friends of the deceased poured into the church, looking for a place to sit down, some going first to the casket at the front of the church to pay respect or to say a few words to Ben's widow. Occasionally someone would pass by their row and say hello to one or more of them. At the front of the church Ben's wife, Sylvia, sat with family and close friends.

Marie craned her neck to get a better look. "I was wondering if his daughter was going to make it. But I don't see her."

"He had a son too, didn't he?" Danielle asked. "I heard he died a couple of years before I moved here."

"Skiing accident. He was the apple of their eye," Marie said. "One good thing, now Ben can see him."

"Did he have children?" Danielle asked.

"You mean Ben's son?" Marie asked.

"Yes."

"Stepkids. He married an older woman who already had children." Marie looked up to the front of the church again. "I don't see the daughter-in-law here, although I heard she moved back East not long after the accident. If any of her kids are here, I don't recognize them. But I doubt it. I don't think they had a chance to get close to Ben or Sylvia considering their stepdad died not long after they married."

"So what about the daughter?" Danielle asked.

"She was always trouble. Got heavily in drugs. I haven't seen her in years, and Ben and Sylvia would never talk about her."

"Who's sitting up in front with Ben's wife?" Danielle asked, looking to the front of the church.

"That's her sister and brother-in-law. They live in Portland."

"I think the service is about to start," Danielle whispered as she nodded to the front of the church.

Pastor Chad walked to the podium. He stood there a few minutes, looking out to the mourners, waiting for them to stop talking so he could begin the service. The sound of voices stilled to a whisper, and then after a moment it was completely silent.

"Oh, there's Adam!" Marie said, breaking the silence. Only the mediums sitting in her row could hear her. She looked at Danielle and said, "I'll see you later, dear." Marie vanished and then appeared a few seconds later, sitting on the other side of the church next to her grandson. He, of course, had no idea his grandmother was at his side.

Midway through the service Ben arrived. Danielle looked to Walt and then down the aisle to Chris and Heather, who looked her way and nodded.

"I wondered if he would show up," Danielle said under her breath.

Ben, who was standing by his casket, looked out into the pews, taking in who was in attendance. When he spied Marie, he froze. A moment later, he was standing by her side and the two began talking. Danielle and her fellow mediums wondered what they were saying, but they were too far away to hear the conversation.

When the service was finally over and Danielle stood up with the others, she was startled when a man touched her arm and said, "Excuse me, are you Danielle Boatman?"

Standing in the row in front of the pew she had just occupied, preparing to step out into the aisle, Danielle looked at the man. She didn't recognize him. Middle-aged and nondescript, he wore a black suit and tie.

"Yes, I am," she said.

"Ben's widow, Sylvia, wanted to know if you would be so kind as to come with me to the church library so she can talk to you privately for a moment."

"She wants to talk to me?" Danielle frowned. She glanced behind her at her friends. They had all heard the man's request and, by their expressions, were as curious as she was to know why Sylvia wanted to talk to her.

"Umm...sure...I guess," Danielle stammered.

DANIELLE FOLLOWED the man to the library. When she entered the room, she found Sylvia sitting in a chair next to a desk, a box of Kleenex on her lap, as she repeatedly dabbed the corners of her eyes with one damp tissue. Sylvia, who was in her eighties, made no attempt to stand, but she smiled up at Danielle.

"Thank you for agreeing to talk to me," Sylvia said.

Danielle was surprised when the man who had brought her to the room did not leave, but entered with her and closed the door behind them.

"You've already met Irvin Brunskill, he's our attorney," Sylvia explained as she pointed to the man who had escorted Danielle to the room.

"We were not formally introduced." Irvin extended his hand to Danielle. "Nice to meet you, Ms. Boatman."

Confused, Danielle shook his hand. "Umm...nice to meet you. Exactly why am I here?"

Irvin motioned to an empty chair next to Sylvia. "I'll explain shortly."

Reluctantly Danielle sat down and watched as Irvin took a seat behind the desk. He opened a manila folder already sitting before him.

"Mrs. Smith wanted to take care of this before she returns to her house for the wake. While you, of course, are most welcome to attend, she just thought it would be best if we take care of this now. She would like to put it behind her."

Danielle frowned. She looked curiously from the attorney to Mrs. Smith.

"I'll cut to the chase, Ms. Boatman. Ben left you his Packard."

Danielle abruptly sat up straight in her chair. "He what?"

The attorney started to say something, but Sylvia stopped him. She looked at Danielle and said, "I think I should explain."

Danielle looked to the elderly woman, curious to hear what she had to say.

"I know what happened between you and some of the museum board members. Ben came home after the police questioned him, and he told me everything," Sylvia explained. "He was so embarrassed—and ashamed."

"I'm so sorry you have to do this, Sylvia," Ben said when he appeared the next moment, standing at his wife's side. Danielle glanced up to him. Ben smiled at Danielle and said, "Marie explained everything. I know you can see and hear me."

"I always knew there was something not quite right with that Packard," Sylvia explained. "I never understood why my father-in-law kept it locked away in his barn. And he would get so angry if Ben would show it to one of his friends."

"I didn't realize at that time what my father had done," Ben explained.

"But even a car stored away for a lifetime and never used begins to age. I will say one good thing about the Packard, Ben and our son spent some wonderful hours working on the car—bringing it back to its former glory. This was, of course, after my father-in-law died." Sylvia paused at the memory, silently reflecting before going on.

"I'll confess, it was why I couldn't bear just giving it to you while I was still alive," Ben told Danielle. "I knew the car rightfully belonged to you, but it held so many memories—memories I shared with my son. I wasn't ready to let that go. But now, now I will be able to see my son again, and I have to make things right before I go."

"It was only after Ben started going through those old boxes of his father did he realize the car had been stolen from Walt Marlow. By that time, he and our son had finished refurbishing the Packard, and as far as he knew, there wasn't anyone left from the Marlow family. While he understood Brianna was technically its owner, he conveniently made excuses why it was no longer relevant. But I suppose deep down he knew it was wrong. That's probably why he didn't take the car out much."

"When did Ben decide to leave it to me?" Danielle asked.

"My client called me a couple of weeks ago," the lawyer said. "He told me he wanted to make a change in his will. I'll admit, I tried talking him out of it. He never explained why he wanted to leave it to you."

"I was ashamed," Ben said, yet only Danielle could hear.

Sylvia smiled at the attorney and then looked to Danielle. "After Ben died, I explained it all to Irvin."

"But the Packard has to be worth a fortune. Are you sure you want to do this?" Danielle asked.

"It's the right thing to do. And what am I going to do with a car like that? I don't even drive anymore. And frankly, I would rather not have to worry about selling it. It's not like I need the money. Plus, there is satisfaction in knowing things have come full circle. And it's what Ben wanted."

NINE

W alt and the others were curious to find out why Ben's widow wanted to talk to Danielle in private. It wasn't until they were all in the car with Danielle driving them to the Smith house for the wake did she tell them.

"Do you have any idea how much that car is worth?" Ian asked from the back seat.

"Not a clue, and it's not like I haven't tried to find out," Danielle said as she steered her car down the road.

"We wondered what it might be worth after I first realized it was my car," Walt explained. "Danielle tried looking up the current value on the internet, with no luck."

"Has to be worth a fortune," Chris said.

"I found a 1924 Packard sedan online. That was as close as I got," Danielle told him. "It was a YouTube video, and the owner was trying to sell the car."

"How much was the owner asking?" Lily asked.

"I don't know," Danielle answered. "I didn't bother watching the video; it was the wrong car."

"What are you going to do with it?" Chris asked.

Danielle looked in her rearview mirror at Chris. "Who are you asking?"

"You."

"Then you're asking the wrong person. It's not my car. It belongs to Walt," Danielle said.

"It may technically be my car, but as far as the good people of Frederickport will know, it belongs to you."

"Yeah, considering what it's probably worth, your pal Joe Morelli might try having you committed if he thought you just gave away something that valuable to Walt," Heather pointed out.

"Can we just not discuss any of this at the wake?" Danielle asked. "I'd rather not have people asking me questions. To be honest, I don't know how I can even explain it without making Ben look bad, and I don't think that's something I want to do to a person at his wake."

Shortly after arriving at the Smith home, Danielle and her friends found themselves greeted by Pastor Chad. Nearby was Millie Samson and Herman Shafer. It was the first time she had seen them together since all that had happened weeks earlier. She assumed Millie and Herman had been at the church for Ben's service, but she hadn't seen them there.

Danielle felt awkward, while Chad and Herman seemed embarrassed. Millie, on the other hand, unabashedly opened her dialogue with Danielle by saying, "I understand you have a new car."

Stunned by Millie's greeting, Danielle flashed her a halfhearted smile and said, "I suppose I do."

"The entire thing is silly, I think. Of course, Ben is free to leave the car to whomever he wants. I just feel a little sorry for Sylvia. I imagine that thing is worth a fortune, and I'm sure she could use the money now with Ben gone, and you certainly don't need it."

"Millie, please. This is not the time or place," Pastor Chad reprimanded.

"I'm not criticizing Danielle," Millie defended. "If someone left me something valuable in their will, I probably would want to keep it too."

"After all that's happened—" Chad began, only to be cut off by Millie.

"I'm sorry for what we did. In fact, I have apologized to Danielle. Didn't I, Danielle?"

"Uhh…yes…" Danielle glanced over to Walt and the others, who appeared as surprised at Millie's opening as she had been.

"After all, we never meant any harm. I think most people could understand us not wanting to flaunt all those old family skeletons. As for that Packard, we don't really know if it belonged to Walt Marlow or not."

"It did," Walt interrupted.

Startled at Walt's comment, Millie stared at him a moment.

"Oh, there's my sister and Joe," Ian interrupted. Danielle used that moment to cut short her conversation with Millie.

THE SIX FRIENDS sat at a large table for twelve at the Mexican restaurant for an early dinner.

"I hope you don't mind that I invited my sister and Joe," Ian said after they all sat down. Since Joe and Ian's sister, Kelly, had also been at the Smiths', Ian found it impossible not to invite the pair to join them all for dinner when Kelly had asked him what they were all planning to do after the wake.

"It's Adam I have a problem with," Danielle grumbled, picking up the menu.

"What are you talking about?" Chris asked. "You knew Adam and Mel were going to join us for dinner."

"That was before I found out Ben left me the Packard," Danielle grumbled.

"What does that have to do with anything?" Chris asked.

Before Danielle had a chance to answer, Joe and Kelly arrived, and a few minutes later, Adam and Melony showed up, with Marie's ghost trailing behind them. The minute Adam opened his mouth, Chris understood Danielle's earlier comment.

Instead of sitting down with Melony, Adam picked up one of the full water glasses from the table. He raised a toast to Danielle. "Here is to Miss Boatman, who has once again fallen into a pot of gold!"

"Oh, sit down, Adam," Danielle grumbled.

Marie chuckled. "You do have to agree, dear, it is amusing."

"What's he talking about?" Kelly whispered to Joe.

Joe looked at Kelly and shrugged.

Adam laughed. "No, seriously, Danielle, how do you do it? Do you have any idea how much that car is worth?"

"Adam, listen to Danielle and sit down," Melony scolded while resisting the urge to laugh.

Ian glanced from Adam to Danielle and chuckled, while Lily

couldn't help but giggle—although she did briefly feel disloyal to Danielle for doing so.

Before taking Melony's suggestion, Adam returned the glass of water to the table and then made an exaggerated bow to Danielle while saying, "Hail to the magnificent Lakshmi. I am not worthy!"

Danielle crumpled her napkin and threw it at Adam; it landed on the floor, missing its mark. Adam bowed several more times while backing up to his chair before sitting down.

Walt silently handed Danielle one of the extra napkins on the table, but stopped her from throwing it at Adam when she started to crumple it up like she had the first one. "No, you're going to need a napkin for dinner. Plus, your aim's not great."

Melony half-heartedly swatted Adam, who was now sitting next to her, and said, "You're such a jerk."

"Would someone tell me who is the magnificent Lakshmi?" Heather asked.

"I believe she is the Hindu goddess of wealth," Lily told her.

"I just want to know what pot of gold Danielle fell into now," Kelly said. "And what car is Adam talking about?"

"You didn't hear anyone mention Ben's Packard at the wake?" Ian asked.

"I heard someone say Sylvia wasn't keeping it," Joe said.

Heather glanced over to Marie, who sat next to her. Since the chair had not been pulled out from the table, and Marie was unable to harness energy, it looked as if the tabletop was cutting the ghost in half. Heather frowned at the sight.

"Ben left the Packard to Danielle in his will," Chris explained.

"And that is one gorgeous car," Adam said with a sigh.

Kelly looked at Danielle. "Why would Ben leave it to you?"

"There's a good chance Ben's father stole the car after Walt Marlow was murdered," Joe explained.

Kelly looked at Joe and frowned. "You never told me that." She glanced to her brother. "Did you know that?"

Ian shrugged. "Those boxes Beverly Klein brought over to Danielle a few weeks ago with the historical documents, there were some articles about how Walt Marlow's car disappeared after he died. It was a 1924 Packard Coupe."

"Just because it disappeared, it doesn't mean Ben's father stole it," Kelly argued.

Heather looked over to Marie again, who was listening intently to the conversation. Abruptly Heather took one foot and shoved Marie's chair out from the table.

Marie let out a little yelp, but looked down and saw her body was no longer going through the tabletop. "Oh, thank you, dear."

Lily frowned at Heather. "Why did you do that?"

"Why do you think?" Heather asked, arching her brows and then nodding toward Adam.

Lily looked from Adam to the seemingly empty chair. "Oh…"

"What are you two talking about?" Kelly asked.

"Oh, nothing." Lily smiled and picked up a menu.

"You people are weird," Kelly grumbled.

"Yes, we are." Ian laughed. He reached over and pulled his wife's chair closer to him and kissed her cheek.

"IS THERE SOMETHING WRONG?" Joe asked Kelly when they drove home later that night.

"I feel like such an outsider these days," Kelly told him.

Joe pulled into their driveway and parked the car. Instead of getting out of the vehicle, he removed his seatbelt and turned to face Kelly, who sat in the passenger seat looking dejected.

"What do you mean?"

"Ever since Ian married Lily, we just aren't as close as we used to be," Kelly said with a pout.

Joe reached out and brushed Kelly's hair away from her face. "He's married now. It's to be expected."

She turned to face Joe. "But doesn't it bug you how they always seem to have some sort of inside joke that we're left out of?"

"Inside joke?"

She shrugged. "Something. Not a joke exactly. But it's like they're all sharing some secret and we're not part of it. Don't you ever feel that way?"

"I'm not sure what you mean. But I figure, considering all that's gone on, I'm just not accepted. It's probably me, not you."

Kelly frowned at Joe. "What do you mean?"

"You have to admit, if Ian wasn't your brother, I would never have been invited tonight."

"That's not true!" Kelly insisted.

"It's no secret I didn't trust Chris when I first met him—and I still don't trust that Marlow character. And while Danielle says she forgives me for arresting her, I suspect she doesn't. And Lily, well, she's always been fiercely loyal to Danielle."

"Are you saying this thing I'm feeling—how I feel like an outsider—is because of how they feel about you?"

Joe shrugged. "That would be my guess."

DANIELLE AND WALT sat alone in the parlor, sitting on the small sofa. Walt sipped a brandy while Danielle nursed a hot cup of herbal tea.

"It was supposed to be our wedding night," Danielle said with a sigh.

Walt wrapped one arm around her shoulders and pulled her closer. She rested her head on his shoulder.

"How do you really feel about inheriting the Packard?" Walt asked.

"Well, it solves two problems," Danielle told him.

"What two problems?"

"You need a car—and I was trying to figure out what to give you for a wedding present."

Walt chuckled. "Are you saying you're giving me the car?"

"Yes, of course. I can't imagine doing anything else with it. But I think we should tell people you bought it from me."

"With what money?" Walt asked.

Danielle shrugged. "No one really knows how much money Clint Marlow had. And no one has to know how much I sold it to you for."

TEN

W alt didn't care for the canned shaving cream Danielle had initially purchased for him. It remained in his medicine cabinet. Instead, he used the shaving soap she had found for him online. He finished shaving and then rinsed his face at the bathroom sink. After removing all traces of the shaving soap, he patted dry his face with a hand towel and looked in the mirror.

He didn't miss the beard he'd had for a short time after claiming Clint's body. Fact was, in his day beards were not in style. The fashion was more toward a clean-shaved face with the exception of a mustache. He had tried wearing a mustache once, yet found the necessary trimming and extra cleaning more annoying than simply shaving each morning.

Looking into the mirror, he smiled. Today was his wedding day. He couldn't recall feeling this happy when he had married Angela. In fact, if he were truthful with himself, there had been some hesitation on his part, yet he had been a man of his word, and at the time he would never have left a woman at the altar. Although, in retrospect, it would have been the smart thing to do.

As soon as that thought came into his head, he dismissed it. Staring at his reflection, he said, "No, all that happened brought me to this moment. This is exactly where I want to be."

Twenty minutes later Walt headed downstairs from the attic. He passed Danielle's bedroom. Her door was open, but the room was empty. Continuing on to the stairs leading to the first floor, he came across Max, who was sauntering in his direction, panther like—a black miniature panther with white-tipped ears.

"Good morning, Max," Walt greeted him.

The cat paused a moment and looked up to him through golden eyes and then meowed.

"Ahh, she's in the kitchen, thanks. We're taking a little drive today, Max. We'll be home later this afternoon."

Max didn't comment, but continued on his way to Danielle's room, where he intended to nap.

In the kitchen Walt found Danielle standing by the coffeepot—wearing a dress he had never seen before, her hair falling in curls several inches above her shoulders. It was obvious she had spent some time with the curling iron this morning. Busy pouring herself a cup of coffee, she hadn't heard Walt walk into the kitchen.

Stopping in his tracks, Walt took in the sight of her. "You look gorgeous."

Surprised by his voice, Danielle looked to him with a smile. Her eyes widened. "Walt! You're wearing that suit you bought in Portland!"

He stepped farther into the kitchen. "It is our wedding day."

Danielle's grin widened as she looked him up and down. "That suit looks great on you."

He eyed Danielle, a crooked smile on his face. "Where did you get that dress? I've never seen it before."

Danielle glanced down at her dress and then looked back to Walt. "You like it?"

"I said you look gorgeous, didn't I?" He walked to Danielle and took her into his arms for a kiss. After their kiss ended, he asked, "When did you get the dress?"

"After we bought the marriage license, that night I came home and started shopping for dresses online. It arrived Saturday. I was holding my breath, worried it wouldn't fit."

Smiling, he looked down at the dress and said, "It fits perfectly."

The landline began to ring.

Danielle looked over at the phone sitting on the counter. "Must be B and B business."

"You go ahead and answer that. I'll be right back."

Fifteen minutes later, when Walt returned to the kitchen, he found Danielle standing quietly by the kitchen counter, looking absently at the phone.

"You ready?" he asked.

Danielle glanced up at him. "That was Chris's uncle Loyd Glandon."

Walt arched his brow. "Don't tell me, he called to make a reservation for Christmas?"

Danielle nodded. "I really wanted to tell him we aren't taking any reservations over the holidays."

"How long are they staying?"

"They're arriving December the twentieth, it's a Tuesday, and leaving the twenty-seventh." Danielle closed the reservation book. It sat on the counter by the phone.

"They're not staying for New Year's?" Walt asked.

"I guess not. I suppose I should tell Chris."

"Might be a good idea."

LATER THAT MORNING Walt and Danielle were off to Astoria. Their first stop would be the jewelry store to see if the rings were finished.

"I was thinking about your Packard last night," Danielle told Walt as she steered her car north.

"What about it?"

"I'm not sure where we're going to park it. We don't have a garage, and it will destroy that car to leave it out in the rain. As it is, I wish I had some place to park my car."

"I'll be honest; I haven't thought that far ahead. I don't imagine Ian will let me use his garage like George did." Walt chuckled.

Danielle glanced briefly to Walt and then looked back down the road. "You used to park your car across the street at the Hemmings' house?"

"Only after the carriage house burned down. I intended to rebuild it. George was nice enough to let me use his garage. I suppose Ben's father wouldn't have been able to steal the car if I hadn't parked it along the side of Marlow House the night I was murdered, instead of taking it over to George's like I normally did."

Danielle frowned. "Carriage house? What carriage house?"

"The one that used to be behind the house. I converted it to a garage."

"You mean where the backyard is?" Danielle asked.

"Yes."

"I didn't even know anything had been back there."

Walt shrugged. "We cleaned the area up after the fire, with the intention of rebuilding. Over the years the grass and foliage took over. I guess I never mentioned the carriage house before, never saw a reason."

"I assume access was by way of the alley?"

"Exactly."

"I did wonder why your Packard wasn't rusted out if you'd left it out in the rain all the time."

"I suppose I need to rethink the Packard."

"Rethink how?" she asked.

"Maybe you should just sell it," he suggested.

"Or maybe I should see about having a garage built where the carriage house used to stand—a two-car garage, for both our vehicles. If there's room."

IT WAS NOT QUITE ELEVEN in the morning when Danielle pulled up in front of Aaron Michael's jewelry store and parked her car. "I have to admit I'm excited to see what the rings look like."

Fifteen minutes later the two stood in front of the jewelry counter and watched as Aaron showed them the rings he had fashioned from the gold coins.

"They're beautiful!" Danielle reached out and picked up the smaller of the two rings. Holding the gold band up to her eyes, she examined it. In turn, Walt picked up his ring and looked at it.

"So when are you two getting married?" Aaron asked.

Danielle froze a moment and looked to Walt, who smiled at Aaron.

"These aren't wedding rings," Walt explained.

Aaron frowned. "I just assumed, since you had matching gold bands made—in your size—"

"As you know, the rings were made out of the gold coins that belonged to my cousin, Walt Marlow, who shares my name."

Confused, Aaron nodded.

"Danielle wanted me to have something from my cousin, especially since we share the same name, and I do bear a remarkable resemblance to the man. That's why, after she decided to have a ring made for herself, she wanted to have one made for me."

"Oh my, that's generous of her." Aaron glanced from Walt to Danielle.

Walt smiled. "I thought so."

"Well, you two go ahead and look these over and let me run to the back, and I'll get the coins I didn't use," Aaron said before disappearing into a back room.

"Where did you come up with that story?"

Walt flashed her a mischievous grin. "Associating with you taught me a lot."

Danielle chuckled. "You brat."

"Plus, I'd like to be able to wear my ring now. I think the story I just told Mr. Michaels is one we can believably pass on to others without raising too much unwanted speculation."

They tried the gold bands on their right hands and then their left hands. Fortunately, the rings slipped easily onto the ring finger of either hand. Instead of wearing them out of the store, Danielle returned them to the velvet boxes Aaron had given them and slipped them into the small shopping bag, which she dropped into her purse. They both agreed they would officially slip the rings on their hands—their right hands—when they exchanged their vows.

Giddy with excitement, Danielle stepped out on the sidewalk from the jewelry store and failed to see the couple walking down the sidewalk in their direction. Chattering away with Walt instead of paying attention to where she was going, she slammed into the man—it was Adam Nichols.

Danielle came to an abrupt stop. "Adam?"

Standing next to him was Melony Carmichael, who curiously looked both Walt and Danielle up and down while making no attempt to disguise her smirk-like smile. "Hello, Danielle...Walt."

Danielle smiled weakly at Melony. "Hello."

"Danielle?" Adam said with a frown, looking from her to Walt Marlow. "What are you guys doing here? You look like you're on your way to church."

"Umm...I just had some errands to run, and I asked Walt to join me," Danielle stammered.

"You dress pretty sharp for errands," he teased.

Melony glanced from Danielle to the storefront then back to Danielle. "You picked up your ring! Can I see it?"

Danielle stood mute for a moment, seemingly confused.

"Oh, Lily told me," Melony explained. "Can I see it? You picked it up, didn't you?"

"Umm...yeah..." Danielle stammered.

"Hey, have you guys eaten yet? We were just on our way to have lunch. Why don't you join us?" Adam asked.

"Oh yes, please do!" Melony insisted.

Before Walt and Danielle knew what had happened, they found themselves sitting in a small restaurant overlooking the ocean, with Adam and Melony.

Reluctantly, Danielle pulled the jewelry bag from her purse. The moment she did, she remembered there were two boxes in the bag.

"You had two rings made?" Melony asked, watching Danielle fumble with the ring boxes, as if trying to decide which one to hand her.

After a moment, Danielle let out a sigh and handed Melony both boxes to look at. "I decided to have a ring made for Walt too. I wanted him to have something that once belonged to his namesake."

Melony flipped open one of the boxes, revealing the larger of the two rings.

Adam peeked over her shoulder. "You made him a wedding band?"

"It's not a wedding band," Danielle insisted. "It's just a gold band."

Removing the ring from the velvet-lined box, Melony said, "It's gorgeous." She showed the ring to Adam, who only shrugged and turned his attention back to Danielle.

"Hey, I found out what you can get for that Packard," Adam told her.

"I'm not sure I want to sell it."

"Fifty thousand."

"Fifty thousand?" Danielle stammered.

"Yep. Of course, it depends on how good a shape it's in. But I talked to a car guy I know, and he said he was pretty sure you could get fifty thousand for it. I swear, Danielle, you really do have the Midas touch."

"Fifty thousand?" Walt muttered. "I'd say that's a pretty good return on the money."

Adam looked at Walt. "What do you mean?"

"The car cost forty-five hundred," Walt said.

"How do you know that?" Melony asked.

DANIELLE AND WALT LEFT FIRST, claiming they had a few more errands to run, leaving Adam and Melony sitting alone at the restaurant.

"There's something going on between those two," Melony said.

"Noooo." Adam shook his head. "No way."

Melony laughed. "Come on, Adam, can't you see the way they look at each other? It's like they're a couple. And what's with those gold wedding bands—matching bands."

"Danielle said they weren't wedding bands."

"I don't care what she said, but something is going on there."

"But he's such a jerk!" Adam insisted.

"You have to admit he's been really nice lately. Maybe he just got off on the wrong foot. And ever since she brought him home from the hospital, they always seem to be together."

ELEVEN

The robotic voice instructed Danielle to turn left.

Walt, who held Danielle's iPhone in his hand, looked at it and shook his head. "Who would've thought road maps would become obsolete."

The voice gave another instruction.

"I wouldn't say they're obsolete, exactly. I suppose some people still use them."

"Maybe we should just get married at the county clerk's office," Walt suggested. "We already know where that building is."

"I'll find the place. And didn't we agree we didn't want to get married by some impersonal county employee?"

Walt looked out the side window. "We're in a residential neighborhood. Are you sure your phone knows where it's going? I haven't seen any churches."

"I'm not looking for a church."

Walt turned to Danielle. "But I thought you said this guy is named Reverend Mike? I assumed he has a church."

Danielle laughed. "No. He was ordained online."

Walt frowned. "Online?"

"Sure. A lot of people get ordained online so they can officiate at weddings. Remember, the chief performed Lily's marriage."

"I just assumed it was because he was the police chief."

"No. Anyone can do it. In fact, it's pretty common for couples who don't have a church wedding to have a friend officiate the service."

A few moments later the robotic voice said, "Your destination is on your right…"

Danielle pulled in front of the small cottage and parked. Instead of getting out of the car, she and Walt stared for a moment.

"Are you sure we're at the right place?" Walt asked.

"I feel like I've stepped back in time—to the sixties. But yeah, it's the address."

Colorful flowers didn't just adorn the perimeter of the property, they covered the exterior of the blue cottage, painted in bright colors. Whoever had painted the flowers had been enthusiastic and imaginative, yet not particularly artistically inclined, considering the uneven petals and paint blotches that looked as if they were covering some prior mistake.

"I guess this is the place," Danielle said as she and Walt unhooked their seatbelts. "But I have to wonder how Astoria's code enforcement missed this."

"Code enforcement?" Walt asked.

Danielle shrugged and opened her car door. "I assume Astoria has a code enforcement, and I find it hard to believe they allow this."

Just as they reached the front gate leading to the walkway to the cottage's entrance, a man came out the front door, waving his hand in greeting. He, like the house, looked as if he belonged in another era, considering his well-worn denim bell-bottoms, bare feet, tie-dyed shirt, a beaded headband, and long curly gray hair that fell to his waist. What he didn't have was a beard or mustache, which surprised Danielle, considering the rest of his ensemble. He looked to be in his sixties, and Danielle wondered if he had been a hippy in his youth and had never grown out of it, or if he'd had some midlife crisis that had sent him back to relive a previous era.

"Hello, hello, are you Danielle?" he greeted her, still waving his right hand as he walked down the walkway to meet them. Between two of his fingers on his right hand, he held what appeared to be a cigarette.

"Yes, and this is Walt. Are you Reverend Mike?" Danielle asked when they reached him midway to the house.

"Yes, I am. Wonderful to meet you, Walt and Danielle." He started to shake Walt's hand but realized what he was holding. He paused a moment, took a puff, and then offered some to Walt and Danielle. It was in that moment that Danielle realized the man was not holding a tobacco cigarette.

"Umm…no, thanks…" Danielle said with a chuckle.

Reverend Mike shrugged, stuck the joint between his lips, and then shook both of their hands before turning back to the house and waving for them to follow him.

Trailing behind the aged hippy, Walt took a sniff and glanced to Danielle, taking note of the pungent odor. She shrugged in reply and smiled.

Inside, the small house was surprisingly clean and tidy, while staying in theme with its exterior. The living room seating was comprised of several beanbag chairs, a fairly new faux-leather couch, and a vintage oak table with an antique Tiffany lamp. Hard rock music posters and a tapestry rug decorated the walls.

Reverend Mike led them through the living room into what he referred to as his wedding room. To Danielle and Walt's surprise, it looked like a mini-chapel. Its one window had been painted to resemble stained glass, adorned with cupids and angels. Danielle was fairly certain whoever had painted it was not responsible for the flowers on the exterior of the house, considering the better quality of the art. Two rows of wooden folding chairs led the way to the oak podium and provided an aisle for the bride.

Standing on either side of the podium, waiting for the would-be bride and groom, were two women. The elder one wore a floor-length tie-die dress, with her gray hair flowing past her shoulders. The other woman was much younger, wearing leggings and a long pink blouse, her brown hair cut in a short bob. On one side of each woman was a faux marble column, and on each column sat a wicker basket filled with artificial flowers.

"This is my wife and daughter," Reverend Mike announced. "They'll be your witnesses. You mentioned on the phone you would need witnesses. That's twenty bucks extra. Each."

DANIELLE BEGAN TO LAUGH. She couldn't stop laughing, which wasn't necessarily a good thing, considering she was driving. The laughter made her cry, and she was unable to wipe away the tears and keep both hands on the steering wheel.

"This is not how I imagined my bride to behave after just exchanging vows." Walt's attempt at a serious tone missed its mark. "I have a hysterical bride."

"We just got married by a stoned hippy. I wonder if the marriage is legal if the officiant is high?"

"You have to give the guy credit; he did try to share."

Danielle giggled. "I know. All through the ceremony he kept handing you the joint."

Imitating Reverend Mike, Walt altered his voice and held out his right hand, pretending he was holding a marijuana cigarette. "We are gathered here today…you sure you don't want a drag?…Do you take this woman…this is really good stuff…"

Danielle started laughing again. "That was the most bizarre wedding ceremony I have ever been to."

"And it was ours." Walt snickered.

"Much more memorable than the county clerk."

"You are right about that," Walt agreed with a chuckle.

Danielle let out a sigh. "There is only one thing I regret."

"What's that?" Walt asked.

"I'm dying to tell Lily about it. Of course, she would be mad because she wasn't there. But she would find it hilarious."

"You'll eventually tell her. I suppose you could tell her now if you want."

Danielle shook her head. "No. For now, I would rather not."

"Are you hungry?" Walt asked.

"Not really."

"I know we were going to go out to get something to eat after the ceremony, but I'm not hungry either," Walt confessed. "That lunch filled me up."

"Which is saying something because you're always hungry," Danielle teased. "When we get home, we could grill a couple of steaks later and toss some baked potatoes in the oven."

"A romantic dinner for two?" Walt asked.

"I'd like that. But what do you want to do now? You want to head home?"

"Would you mind if we stop at that hat store we passed earlier?" he asked.

"Hat store?" Danielle frowned.

"To be honest, I feel strange going out without a hat. I'm not completely dressed."

"I never saw you wear a hat before."

Walt laughed. "From the first time I met you until Clint's accident, the only place you ever saw me was inside the house. A gentleman doesn't wear a hat indoors."

DANIELLE SAT on a wooden stool in the corner of the quaint hat store and watched Walt try on one hat after another. The shop offered a variety of hats—beach hats, cowboy hats, baseball hats, and hats that Danielle suspected were worn more at costume parties. A number of hats Walt tried on fell into that category— headgear popular in the 1920s, such as flat caps, the panama, the derby, the straw boater—and the fedora. It was the fedora Walt seemed drawn to, and Danielle had to admit he wore it well. It looked sharp with his suit, and when he stood there adjusting the fedora on his head while looking in the nearby mirror, she had the whimsical thought that he had just stepped out of *The Great Gatsby* movie. She smiled at the thought.

THEY WERE BARELY HOME for ten minutes when Lily came knocking at the kitchen door. The door wasn't locked, so she walked in after knocking, finding Danielle alone in the kitchen. Walt had left minutes earlier to use the bathroom.

"Wow, nice dress. Are you going somewhere?" Lily asked, taking a seat at the kitchen table.

"Umm…no, I just got home. We just got back from Astoria."

"That's why I'm here. I saw Melony at the grocery store, and she said she and Adam ran into you and Walt in Astoria. You were picking up the rings. I'm dying to see them."

Danielle let out a sigh and walked to the table. She held out her right hand for Lily to see.

"Oh, take it off! I want to try it on!"

Reluctantly, Danielle twisted the ring off her finger and handed it to Lily.

Examining the ring, Lily said, "It's really pretty. He did a great job. But Mel is right. It does look like a wedding band."

Danielle shrugged. "It's just a gold ring."

Lily slipped it on and held out her hand, looking at Danielle's ring on her finger. As she wiggled her fingers while tilting her right hand from side to side, examining the ring, Walt walked into the room.

"Hello, Lily," Walt said, glancing from Lily to his bride.

Lily looked up to Walt and held out her hand. "I want to see yours!"

Minutes later, after Lily had finished inspecting the rings and had handed them back to their respective owners, Ian came breezing through the back door.

"I was just coming home," Lily said as she stood up.

"That's okay," Ian said. He looked at Walt and Danielle. "Hey, Chris just called and wanted to know if we all want to meet them for Chinese food."

"Oh, Chinese!" Lily said.

Danielle and Walt exchanged smiles, and Danielle looked to Ian and said, "Thanks, Ian, but I did a lot of driving today, and frankly, I don't really feel like going out again. In fact, I was just heading upstairs to change my clothes."

"Have you eaten yet?" Lily asked.

Danielle shrugged. "No. We had lunch with Mel and Adam in Astoria. I'll just make a sandwich later, but you go."

The next moment Ian's cellphone rang. He answered it.

"No, Danielle is tired; she doesn't want to go out again," Ian told the person on the phone. He then looked at Walt and asked, "Do you want to go?"

Walt shook his head and said, "Thanks for the offer. I'll stay home and keep Danielle company. I feel guilty she had to do all the driving today."

"No, he's going to stay here, keep Danielle company. What? That's a good idea. See you then."

Ian got off the phone and said, "That was Chris. He's going to pick up the Chinese food and bring it over. Heather's coming too, and so are Adam and Mel." He looked at Danielle and added, "You go ahead and change your clothes. We'll take care of everything."

AT LAST THEY WERE ALONE. All their friends had left.

"This really was a funny day," Danielle mused. She stood at the

THE GHOST OF CHRISTMAS SECRETS

base of the stairs on the first floor, Walt by her side as they prepared to go upstairs.

"I got to meet my first hippy," Walt said as they started up the stairs together.

"I got married by a stoned senior citizen," Danielle added.

They continued up the stairs.

"We had a lovely wedding reception, with most of our friends in attendance," Walt said.

"They just didn't know it was a wedding reception," Danielle added with a laugh.

"But you know the best thing about the day?" Walt asked.

Danielle paused on the stairs and turned to Walt. "I know what was the best for me."

Walt took Danielle in his arms. "What?"

"I got to marry you," she whispered.

After a brief kiss they continued to the second floor. When they stepped on the landing, Danielle said, "Umm…I'm going to go take a shower."

"I'm going to take a shower too. It's been a long day."

"Yes, it has. I plan to hit the bed as soon as I get out of the shower," Danielle told him as they walked toward her bedroom.

"Me too." Walt gave Danielle a quick kiss and then continued down the hallway to the stairs leading to his attic bedroom, while Danielle entered her bedroom and headed for her bathroom.

When Walt and Danielle each finished their showers some twenty minutes later, they went to bed—first in Danielle's room—and then in Walt's.

TWELVE

DECEMBER 2 FRIDAY

A string of Christmas lights weaved its way up main street, arching from one streetlamp to the next. Holiday shoppers hurried on their way, pelted by the gray sky's persistent drizzle. Many of the evergreen wreaths adorning the shop doors hung crooked, battered by the hastily opening and closing from customers seeking shelter from the inclement weather. Christmas carols intermittently drifted out to the street from random businesses playing music inside. On one corner Santa stood, ringing his bell and collecting goodwill in the form of loose change and an occasional dollar bill or two.

Adam Nichols hurriedly pushed open the front door of Lucy's Diner, letting Melony Carmichael enter first as he followed her in, giving a perfunctory shiver as he removed his coat, shaking off the moisture.

"Why doesn't it just rain and get on with it?" Melony asked as she removed her jacket before taking a seat in a window booth.

"I thought it was?" Adam sat down across from her.

"That's not a respectable rain, just annoying moisture on steroids." She picked up one of the menus sitting on the table and opened it. Adam chuckled. A few minutes later the server brought them coffee and took their order.

"Well, look at that!" Melony said, looking out the window.

Adam turned to see what she was talking about. The sky, no

longer gray, appeared to have opened up, a bit of blue showing while sunshine rained down on the street below.

"It took my advice. If it's not going to give us a proper rain, then give us sunshine," Melony said.

"I am a little tired of all the rain we've been getting," Adam grumbled.

"You and me both."

Still looking out the window, something caught Adam's attention. "Look who's here."

Melony looked out the window again and spied the black vintage Packard coming down the road. She watched as it pulled in front of the bank across the street and parked—directly under the opening in the clouds. Golden sunlight dramatically poured down on the car.

"I still can't get over Walt Marlow," Adam mused.

They watched as Walt got out of the car. Over his suit he wore a long, double-breasted overcoat jacket; its hem fell mid-thigh. He adjusted his fedora as he made his way to the bank.

"I love how he dresses," Melony said with a sigh. "He just goes with that car."

"It's weird," Adam grumbled. "I swear, the guy dresses like a freaking gangster." He turned from the window and faced Melony.

She laughed. "He does not. There is something sexy about a guy in a classy overcoat. The way it brushes against his thighs when he walks."

Adam frowned. "Now you're being weird."

Melony laughed again. "Oh, come on. What do you have against Walt Marlow? He apologized ages ago for being rude when you first met. And you have to admit, any worries we initially had about him trying to take advantage of Danielle by staying here were unfounded, considering how things have turned out."

Adam slumped back in the booth seat while his right hand absently fidgeted with the handle of his coffee cup. "Maybe it's the house."

Melony wrinkled her nose "What do you mean, maybe it's the house?"

"You know how some things are cursed?" Adam asked.

Melony shrugged. "Yeah, I guess."

"Maybe Marlow House is the opposite of cursed. Just think

about it; everyone who has lived there has not just had good luck—they have great luck."

"I don't think the original Walt Marlow had terrific luck," Melony reminded him. "He was murdered in the house."

Adam leaned forward and rested his elbows on the tabletop. "Maybe not that kind of luck…"

"No, I'd say being murdered wasn't any kind of luck." Melony snickered.

"I'm talking financially. Let's start with Frederick Marlow. He built the house. He was rich. Richest man in town back in his day. So was his grandson, Walt, who inherited all the money. Brianna and her mother don't count; they never lived in the house. Danielle has fallen into one inheritance after another since she moved in—to the point that it is utterly ridiculous."

"Utterly ridiculous?" Melony laughed.

"Lily lived at the house, and she didn't just marry a wealthy guy, she got a lot of money from that lawsuit."

"I certainly wouldn't call that lucky. Lily could have been killed."

"But still, she scored on the finances. And I'm not saying anyone who stays there gets rich, just the people who live there long term. I would include Chris, but he was already rich. Although, I suppose I could argue his foundation got richer, since Danielle dumped a lot of money into it."

"What about Heather? She lived there for a while; she's not rich."

"No. But her finances have certainly improved, considering her job with the Glandon Foundation. And now we have Walt."

"Come on, you aren't serious?" Melony frowned.

"From everything I know about that guy, he didn't have much when he showed up here. Not sure how he was planning to finance that trip to Europe. But now he's driving a fifty-thousand-dollar vintage car."

"He must have had some money. After all, he did commission that artist to reproduce those paintings, and that must have been expensive," Melony reminded.

"Maybe. But to come up with fifty thousand cash to buy a car like that?"

"You know how he did it."

"Right. He sold his book, which is now a bestseller, and there's talk it could be made into a movie. Tell me, how many first-time authors sell their first book for over seven figures, and then get producers interested in a movie deal within six months? Just how many? Tell me!"

Melony's eyes widened. "Gee, Adam, settle down. Not sure why you're so worked up. Anyway, if Ian hadn't given the book to his agent, I doubt Walt would even have a publisher now. Success is often about who you know, not what you know."

"It's that house, Mel! It's like this big o' leaky good-luck charm."

Melony cocked her head slightly and smiled. "How do you know it's leaky?"

Adam leaned back in the seat again. "Bill told me. He has to go over there and replace some shingles on the roof."

"That is an interesting theory. A little wacky, but interesting."

TO CELEBRATE the beginning of Christmas vacation, Lily met Ian at Pier Café after she got off work on Friday. They waited for Heather and Chris to join them. Lily had invited Walt and Danielle, but Danielle declined; she was in the middle of holiday baking.

"I say we stop at Marlow House after we eat here," Lily suggested. "I think Dani's baking her chocolate drop cookies today. They're killers."

"Oh, I do like those," Ian agreed.

A few minutes later Chris and Heather arrived. After removing their jackets, they joined Ian and Lily in the booth.

"Sorry we were late," Heather said as she picked up one of the menus.

"Her mean boss wouldn't let her go," Chris said.

Looking at the menu, Heather rolled her eyes.

"I heard he is pretty demanding," Lily teased.

"Guess who has a hot date tomorrow night?" Chris asked.

Heather flashed Chris a frown. "Shut up."

He laughed.

Ian arched his brows at Heather. "You?"

Heather closed her menu and tossed it on the table. "It's not a hot date. Just a friendly dinner out."

"To Pearl Cove." Chris snickered.

"Oh, who with?" Lily asked.

Heather shrugged. "Just a guy. No big deal."

"He's the electrician who did some work around the office. He kept dropping by, making sure everything was okay." Chris looked mischievously at Heather. "What he really wanted was to see if Heather was okay. He finally got the nerve to ask her out."

"Pearl Cove, pretty classy for a first date," Lily said.

"I haven't been out on a date in…well…it's been a long time," Heather said with a sigh.

"You'll do fine. It's like riding a bicycle," Chris told her.

"How would you know? When was the last time you went out?" Heather asked.

Chris shrugged. "I'm too busy to get involved with any woman right now."

Lily flashed them her Cheshire cat grin. "You know who else has a date tomorrow?"

"Who?" Chris asked.

"Dani and Walt. In fact, I think they may also be going to Pearl Cove," Lily said.

Heather shrugged. "Big deal. They've gone to Pearl Cove lots of times. Anyway, they're always hanging out together."

"No, but this time it's an official date," Lily insisted.

Lily didn't see Carla had just walked up to their table to take their order. She looked at Lily and asked, "Who's going on an official date?"

"Walt and Danielle," Heather answered for Lily.

Carla laughed. "That's hardly news. They've been dating for months."

"No, they haven't," Lily argued. "They were just together a lot because he was staying at Marlow House. But now, after getting to know each other all these months, they've decided to go on a date."

Carla looked down at Lily and smiled. "Oh, honey, I thought you were Danielle's best friend."

Lily frowned at the server. "I am."

"Maybe you are. But one thing I know, she obviously doesn't tell you everything."

"What is that supposed to mean?" Lily asked.

"I just know those two have been fooling around for at least six months," Carla said.

"What do you mean fooling around?" Heather asked.

Carla quickly looked around to see who was listening, and then she turned her attention back to the table and said in a conspiratorial whisper, "All I know, they were seen over at Pearl Cove getting all busy right there at a table, for anyone to see."

"Getting busy?" Ian asked.

Carla shrugged. "You know. They were all over each other making out."

"Who told you that?" Lily asked.

"The hostess at Pearl Cove. You can ask her if you want. Not that it really matters. They're both adults. I'm just saying they are way past the first-date stage."

"Do you think Carla is right?" Heather asked after the waitress left the table.

"It doesn't sound like Dani," Lily insisted.

Chris shrugged. "I don't know. Doesn't surprise me. That place is pretty dark. I don't imagine they thought anyone could see them if they were *getting busy*."

"I hate that expression," Heather grumbled.

"We all know those two were only biding their time until people came to accept Walt," Ian reminded them.

"Now he's almost a local celebrity with his book making the bestseller list," Heather said. "Most of the town freaking loves him."

"I know Dani and Walt have feelings for each other, but I thought they were taking their time..." Lily began.

"Taking their time for what?" Chris asked.

Ian looked at Chris and chuckled.

Chris looked back to Ian. "What?"

"You're the one among us that I'd expect to have more of a problem dealing with this."

"Hey, I accepted months ago Danielle and I would only be good friends. And seriously, haven't you guys seen how those two look at each other? I noticed it when I first met them—in the beginning I tried to ignore it; after all, he was a ghost back then. But now... well..." Chris shrugged.

"Are you saying—you think they have—I mean—" Lily stammered.

Ian began to laugh. "Seriously, Lily, you of all people shocked at the prospect Walt and Danielle might now be lovers?"

Lily scowled at Ian. "Just exactly what is that supposed to mean?"

"Come on, we didn't exactly wait until our wedding night."

Lily gasped and smacked Ian's arm, only to be met with a chuckle.

"Babe, I'm not saying there was anything wrong about that. I'm just curious why you find the prospect of Walt and Danielle moving to the next level in their relationship difficult to believe."

"Because…because she is my best friend!"

"So?" Ian asked. "What does that mean?"

"She would have told me!"

THIRTEEN

M arie Nichols thought it would be nice to be able to taste food again, especially now that Danielle was in baking mode for Christmas. Marie had never been fond of baking when she had been alive. But she had loved cake, cookies and cinnamon rolls, which was why she had been such a faithful Old Salts customer. She did have one thing in her culinary repertoire: Christmas candy. Specifically, her homemade divinity and peanut brittle she had made once a year. This would be the second year she hadn't made the candy.

Marie stood alone in the Marlow House kitchen, eyeing the chocolate drop cookies Danielle had made the night before. Most of the cookies were stored away in a covered roasting pan in the pantry, yet a dozen or so Danielle had arranged on the cake plate, covered with a glass dome. It sat on the center of the kitchen table. Even if Marie had been able to eat cookies, she didn't have the power to remove the glass dome to liberate one. All she could do was look at them and remember what they had tasted like.

From what Danielle had once told her, the chocolate drop cookie recipe was passed down in the Boatman family. If overbaked, the cake-like cookies became dry and mediocre, yet if taken out of the oven at precisely the right moment, they were moist and irre- sistible, a fudgy bakery concoction smothered in homemade fudge frosting—nirvana for chocolate lovers.

Marie wondered what Danielle would be baking today. She glanced at the clock and thought it odd Danielle had not come downstairs yet. The next moment she stood at Danielle's bedroom door; it was ajar. Knocking was not an option. If she couldn't move a glass dome from a cake plate, she certainly could not make a knocking sound.

"Danielle!" Marie called out through the opening.

From the bedroom came a meow. *Marie, I'm in here.*

The next moment Marie stood beside Danielle's bed, where Max lounged. By the looks of the bed, Danielle had made it after getting up that morning.

"Is Danielle in the bathroom?" Marie asked the cat as she glanced toward the master bath.

Max stared intently at Marie.

Marie frowned. "What do you mean she's been gone all night. Gone where?"

The next moment the closet door opened, and Danielle stepped out. She wore pajama bottoms and an oversized T-shirt, her hair tousled as if she had just gotten out of bed. The moment she spied the elderly woman—or more accurately, ghost—standing by her bedside, she groaned.

"Danielle Boatman! Did you spend the night with that man!" Marie snapped.

"That man? You mean Walt?" Danielle couldn't help but smile.

"I know things have changed since I was a young woman, but Walt is your tenant, and if word gets around that you have allowed yourself to get so familiar with your tenant—"

"He is not just a tenant," Danielle said wearily, taking a seat at her dressing table.

Marie moved to Danielle's side and watched as the young woman began brushing her hair. "I understand you two have feelings for each other," Marie said in a gentler tone. "And I suppose this explains the times I popped in during the mornings and found you gone with your bed already made."

Danielle set her brush on the dressing table and turned to Marie. "I'm going to tell you something. I want you to promise not to tell anyone."

"Of course; what is it?"

"Walt's not my tenant. He's my husband."

Marie's eyes widened. She stumbled backwards until she

reached the foot of the bed and then sat down. "You got married? When?"

"The day after Memorial Day. But you have to promise not to tell anyone. Not yet."

"Lily knows, doesn't she?"

Danielle shook her head.

"I don't understand. Why the big secret?"

"Because everyone would think I had lost my mind if I suddenly married someone who was virtually a stranger. A man who reportedly had amnesia, who had just lost his fiancée."

"Dear, I don't think anyone considers Walt a stranger anymore. He's been here for over seven months. Most people seem quite taken with him now."

"Not everyone. Your grandson can barely stand Walt. I swear, he thinks Walt's trying to rip me off."

Marie shrugged and said, "I suppose my dear grandson imagines he sees a bit of himself in Walt, in that respect."

Danielle's eyes widened. "What are you saying?"

Marie chuckled. "I love my grandson, and he has always been good to me. But, dear, I am not blind. I know he's wasted a great deal of time looking for a fast buck, trying to work some angle. I know full well had it not been for my intervention, he would have fought tooth and nail to keep those gold coins, which he had no right to. I also know about the time he broke into Marlow House, looking for the Missing Thorndike."

"You do? How long have you known?"

Marie let out a sigh and said, "Not long. I overheard him telling Melony about it. You have no idea how I wanted to give that dear boy a good smack when I found out!"

"I forgave Adam long ago."

"I'm grateful for that—for you giving him another chance. Adam needs friends like you in his life. I've tried to help keep the boy on the right track. Sadly, his parents made one mistake after another. But Adam has come a long way, and I know he sincerely cares about you, and in his own way he's looking out for your best interests."

"Then you should be able to understand how announcing my wedding would make people like Adam, who doesn't know Walt's real story, flip out and just cause me grief. We have been letting them get used to Walt being here—letting them see—or think they are seeing—our relationship progress naturally. Tonight Walt's taking me to Pearl Cove, and we're going to let it be known it is a date—not landlord and tenant sharing a meal. And after a while we'll announce our engagement, and we'll have another wedding. With all our friends there."

"I still don't understand why you didn't tell Lily. Why you didn't tell me sooner."

Danielle smiled softly and glanced to the closet and the hidden staircase leading to the attic bedroom. "Walt and I did not get to have a real honeymoon. Instead, we've had this time together—time we didn't have to share with anyone. But now, like you just said, most people have come to accept Walt, and we're ready to move forward."

"When are you going to tell Lily?"

"I'm not sure."

"Why did you tell me?"

Danielle shrugged. "I guess since you caught me coming out of the closet from Walt's room, it was one way to avoid one of your relentless lectures."

"I don't lecture," she said defensively. "And certainly not relentlessly."

In response, Danielle arched her brow.

Marie shrugged. "Okay. Maybe a little."

The cellphone began to ring. Danielle stood up and pulled it out of her pajama-bottom pocket. She looked at it a moment before answering. It was Lily.

When she finished with the phone call a minute later, she said, "That was Lily. She's on her way over. Now promise, please keep my secret and don't tell Eva."

"I WANTED to come over last night." Lily sat down at the kitchen table and lifted the glass dome off the cake pan without asking.

"Cookies for breakfast?" Danielle teased.

"One of these includes all the basic food groups." Lily snatched a cookie.

"Fruits and vegetables?"

"It has chocolate, doesn't it? That comes from a plant."

"True. You want some milk with that?" Danielle opened the refrigerator.

"Of course, you know me." Lily looked down at the cookie she had just placed on a napkin. "How did they turn out?"

"You tell me." Danielle poured cold milk into a tall glass.

Lily swiped a bit of the frosting with her fingertip and stuck it in her mouth. "I love this frosting. So much better than that canned junk they sell in the stores."

Danielle walked to the table and set the glass of milk by Lily and then sat down.

"The original frosting recipe called for whipped raw egg, but I leave that out," Danielle told her.

"Why is that?"

"I don't want to get someone sick by eating raw egg."

Lily took a bite and then moaned. With frosting on the edges of her mouth, she looked at Danielle and said, "It is so moist."

Danielle smiled. "Thank you."

After Lily finished the cookie, she said, "You know what I don't understand?"

"What?"

"My mom told me that when she was a kid, Grandma used to make her homemade eggnog—with raw eggs—and no one got sick. I've seen lots of old recipes where you don't cook the eggs. Like homemade meringue. So why now? Did people get sick back then and just didn't know what caused it?"

"I looked it up once when I started using Mom's old recipe books. I wondered that too," Danielle explained. "I guess it wasn't even an issue until the 1970s. Until then, people rarely got sick from eating raw eggs. Heck, my mom told me she used to make herself health drinks in a blender with raw eggs."

Lily wrinkled her nose. "Ick."

"But around the seventies, something changed. Not sure if it was a sanitation issue or a new strain of salmonella. I just know it was no longer as safe as it used to be to eat raw eggs."

Lily licked frosting off her fingers and said, "I think your frosting tastes delicious without the egg."

"If you want to take some cookies home with you, help yourself."

"Thanks, but that would be dangerous. I'll just come over here and mooch them." Lily grinned.

"So how was dinner last night? Sorry I missed it."

"It was fine. But Carla said something interesting." Lily studied Danielle.

"Who was she talking about now?"

"You."

Danielle arched her brows. "Me?"

"According to Carla, someone saw you and Walt getting busy at Pearl Cove not long after he moved in."

"Getting busy?"

Lily nodded.

Danielle groaned. "I didn't think anyone saw us."

"So what's going on with you and Walt?"

"You know how I feel about Walt."

"Do I? You don't really talk about it. Back when he was the local friendly ghost, you often reminded me he was just a friend. Not that it wasn't obvious how you really felt."

Danielle was saved from answering the question when the land-line rang. She immediately stood up. "I have to get that."

Lily sat quietly at the table and listened to Danielle's side of the conversation. It was obvious to her Danielle was taking a reservation. When Danielle got off the phone, she finished writing something in the reservation book before turning back to Lily.

"So when was that for?" Lily asked.

"It was another Christmas reservation."

"I thought you weren't going to take any reservations this Christmas—except for Chris's uncles."

Danielle walked to the table and sat down. "I wasn't going to. In fact, I turned down a few."

"So why did you change your mind? Is this someone special?"

"Last night when I was making cookies, Walt and I were talking about how it's going to be kind of awkward having Chris's uncles stay here."

"So more guests will make it less awkward?" Lily asked.

"Yeah, maybe. We started talking about how it might be a nice buffer if we had some other guests staying here. That way, it's not just Walt and me trying to make conversation with the uncles around the breakfast table. Considering the circumstances, I don't really have a favorable opinion of the men, and I haven't even met them yet."

"So who are the other guests?"

"Newlyweds. Apparently they had reservations in Depoe Bay, but something happened with the property, she didn't tell me exactly, so now they're scrambling to find someplace to stay since it's such short notice. She seemed thrilled we had a vacancy."

"I bet she did. What are their names?"

"Zara and Noah Bishop."

FOURTEEN

DECEMBER 19

"I wish you'd have come to me before going to the Glandons," Noah told Zara—again. He sat with her in his car, looking up at Marlow House. They had arrived minutes earlier.

"I'm so sorry, Noah. We don't have to do this."

"Yes, we do. They didn't give us any choice," Noah reminded her.

"I just don't know how we're going to pull this off. Maybe you should just forget about me and go talk to Chris. Tell him everything."

"What if he doesn't believe me? If he doesn't believe you? Why should he? We're strangers to him," Noah reminded her.

"Then don't tell him everything," she suggested. "It's my fault all this happened. I'll deal with the consequences of my actions. You don't have to worry about me. I don't want you risking your life, and this could be dangerous."

"Do you honestly think I would walk away from you now?" he asked. "Plus, if I don't tell him everything—or if I tell him everything too soon, it could cost him his life."

Zara let out a sigh and slumped back in the car's seat and closed her eyes. "Imagine what would have happened had I not got lost and ended up in Silverton."

"I just hope this Ramone knows what he's talking about. You sure the Glandons are arriving tomorrow?" Noah asked.

84

"That's what they said."

"I think I'd better go up first. I'll tell them you're in the car on the phone. And then when I come back to get the rest of the luggage, you can come up with me."

"Sounds good."

Noah opened the driver's door and stepped out of the car. He paused a moment before closing the door and said, "Whatever you do, stay in the car until I get back. Promise?"

"Don't worry. I'm not going anywhere."

———

THE SCENT of pine permeated the interior of Marlow House. It came from multiple sources—the towering noble pine in the living room—festive evergreen wreaths hanging in various rooms throughout the house—and diffused essential oils, a holiday gift from Heather.

Danielle had been humming Christmas carols all afternoon. She stood in the living room, admiring the Christmas tree, its limbs weighed down with gold and red shiny balls. Hidden in the branches were strands of white twinkly lights. They had decorated the tree earlier in the month—the Sunday after her and Walt's first official date. Most of their friends had helped with the tree, including Ian, Lily, Chris, Heather, Adam, Melony, and even the chief and his boys, along with the guests who had been staying at Marlow House that weekend.

There was no denying the Christmas spirit after the tree-decorating party. The holiday spirit continued with each new round of guests, who usually arrived on Thursday or Friday and checked out by Monday. However, today was Monday, and while guests had checked out this morning, more were arriving this afternoon.

"Everything looks beautiful," Walt said when he walked into the living room. "I think this tree is even better than last year's."

Danielle turned toward him and smiled. "Times like this I wish I would have listened to you, and didn't start the bed and breakfast."

"I'm surprised to hear you say that. You seem to really enjoy it. Meeting new people—giving you an excuse to bake ten dozen cookies."

Danielle grinned. "I know. But I really wish we weren't having any guests this week. I don't want to share our first Christmas with strangers."

Walt walked to Danielle and took one of her hands in his, giving it a reassuring squeeze. "If we're lucky, we'll have many Christmases together. And it's a little too late to close up shop now. I believe the newlyweds have arrived."

Danielle glanced toward the front window, but she couldn't see the street from where she stood. "They haven't rung the bell."

"They're just sitting in the car. I saw them from my window upstairs."

Danielle frowned, still looking toward the window. "Maybe it's not them, just someone lost and trying to figure out where they are," she suggested.

The doorbell rang.

"See," Walt said.

Several minutes later Danielle opened the front door, Walt by her side. Standing on the front porch was a man, suitcase in hand. He appeared to be in his late forties or early fifties, and by Danielle's estimation, fairly good-looking, with an athletic physique, sandy-colored hair, and twinkling blue eyes.

"I hope I'm at the right place. This is Marlow House, isn't it?" the man asked.

"Yes, it is. I'm the proprietor, Danielle Boatman, and this is one of our full-time residents, Walt Marlow," Danielle introduced. "I assume you're Noah Bishop?"

"Yes, I am. Nice to meet you." Noah turned toward Walt, prepared to shake his hand when he paused and said, "Wait a minute…you're that Walt Marlow the author!"

Walt shook his hand and smiled. "Guilty as charged."

"I recognized you from the picture on your book cover! I just finished your book. I absolutely loved it!"

"Thank you."

"Wow!" Noah looked at Danielle and grinned. "I had no idea a celebrity lived here."

Danielle glanced at Walt and smiled. "We are proud of him."

"I heard they were already talking about making a movie out of your book. It would make a great movie."

"There is talk, but it's a little soon to say for sure," Walt told him.

Danielle craned her neck to get a better view of the street. "And your wife? I believe I talked to her on the phone when she made the reservation."

"She's in the car, on the phone. It rang right when we pulled up," he lied. "She'll be a few minutes."

Danielle opened the door wider and welcomed him in. "There's no reason for us to all stand out here. Please, come in."

Still holding the suitcase, Noah walked into the house and glanced around the impressive entry hall and asked, "Do you have a lot of guests staying here?"

"At the moment, just Walt—and now you and your wife," Danielle said. "We have two other guests arriving tomorrow, who'll be staying through Christmas, like you. I can take you to your room now unless you'd rather wait for your wife," Danielle asked.

"I'd like to take this suitcase to my room, if you don't mind, but first, I need to tell you something." He glanced to the front door and then back to Danielle.

"Yes?" Danielle asked.

"I wanted to warn you about my wife before she gets here. I don't want to embarrass her, but I think I should explain."

"Is there a problem?"

"Zara, my wife, is painfully shy. And she has a few—umm—issues she's trying to work through. I don't want to say she sufferers from mysophobia exactly…"

"She has a fear of germs?" Danielle asked.

"Mostly, she doesn't like shaking hands. And touching doorknobs is a problem for her."

Walt resisted the temptation to say that might present a problem getting in and out of rooms.

"I'll confess, she wasn't thrilled about staying at a B and B. I talked her into it after the house we rented fell through. You see, if we rented a house, she would just go through and sanitize all the doorknobs, and then she would feel comfortable opening them."

"If your wife feels more comfortable wiping down my doorknobs, I won't be offended. And I understand not wanting to shake hands. I know a number of people who feel the same way," Danielle said.

"Thank you, that's kind of you. She usually keeps some wipes in her pocket. But she only uses them when people aren't around, because she's self-conscious. That's normally not a problem, because when we're together, I just open the door for her and no one thinks anything about it."

"There was a time most gentlemen did that anyway," Walt noted.

Noah looked at Walt and smiled. "True."

"Is there anything else?" Danielle asked.

"Like I said she is shy—self-conscious. So if she doesn't talk to people, please don't take it personally."

AFTER DANIELLE SHOWED Noah to his room upstairs, where he left his suitcase, the two returned to the first floor. Danielle stayed in the living room with Walt while Noah stepped outside to retrieve his wife.

"I knew a guy once who refused to shake hands," Walt mused. He sat with Danielle on the sofa.

"Was it the germ thing?"

Walt shrugged. "He never said; I never asked. But I do remember Hal Tucker went to shake the guy's hand when they first met, and Hal took exception to the guy's refusal. Almost broke out into a fistfight."

"I wouldn't want to shake Hal Tucker's hand either, and it has nothing to do with germs," Danielle grumbled.

Walt chuckled in response.

Danielle glanced to the doorway leading to the hall, listening for Noah to return with his wife. "I will admit, I expected him to be much younger."

"Why's that? Did his wife sound young on the phone?"

"In a way, but that's not why. They're newlyweds, so I just expected them to be younger."

"It might be their second marriage—like us."

"He's older than us—well, at least he's older than me." Danielle grinned mischievously.

"I'd remind you that you're technically older, if we go by my age at death—yet considering Clint was older—I don't know how old I am anymore."

Danielle laughed. "Aw, come on, Walt, we know exactly how old you are. You were born in 1899, so on your next birthday you will be, what, one hundred eighteen? I think you look darn good for your age, old man."

"In my day, young lady, an impertinent wife would find herself over my lap while getting a sound beating."

Danielle smiled at Walt. "I know you better than that. Even back then you wouldn't have struck a woman."

"True," Walt said with a sigh.

They heard the front door opening. Danielle stood up.

"You coming?" Danielle asked.

"In a minute," Walt said.

Danielle turned from Walt, but before she took a step toward the door, he reached up and gave her backside a firm swat with the palm of his hand.

Danielle jumped in response and gave a little squeal. She turned quickly to face Walt while her right hand went back to touch the seat of her pants. "You brat!"

"I couldn't resist," he said as he stood up from the sofa.

"I'll get even with you later," Danielle whispered to Walt as they made their way to the door.

"I'm counting on it," he teased, reaching out and giving her backside another swat, this one much gentler.

───────

WHEN DANIELLE MET Zara a few minutes later, she wondered briefly if the woman had been a model. Dressed in a black turtleneck sweater and dark slacks, Zara was tall and thin, with a pretty face and shortly cropped hair, with big blue eyes. Danielle had always been envious of taller women, because they were able to carry additional weight. Zara lacked Danielle's curves, although Danielle never considered herself especially curvy, not when standing beside Lily. She guessed Zara was in her forties and suspected Walt might be correct; this was probably a second marriage for one or both of them.

Danielle noticed Zara wasn't carrying a purse, and thought, *A girl after my own heart*. There were many times Danielle had refused to carry a purse, often using one of her pockets to hold her phone and ID, yet in the last year or so she had begun carrying a purse more frequently.

"Would you like a quick tour around the house?" Danielle

offered after introductions were made. "So you'll know your way around."

"That would be lovely," Zara told her.

Danielle started with the parlor and then went to the living room, pausing a moment at the downstairs bedroom.

"I normally save this room for guests who have difficulty with the stairs," Danielle explained. "Tomorrow we have two gentlemen arriving, and one of them will be staying in this room."

She gave them a quick tour of the kitchen and then took them into the library, Walt trailing behind them. Displayed where the original portraits had once stood were Clint's reproductions. Danielle explained the paintings' history.

Zara studied the portrait of Walt and then looked over to him. "She's right, you do look just like your cousin."

"That's what I've been told."

Zara turned her attention back to the painting and cocked her head slightly. Still looking at it, she said, "I can almost imagine you stepping out of that painting. That you are Walt Marlow. This Walt Marlow."

FIFTEEN

A fter coming into the kitchen, Danielle slipped on a Christmas apron over her jeans and blouse, its front adorned with an appliqué red-nosed reindeer. The apron had belonged to her cousin Cheryl. They had all had one—her parents, her aunt and uncle, and Cheryl's younger brother. But now they were all gone—there was no one left from her family, but she now had Walt. Walt was her family, as were her friends.

A Santa appliqué decorated her apron, but it needed mending, which was why she had decided to wear her cousin's apron today. Perhaps tomorrow she would wear her mother's, and the next day, her aunt's. The Christmas aprons had been a family tradition, and they had all been wearing them the last time she had seen them—in her Christmas dream hop two years ago, courtesy of Walt. Danielle smiled at the memory, reminding her of another reason she had fallen in love with a ghost.

"Do I smell cookies?" Walt asked as he walked into the kitchen.

Danielle, who had just pulled a cookie sheet from the oven, paused a moment and looked back at Walt. "I swear, you have a sixth sense when it comes to cookies."

"It hardly takes a sixth sense. I can smell them. And I'm fairly certain my sense of smell is included in the standard five." Walt tried to snatch a chocolate chip cookie from the hot sheet, but Danielle swatted him away.

"Stop that, you're going to burn yourself, and they need to firm up anyway." Danielle set the cookie sheet on the hot plate while Walt stood by, waiting anxiously for a taste. "And I meant you have a sixth sense when it comes to knowing when they're coming out of the oven. You always seem to know."

"It's a gift." Walt took a seat at the kitchen table, his eyes still on the warm cookies.

"What do you think of our new guests?" Danielle gingerly removed the cookies from the pan and set them on a plate.

"His wife didn't seem that shy to me," Walt said.

"Maybe she's just shy in large groups," Danielle suggested.

"Perhaps. But I do believe she has that germ phobia. I noticed she didn't use the handrail going up and down the stairs."

Danielle cringed. "That doesn't thrill me. We've already had one disastrous fall down our stairs."

"In all fairness, she didn't trip or just fall, she was pushed," Walt reminded her.

"Still. It's not safe walking up and down stairs without holding onto the rail."

"I don't think you need to worry about that right now. She made it back down the stairs safely, and they just left the house. Noah told me they were going to take a walk along the beach."

"I hope they brought their jackets." Danielle shivered at the thought.

"Yes, they were both wearing jackets," Walt assured her. "Now, what about that cookie?"

Danielle grabbed a napkin and used it to plate one warm cookie. She handed it to Walt and then returned to the counter to place more cookie dough on a fresh cookie sheet.

"Have I told you I love you lately?" While his words of affection were directed at her, his gaze was focused on what Danielle had just given him.

"Are you talking to me or the cookie?"

"A little of both." He laughed.

"You only love me for my cooking," Danielle teased, her back to him.

"They do say the way to a man's heart is through his stomach." He bit the cookie in half and then glanced over to Danielle, who was focused on her task at hand. He turned his attention to the cookies she had set on the plate.

Finishing the freshly baked treat, he licked the warm chocolate off his fingers and glanced at Danielle and then to the plate again. The next moment, one of the cookies lifted up and off the plate and began floating across the room to him. Just as it reached his hand, Danielle, her back still to him, said, "I saw that."

OVERHEAD, the sky was gray yet free of drizzle and rain. Noah wrapped his arms around his waist, pressing his jacket closer to his body, attempting to ward off the chill. Zara, who walked beside him up the road as they headed north, seemed more interested in what was on the other side of the street.

"I had no idea he was the author," Noah told Zara. He tucked his hands in his coat pockets and shivered.

"That's the book you just finished reading?" she asked.

"Yes. It hasn't been out long, but it's been number one on the bestseller list for a couple of weeks now, which is pretty amazing considering this is his first book. Of course, I imagine part of it goes back to it's all about who you know."

"What do you mean by that?" she asked.

"In one of the reviews I read about the book, it mentioned how Marlow's neighbor is Jon Altar. According to the article, Altar read the book and passed it on to his agent. The rest is history."

"I've always loved Jon Altar's work." Zara stopped walking a moment and then looked down the street toward Marlow House. "That must mean Altar lives around here. That's strange, when I checked the houses on this street, I didn't come across his name."

"I'm pretty sure it's a pen name."

Zara let out a sigh and turned her attention back to where they were headed. "We could use someone like Jon Altar."

"Knowing what I know now, Marlow's book makes sense."

"I never realized how bizarre this world was," Zara noted.

"That's for sure."

Zara stopped abruptly and looked across the street. "There it is."

Noah looked at the house that had Zara's attention. "That's where Chris lives?"

She nodded. "Yes. And the woman who works for him, she lives a couple of houses down from Marlow House, going the other way."

"I wonder if he's home," he asked.

"There's no car in the driveway, but I would expect him to park in the garage."

"You certain he didn't get a good look at you?"

"Like I said, I only saw him from a distance. I didn't want him to get a good look at me. I figured it might complicate things if he recognized me," she explained.

"But the woman who works for him, she saw you?"

"Yeah. Which is why I need to avoid her if possible."

"Maybe you should have dyed your hair or worn a wig?" he suggested.

"Funny, Noah." She didn't sound amused.

"Sorry. But if you can't avoid her, you'll just have to make her think she must have seen your double. They say everyone has one."

A moment later a car came driving down the street and turned into Chris's driveway.

"There he is," Zara whispered.

"Let's cross the street, like we're going to the beach," Noah suggested.

By the time they reached the sidewalk on the other side of the street, Chris was already out of his car, getting something out of the trunk.

"Hello. It's a beautiful day, isn't it?" Noah cheerfully greeted Chris, Zara by his side.

Chris, who had just closed his trunk, paused a moment and looked up at the dismal gray sky. "Where are you from, the North Pole?"

"I guess I just love this type of weather," Noah lied, feeling foolish for his opening statement.

Chris turned to the pair and smiled. "Yeah, a lot of people don't have a problem with the gloom, but I wouldn't mind a bit more sunshine this time of year. So, are you new in the neighborhood or just visiting?"

"Just visiting for the holidays. We're staying at Marlow House through Christmas," Noah explained.

"Ahh, so you're the other guests. Danielle told me you were coming in today."

"You're friends with Danielle Boatman?" Zara asked.

"Yes." Holding the bag he had removed from his trunk, Chris walked down his driveway toward the pair, who stood on the sidewalk. "Marlow House is where I stayed when I first arrived in Frederickport. In fact, it was also Christmastime, two years ago. Marlow House is always quite festive this time of year, and if you like Christmas cookies, you came to the right place," Chris said with a chuckle.

"Good to know. I haven't tried any of her cookies yet. I'm Noah Bishop, by the way, and this is my wife, Zara."

"Chris Johnson," Chris said and then shook Noah's offered hand. After the handshake ended, Chris turned to Zara, but her arms were firmly folded across her waist as she nodded to him and smiled. It was obvious to Chris she wasn't interested in shaking his hand.

"Nice to meet you, Chris. Maybe we'll be seeing you around while we're here," Noah said.

"You will. I'll be having Christmas dinner with you all at Marlow House, but I imagine you'll see me again before then. My uncles are the other guests staying there this week. They're arriving tomorrow."

"Danielle mentioned that," Zara said.

The sound of barking came from Chris's house. All three turned toward it. In the window, her head shoved between an opening in the curtains, was a pit bull barking furiously.

Chris looked backed to Noah and Zara and said, "I'd better get going before Hunny starts eating the furniture. Nice meeting you both. Enjoy your time in Frederickport."

"Thank you," Noah said.

"See you later," Chris called out as he turned toward his house and started up the driveway.

"Do you have any doubts now?" Zara asked after Chris went into his house, and they started down the street.

Noah shook his head. "No, it's him."

WALT WAS STILL SITTING at the kitchen table when Chris knocked on the back door twenty minutes later. Chris didn't wait for a response, but just walked in. He hadn't seen Danielle in the kitchen when he had first peeked in the window, but he found her standing at the kitchen sink, washing a mixing bowl, when he walked in.

"Rumor has it you're baking cookies," Chris said.

"You'd better hurry before Walt eats them all," Danielle teased as she turned to face him.

"Even I couldn't eat all the cookies you bake," Walt said as he gave Chris a nod and pointed to the plate of cookies, silently suggesting to help himself. "Although, I am giving it my best shot."

Chris grabbed a couple of cookies from the plate and then headed for the table to sit with Walt. En route there Danielle stopped what she was doing and handed him a paper napkin.

"I met your guests," Chris said after taking his first bite of cookie.

"The Bishops," Danielle said. "They arrived this afternoon. I suspect you met them while they were taking their walk?"

"Yes, they were down by my house. He seemed pretty friendly, but she didn't say much."

"According to him, his wife's extremely shy, but she didn't seem particularly shy when we met her," Walt said.

"When do you think my uncles are going to arrive?" Chris asked.

Danielle dried her hands on a dishtowel and then tossed it on the counter as she headed to the table. "They're flying into Portland. I don't expect them until later tomorrow afternoon." Danielle sat down at the table.

"There was something familiar about him," Chris said after finishing his first cookie.

"You mean Mr. Bishop?" Danielle asked.

Chris nodded and broke his cookie in half. "It was something about his laugh. Driving me nuts, I'm trying to place it."

SIXTEEN

E arly Tuesday morning Danielle turned off the baby monitor and put it in her top dresser drawer. She wondered what people would think if they found it in her room. She smiled at the thought. She and Walt hadn't been married long when they realized the attic bedroom suited them best. The attic suite was larger than her room, and its modern bathroom and larger shower was much nicer than hers on the second floor.

However, there was one problem. If they had guests and one needed her in the middle of the night, there would be no one in her room to hear the knocks. It didn't take her long to find a solution—a baby monitor. Each night she would set it on the table by her locked bedroom door and turn it on. Upstairs by their bed was the receiver, and if anyone knocked or called her name outside her door on the second floor, she would hear them.

Danielle felt a little guilty knowing that when Joanne stripped her bed each week, she was removing clean sheets—washing clean sheets—and then remaking a bed that didn't need to be made. She was tempted to tell Joanne that she would be doing her own sheets, but she was reluctant to do that, since the housekeeper was sometimes a bit territorial over her household duties.

After dressing for the day, Danielle headed downstairs. She found Walt in the kitchen, standing by the sink. He had already made coffee and picked up the newspaper from the front porch.

"Good morning," Danielle said as she breezed into the room.

"Hmmm…didn't I just see someone who looked a lot like you… but she was wearing a sexy little nightshirt and her hair was all messy, rather adorable."

Danielle shushed Walt and glanced back to the door leading to the hallway, yet she was unable to suppress her grin. "Shhh, someone might hear you!"

"We're the only ones downstairs. Your guests are still in bed."

Danielle gave Walt a quick kiss before filling her cup. "Thanks for making the coffee."

"My pleasure." He gave Danielle a little salute with his cup and then turned and walked to the kitchen table, where he sat down with the newspaper and his cup of coffee.

Still standing by the counter, about to take a sip from her cup after adding cream, Danielle looked down into her coffee and to her annoyance found red and green glitter floating with the cream, with more falling from the ceiling into the cup.

"Eva! Please not in the coffee!" Danielle begged.

The next moment Eva fully materialized. "Sorry, Danielle."

Danielle looked down into her coffee cup and found the glitter gone. "Thank you." She walked to the table and sat down with Walt, who had just looked up from the paper at Eva's arrival.

"I'm in the Christmas spirit!" Eva said with a flair as she threw her arms in the air, tossing more green and red glitter. Fortunately, this time none landed in the coffee.

Dressed in a formfitting, full-length green velvet dress, with a wide skirt and white fur collar and hat, Eva Thorndike—the onetime silent screen star who bore a striking resemblance to the Gibson Girl, and who was now a ghost—twirled round and round merrily in the center of the kitchen while Walt and Danielle watched.

The next moment Marie appeared. "Are you done with the glitter yet?"

Eva stopped twirling and frowned at the three, none of whom seemed to appreciate her festive entrance. "You are all such party poopers."

"Sorry, dear," Marie said. "But ghostly glitter is not much better than real glitter—and real glitter should be outlawed."

Eva was about to respond to Marie's commentary when Noah walked into the kitchen.

"Good morning," he said brightly.

Marie turned to the man and eyed him up and down. "So this is one of your new guests?"

"I'm more curious to see what Chris's uncles look like," Eva said.

"Good morning," Danielle called from the table. "Help yourself to some coffee. Everything's right there." She pointed to where the coffee pot sat on the counter. Several clean mugs and spoons and a creamer and sugar bowl sat nearby, along with several flavored creamer options.

"Thank you." Noah poured himself a cup.

"Is your wife up?" Walt asked.

"No. She's still sleeping." Coffee cup in hand, Noah headed to the table and walked through Marie, who failed to get out of his way soon enough.

"I hate when that happens," Marie grumbled.

"I was just about to start breakfast, but I can wait until she wakes up," Danielle offered.

"You do the cooking?" Noah asked.

"Sometimes. My only employee is Joanne, who does house cleaning and some of the cooking. But she's not going to be here this week. She left yesterday to go visit her family for Christmas," Danielle explained.

"I know you don't mind the cooking—which I would hate…" Marie shivered at the thought. "But, dear, are you going to be doing the housekeeping this week too?"

Noah, who had been looking at Danielle, failed to notice Walt tilting his head slightly at Marie to get her attention. Once Walt caught the ghost's notice, he nodded toward the broom sitting in the corner of the kitchen, behind Noah.

"To be honest, Zara isn't much for breakfast, so don't worry about her," Noah told Danielle. "I doubt she'll come down for breakfast while we're here."

"Walt, are you saying you're going to help with the house-keeping chores?" Marie asked.

Walt grinned as the broom rose in the air and did a little dance before setting back down. Noah saw none of it.

"That's cheating." Marie laughed. "But I wish I could have done that when I was alive! Heavens, I wish I could do it now that I'm dead!"

"WE HAVE one less thing to worry about," Noah told Zara when he returned to their room after breakfast.

"What's that?" she asked.

"The housekeeper you told me about, Joanne Johnson, she's not working this week. That means the only people staying in the house are Walt and Danielle—and, of course, the Glandons."

"That's a break. I'll admit that one was stressing me out. But there's still her friends across the street," she reminded him.

"We just have to be diligent."

"You mean I have to pull off this recluse act."

Noah glanced at his watch and said, "What time did you say the Glandons will be here?"

"Loyd said they should arrive by four. Maybe sooner, depending on traffic. They're flying into Portland, and then they're renting a car."

"Would you like to do something until then?" he asked.

"I suppose I could give you a tour of Frederickport, show you where Chris has his office."

"Sounds good."

EVA THORNDIKE, still clad in her green velvet gown, stood alone in Marlow House's living room, looking out the front window. Minutes earlier it had started to rain.

Danielle, who was just checking on the downstairs bedroom to see if everything was in order, peeked into the living room and spied Eva.

"Where did Marie go?" Danielle asked as she walked into the room.

Eva turned from the window to Danielle. "She went off to see what her grandson was up to."

"I wonder what Adam would think if he knew his grandmother was always keeping an eye on him."

"I imagine he might be embarrassed." Eva laughed.

Now standing next to Eva, Danielle said, "I've always been told spirits didn't watch their loved ones in—well, embarrassing situations."

Eva cocked her brow and looked at Danielle. "Oh really? And didn't you have to get Walt to agree the bathroom was off-limits because he saw a little too much when you first moved in?"

Danielle frowned. "How did you know that?"

Eva smiled and looked back out the window. "You'd be surprised at what I know."

"So you're saying it's a myth that our deceased loved ones don't —look in on our wedding night, for example?"

"That—myth, as you call it—is something the living say to make themselves feel better. But I suppose it is generally true. An earthbound spirit—one cognizant of his or her reality—typically doesn't do something he or she wouldn't do when alive, such as intrude on a love one's private moments."

"I suppose you're right," Danielle agreed. "Fortunately, since I can normally see ghosts when they're lurking around, I have a little more control over what they see."

"Ahh, but that's not always the case; remember Walt," Eva reminded her.

Danielle flashed Eva a smile. "True, but Walt was a clever ghost when it came to harnessing energy. I suspect most spirits can't conceal themselves from me."

Eva nodded. "True."

Looking back out the window, Eva said, "It's raining pretty hard now. Not safe to drive in this type of weather. I wonder…if Chris's uncles were to get into a car accident and died on their way here, will their spirits show up?"

"I would prefer not to consider that possibility."

Eva shrugged and didn't look apologetic. "From what Chris told me about his uncles, they don't seem like very nice men. I wish they wouldn't show up at all."

"According to Chris, they regret challenging his parents' will. They explained why they did it. Maybe they are sincere. After all, what do they have to gain now?"

Eva looked to Danielle. "You can't seriously ask that question. Chris is worth a fortune; he's extremely vulnerable to exploitation."

"But his uncles are old men. They have their own money; they don't need his."

"Danielle, when was there ever enough money for a greedy person? And age means nothing. For some, getting closer to the end heightens the need—the desire to have more—to get more."

LATER THAT AFTERNOON Zara stood at the window in her room, looking down at the street below.

"I think they're here," she announced.

Noah rushed to the window and looked out. A car had just pulled up and parked behind his. A moment later the passenger and driver doors opened, and two men stepped out of the vehicle, one onto the street and the other onto the sidewalk.

"So that's them?" he asked.

"Yes. Loyd is the oldest brother, the shorter one; he's the one who just got out of the passenger side of the car. The other one is Simon, the middle brother."

"I think I'll go downstairs, have a proper introduction."

"You can tell them I'm napping," she suggested.

"When are you going to see them?"

"I'd rather do it when they're together."

SEVENTEEN

W alt and Danielle were alone in the living room when the uncles arrived. Walt spied them first, coming up the front walkway. Danielle glanced at her watch and said, "I really thought Chris would be here when they arrived."

"You want me to call him?" he offered.

"Would you, please?" Danielle asked before heading to the door leading to the entry hall.

When Danielle opened the door, the most peculiar thought popped into her head. They reminded her of defective bookends. Identical in appearance and dress—conservative dark slacks, loafers, and tweed jackets—yet mismatched in size, with the smaller one slightly hunched over and more aged. He walked with a cane, which he also used to nudge his brother to the side, allowing him to step into the house first.

They had just exchanged names and were still standing in the entry when Noah came walking down the hallway from the direction of the staircase.

"More guests?" Noah asked cheerfully.

Danielle turned to Noah and smiled. She then looked back to the Glandon brothers and said, "Gentlemen, this is one of the other guests, Noah Bishop. He and his wife are also staying with us. Mr. Bishop, this is Loyd and Simon Glandon. They have come to spend Christmas with their nephew, Chris, who is a neighbor of mine."

After introductions, Noah excused himself, saying he was going to take a little drive, while Simon Glandon made it clear he wasn't anxious to make the journey up the stairs to see his room, considering he had just driven in from Portland after their flight. He expressed a desire to sit down and have something to drink and perhaps a snack before going upstairs.

Danielle showed them to Loyd's room on the first floor, where they set their suitcases, and then she took them into the living room. The brothers each sat in one of the matching easy chairs, where she left them with Walt while she went to the kitchen to prepare some hot tea and a plate of cookies.

Twenty minutes later, she sat on the living room sofa with Walt, facing Chris's uncles.

"I understand our nephew lived here when he first came to Frederickport," Simon said.

"That's correct, two Christmases ago. He liked Frederickport so much he decided to stay," Danielle explained.

Loyd nibbled a chocolate chip cookie while studying Danielle through narrowed eyes, shifting his gaze from Danielle to Walt, back to Danielle. "I was under the impression you were seeing our nephew."

"Chris and I are just good friends," Danielle explained.

"Good enough that he moved here. Bought a house on your street," Loyd noted.

"It's a good neighborhood," Danielle said primly.

Loyd looked at Walt and asked, "You said your last name is Marlow—is this house yours?" He looked to Danielle and added, "I thought it was hers?"

"This house was originally built by Frederick Marlow, a distant cousin," Walt explained. "I happen to be named after his grandson. But Danielle is the owner of Marlow House. I rent a room on the top floor."

"Interesting," Loyd grumbled under his breath. "How long have you lived here, Marlow?"

"I came for a visit last spring. Like your nephew, I decided to stay."

"You could afford to just pick up and move here?" he asked.

"Actually, Walt's a successful author," Danielle interjected. "He can basically work anywhere."

"I always thought I could be a writer," Simon mused.

Danielle stood up and smiled at the men. "If you will excuse me, I have something I need to check in the kitchen." She looked at Simon. "When you're ready to go to your room, let me know, and I'll take you up. I hope you enjoy your stay, gentlemen."

After Danielle left the room, Walt stood up and started to excuse himself when Loyd waved his hand, motioning for him to sit back down. "I would like to talk to you a moment, young man."

Walt sat back down and asked, "Yes?"

"I assume you know my nephew?" Loyd asked.

Walt nodded. "Yes."

Loyd picked up the cane he had resting against his chair. He pointed it at the doorway, where Danielle had just walked through. "Is there anything going on between those two?"

Walt arched his brow and smiled. "Chris and Danielle? No. As she said, they're just good friends."

"I worry about my nephew. He's always been a naive and sheltered boy. I blame his mother for that; she coddled the lad," Loyd told him.

Simon nodded in agreement.

"Far too easy for a pretty face, like Miss Boatman, to take advantage of an impressionable young man like my nephew. I just want to make sure she's not someone we need to be worried about."

OUTSIDE, Chris moved past the living room window, yet not without first seeing his uncles sitting in the room talking with Walt. He hurriedly made his way to the side yard and up the driveway, to the back door leading to the kitchen. Once there, he peeked in the window and spied Danielle standing at the sink. Without knocking, he opened the door and slipped inside.

"They're here," Chris said in a hushed voice.

Danielle turned from the sink and faced him. "What are you doing in here? Why didn't you go in the front door and say hi?"

Chris took a seat at the table and snatched a cookie from under the glass dome. "I wanted to see how they were first." He took a bite of the cookie.

Danielle walked to the table and sat down. "Don't you think you need to go and say hi, so you can find out for yourself?"

He shrugged. "Not really. I want to get the lay of the land first."

She cocked a brow. "Lay of the land?"

"Yeah, see what kind of mood they're in."

"Well, they did come out and ask me if I was seeing you," she told him.

"What did you tell them?" He popped the rest of the cookie in his mouth and listened intently, waiting for her response.

Danielle stared at Chris a moment and then let out a sigh. "I told them we were lovers and you enjoy spending money on me."

"No, come on, I'm serious. What did you say?"

Danielle rolled her eyes. "What do you think I told them? I told them the truth, that we're just good friends."

"I really wish I hadn't talked you into this. I don't want to deal with them." Chris picked up the glass dome and took another cookie.

"Why do they make you so nervous?" she asked.

"Aside from the fact they dragged me through court and made me feel as if I really wasn't a member of the family, that I was no more than some mutt my parents picked up at the pound, and I had no more right to their estate than a dog?"

"Then why did you agree to this?"

He shrugged. "I don't know. I suppose I was feeling guilty after he called. To be honest, until my parents died, I never considered them anything but family. They were my uncles—a little odd sometimes, but they were my father's brothers. They're the only family I have left. Does that make any sense?"

"I understand. Some people wondered why I didn't kick Cheryl out when she first showed up here. I wasn't under any obligation to let her stay, and she was acting pretty obnoxious."

Danielle paused a moment and looked up, as if talking to the heavens. "Sorry, Cheryl, but it's true. You were acting like a brat."

She looked back at Chris and said, "but Cheryl was family—and like your uncles, she was all I had left. I don't know what your relationship was like with your uncles before your parents' death, but it wasn't all bad between me and Cheryl. Looking back, in many ways we were more like sisters—sisters that got on each other's nerves."

"Any regrets?"

"Aside from the fact she was murdered because she stayed?"

Chris winced. "Yeah—well, that didn't work out terrific, especially for her."

"I'm glad I never cut her off. There were times I avoided her, but I never shut her out of my life completely—I always left the door open. For that, I don't have any regrets."

"Would you and Walt go out to dinner with us tonight?"

"I assume you mean with you and your uncles?"

"And with Heather too," he told her. "I asked her if she would go with me. I'd rather have you all there as a buffer. At least until I get a feel for what they really want."

Danielle began to laugh.

"What's so funny?"

"Your uncles are going to assume Heather is your date. No offense to Heather, but I think your uncles might take an exception to someone who dresses like Heather dating their only nephew."

Chris grinned. "Yeah, that's what I figure too."

Danielle laughed again. "Seriously? You're trolling them?"

Chris shrugged. "Not trolling them exactly."

ZARA WONDERED how long she was going to have to wait. It had been relatively easy sneaking into the downstairs bedroom unde-tected. When Danielle had brought the Glandons to the room to leave their suitcases, she had hidden in the closet, where she had remained. She needed to see the brothers together—and alone. The last thing she wanted was for Danielle Boatman to catch her hiding in one of the closets in another guest's room.

After what seemed like an eternity, she heard something—it sounded like squeaky door hinges. Peeking through the narrow opening of the closet door, she watched as the bedroom door opened. She was prepared to step out of the closet, assuming it was Loyd or Simon, when she froze. It was Chris Glandon.

"This was my room," she heard Chris say. Following him into the bedroom were Loyd and Simon—Danielle Boatman was nowhere in sight.

"I suppose it was an improvement after living on that sailboat," Loyd suggested.

"Now, Loyd, the boy likes a good adventure. What young man doesn't?" Simon chastised. "You have to admit, when you were his age, the prospect of living on a sailboat would have been tempting."

"I prefer someplace that isn't always rocking," Loyd grumbled. Reluctantly he glanced around and shrugged. "It's a nice room."

"I'll take Simon upstairs and show him his room and then—" Chris began, only to be cut off by Simon.

"Shouldn't Miss Boatman do that?"

Chris smiled. "I don't think Danielle will have a problem with me showing you to your room."

"What exactly is the relationship between you and that young woman?" Loyd asked.

"Danielle? She's a good friend."

Simon reached out and gently touched Chris's arm. "If Loyd seems a little abrupt, don't take it personally."

Loyd sat down on the edge of the bed. "You don't have to make excuses for me."

"The thing is," Simon continued, ignoring his brother, "we're just worried about you. That disastrous court case was our misguided attempt to protect you. We want to make it up to you; we want you in our lives again. But that doesn't mean we can suddenly stop worrying about you."

"Worry about me how?" Chris asked.

"We've done a little digging on Danielle Boatman," Simon explained.

"Are you saying you had her investigated?"

"You can't blame us. You come here for a holiday and you end up staying, locating your foundation here. Do you know that woman has profited off some questionable inheritances?"

Chris arched his brow. "Umm…when you say that woman, you mean Danielle?"

"We met Mr. Marlow; the man is renting a room here. He's a rightful Marlow and somehow the Boatman woman managed to get her hands on his family's money," Loyd said.

"And then she inherited her cousin's entire estate—a cousin she was estranged from—in spite of the fact this cousin had other relatives, relatives she got along with, she left all her money to Danielle Boatman. Don't you find that odd?" Simon asked.

Chris shrugged. "Not particularly. What do you think is going to happen?"

"We're worried that Miss Boatman is going to find some way to convince you to get married, and then become a very young widow —for the second time," Simon said.

"They call them black widows," Loyd said.

EIGHTEEN

A fter sending the text message telling Heather he was outside, Chris sat in his car and thought that if his mother were here, she would be lecturing him about how a gentleman always walks to the door to get his date. A real gentleman doesn't wait in his car for her to come to him. Of course, this was not a date, and if his mother were here, he wouldn't be. Or more accurately, if his mother were still alive, he wouldn't be picking up Heather so he could meet his uncles for dinner.

A few minutes later Chris watched as Heather's front door opened and she stepped outside. Bella, her calico cat, dashed out between her legs, attempting an escape, but Heather leaned down and scooped her up, tossing the cat back in the house before closing and locking the door.

He watched as Heather came down the walkway in his direction. Normally, he found her fondness for goth fashion last century, yet this evening he thought it might serve as a nice distraction, taking his uncles' focus off him and putting it on what they might see as a curiosity—Heather. He didn't feel guilty using Heather in this manner, considering he had already discussed it with her. Chris had to give her credit, she had out-Gothed herself, with a floor-length transparent lacy jacket over what appeared to be a leather bustier, miniskirt and knee socks—all in black. She wore her straight dark hair down tonight, and her eye makeup heavier than usual, with black lipstick and matching nail polish. The army boots were a nice finishing touch.

When she reached the passenger side of Chris's car, he leaned over across the seat and pushed opened the door for her. As she climbed in, he said, "You look nice tonight."

"You're full of crap," she said dryly as she got into the seat, shut the car door and buckled up.

"If you don't believe you look nice, then why not wear something else?" he asked.

She looked at him. "I never said I don't like the way I look; I just know you don't like it. Even though you're the one who encouraged me to go full Goth tonight. Although, I don't think of it as Goth. I'm not Goth."

"Whatever you want to call it, you do it with flare."

Heather grinned. "Okay, that's a compliment I'll accept—because I believe it was delivered in sincerity."

Chris chuckled and turned on the engine.

"Are you picking up your uncles?"

"No. They wanted to drive themselves. They're following Walt and Danielle to the restaurant."

"Did you see them yet?" She scooted around in the seat, readjusting her seatbelt so she could look at Chris.

"I stopped over there right after they arrived. Stayed for about twenty minutes."

"And?" she asked.

"And what?"

"How did it go? Do you think they're sincere or after something?"

"Apparently they had Danielle investigated."

Heather frowned. "Why?"

Chris shrugged. "I guess they thought we were an item."

"You almost were. What was their verdict?"

"They were afraid Danielle was a black widow."

Heather scrunched up her face. "She what?"

Chris then recounted the conversation he'd had with his uncles involving Danielle.

After he finished the telling, Heather sat quietly for a moment, considering the uncles' reaction. Finally, she said, "Well, maybe it proves they really care."

"What makes you think that?"

"If they're worried about someone like Danielle bumping you off for your money, maybe they really do care."

"I still don't follow you."

"My mom always freaked over some of my friends, worried they were bad influences. The truth was, I was probably the bad influence. But my point being—"

"Yeah, what is your point?"

"That after Mom was gone, I realized she imagined all those worries because she loved me. Of course, I could be totally wrong, and maybe your uncles are the jerks you always thought they were. If that's the case, just be glad they aren't biological uncles. Trust me, knowing the blood of someone who could practically be considered a serial killer, like my great-grandfather, is running through my veins —well, that sucks. Big time."

"I don't think his blood is actually running through your veins," he gently teased.

"Maybe not his blood, but his crappy DNA."

"Maybe not even his DNA."

"If you're suggesting I might be adopted, no. I'm not that lucky," Heather scoffed.

"I wasn't talking about adoption. Danielle told me something interesting about DNA results she learned when researching on that genealogy website. Each of your parents gives you fifty percent of your DNA. But that doesn't mean it's necessarily an equal portion of whatever they had. For example, maybe your mom is half Irish and half Italian. The fifty percent she gives you might be all Irish— or all Italian. So the other half doesn't even show up in a test. It's entirely possible the DNA your mom passed on to you came from just one of her parents—the parent not related to the killer. And it's also possible your mother didn't have any of his DNA either, maybe her father passed her just the DNA from his mother, not his father."

"Or it's possible the fifty percent my grandfather gave her was from his whacked father—and the fifty percent she gave me was from her father. So that would make me fifty percent serial killer."

Chris let out a sigh and said, "Sometimes you're not the most positive person."

LOYD SAT in the passenger seat of the rental car, his body hunched over as he gripped the top of his cane, its bottom end resting by his feet on the floor mat. In the driver's seat was his brother Simon, who drove the vehicle, following Walt and Danielle to the restaurant.

"I don't understand, if Chris isn't in a relationship with the woman, why is she the executor of his will?"

"Maybe the private investigator got it wrong?" Simon suggested.

With a grunt Loyd said, "Considering his fee, his information had better be accurate."

"I'm not sure our plan is going to work now. There's clearly something going on between her and that Marlow character."

"I could have told you that when I caught the guy patting her butt when they were coming down the stairs and didn't know I could see them."

"It just doesn't feel right. Too much could go wrong now…" Simon muttered.

"I'm in this to win." Loyd lifted his cane briefly before smacking it back down on the floor mat. "We've come too far to turn back now. I don't believe Zara is the last cockroach to come scurrying out of Chris's woodpile. Everyone is taking those gall darn DNA tests these days. It's only a matter of time before Chris does—if he hasn't already. We need to get this fixed before we have to stomp another interloper."

They drove in silence for a few minutes, each thinking of why they had come to Frederickport and their impressions of Marlow House. Finally, Simon said, "That Packard of his is in pristine condition."

"Thing must have cost him a fortune," Loyd grumbled.

THE UNCLES and Walt and Danielle arrived at Pearl Cove first. The hostess sat them at the large booth overlooking the ocean, which Chris had called to reserve earlier that day. The four had just ordered their cocktails and hadn't yet looked at their menus when Chris and Heather showed up.

Loyd's eyes widened when he spied Heather walking toward the table with Chris. "Who is that with our nephew?" he asked Walt.

Walt glanced over at Heather and smiled. "Her name is Heather

Donovan. She lives a couple of doors down from us and works for Chris at his foundation office."

Before Loyd could ask more questions, Chris and Heather arrived at the table. Walt and Simon stood up to greet them, yet Loyd remained seated and hammered the bottom end of the cane against the floor a couple of times. Danielle wasn't sure if it was a gesture of greeting, if it was his way of expressing his inability to stand with Walt and Simon, or just an annoying habit.

After Chris introduced Heather to his uncles, the server arrived with some cocktails. The moment he left the table, Loyd reached into the inside pocket of his jacket, pulled out a cigar, and bit off one end.

"Where's the ashtray?" Loyd asked, looking around the table, the unlit cigar hanging out of his mouth.

"You can't smoke that in here, Uncle Loyd," Chris told him.

Scowling at his nephew, he said, "I always have a cigar when I have a cocktail."

"Maybe you do, but you can't have one in here," Chris said.

Simon reached over and touched his brother's sleeve. "It's the law, Loyd. You can't smoke in a restaurant anymore. You know that."

Begrudgingly Loyd shoved the cigar back in his pocket and mumbled how it was a stupid law. He then looked at Walt and asked, "You look like a man who might appreciate a good cigar."

Walt smiled. "I used to."

Loyd patted the pocket holding the cigars. "When we get back to Marlow House, you can have one with me."

"Thank you for the offer, but I don't smoke anymore," Walt told him.

"Nonsense, one cigar won't hurt you."

"Anyway, Marlow House is nonsmoking," Walt added.

Loyd frowned and looked over to Danielle, waiting for her to contradict Walt.

"Uncle Loyd, if you want to smoke a cigar, you'll have to do it outside," Chris said.

Loyd frowned. "In this weather? I'll freeze to death!"

Looking to change the subject, Simon asked Heather, "How long have you worked for my nephew?"

"Umm..." Heather glanced at Chris for a moment and then back to Simon. "I guess about a year and a half."

"I'm curious about your background. Have you worked with other nonprofit organizations before? Perhaps you have some corporate experience?"

Heather took a sip of her water and studied Simon. "Are you asking why Chris hired me?"

"I suppose I am." Simon picked up his martini and took a drink, his eyes never leaving Heather as he waited for her answer.

Heather grinned at Simon and said, "I suppose he hired me because I ran into his car."

"You what?" Loyd barked. "What do you mean you ran into his car?"

"It wasn't just any car." Heather took another sip of her water and added, "It was his brand-new car. And wham! I plowed straight into it, right in front of Marlow House. I think he felt sorry for me."

Chris nodded. "I did feel sorry for you. You're not pretty when you cry."

Heather turned to Chris and said, "Oh, shut up."

"Do you always tell your employer to shut up?" Loyd asked.

Heather looked at Loyd and shrugged. "Only when I think he needs to shut up."

Chris laughed at Loyd's sour expression. "You have to understand, Uncle Loyd, Heather and I were friends before I hired her. So we don't have a particularly formal relationship."

Heather's eyes widened in surprise. "Seriously, you considered me a friend even before I slammed into your car?"

Chris shrugged. "Sure."

Heather looked at the uncles and said, "You know, that really means a lot to me. After all, I did accuse him of murder once. That's when I was living at Marlow House."

Walt and Danielle sat silently and listened to the peculiar banter between Heather and the uncles. Since no one was paying attention to them, Walt slipped his hand under the table and onto Danielle's knee. She glanced over to him and smiled; he smiled back, his hand gently massaging her knee, the fabric of her leggings separating his touch from her skin.

He leaned over and whispered, "One reason I prefer dresses." Only Danielle heard. She responded with a giggle.

Chris heard the giggle and became momentarily distracted as Heather went on to explain to the uncles why she had been living at Marlow House. While the ridiculous chatter between his uncles and

Heather filled his head, he tuned them out for a moment, focusing instead on Walt and Danielle. The pair seemed oblivious to what was going on around them, only paying attention to each other. Chris couldn't help but notice the way they looked at each other, neither aware he was watching. It was in that moment he felt an intense pang of regret for what he had once imagined he could have with Danielle. Yet, looking at Walt and Danielle now, he knew—as he had always known—he would never be able to compete with Walt, even if Walt had remained in the spirit world.

NINETEEN

L oyd was already dressed when his brother knocked on his door Wednesday morning. Loyd threw the door open and motioned him in.

"Don't you want to go have breakfast?" Simon asked.

"I want to talk to you first." Leaving the door open, Loyd turned his back to his brother and walked to one of the chairs by the bed.

With a sigh, Simon walked into the bedroom and shut the door behind him.

"Did you sleep okay?" Simon asked.

"I slept fine." Loyd pointed to the empty chair. "Sit down. I want to talk to you about something."

Simon sat down and waited.

"I've been thinking a lot about that Heather woman."

"You don't think Chris is really seeing her, do you?" Simon asked.

"It would be good for us if he was."

Simon furrowed his brow and stared at his brother. "Exactly what are you thinking?"

After Loyd explained what he had in mind, he added, "It might actually be the better option. And I don't think our original plan is going to work."

Simon glanced at his watch. "I think we'd better discuss this

THE GHOST OF CHRISTMAS SECRETS

later. Chris mentioned he was coming over to have breakfast with us, and he should be here any minute."

"I suppose we can talk about this when we go out this afternoon."

Simon frowned. "Where are we going?"

"To get our nephew a Christmas present. If we want to pull this off, I think it might be a good idea if we have something under the tree for the boy. But first, I'd like Chris to show us his house and then the foundation office."

"Ahh, to give us an idea of what to get him for Christmas?"

Loyd scowled. "Are you an idiot, Simon?"

"Obviously you think I am," Simon snapped. "So why do you want Chris to give us a tour if it's not to help us figure out what to get him?"

"Because I'd like to see the properties. When we're done with this, those properties will belong to us, and I'd like to see what he's spent our money on."

"MORNING, Walt, are my uncles up yet?" Chris asked when he walked in the back door with Hunny by his side.

"I believe so. I heard Simon this morning, and I assume he's in his brother's room since I haven't seen him since he came downstairs."

Hunny, her tail and butt wiggling in excitement, went to greet Walt, who put down the newspaper to give the pit bull his full attention. Chris walked over to the coffee pot and poured himself a cup before returning to the table with Walt.

"It was an interesting night last night," Walt said. "Not sure your uncles knew what to make of Heather."

"I'm surprised you noticed." Chris sipped his coffee.

Walt looked inquisitively at Chris. "Why wouldn't I notice?"

Chris shrugged. "I guess I just thought you and Danielle were in your own little world last night."

Walt set his cup down and studied Chris. "Are you okay with this?"

"You mean you and Danielle?" he asked.

Walt nodded.

"And if I wasn't?"

"I'd feel bad for you."

Chris chuckled. "No, I'm okay, Walt." Chris sipped his coffee and then asked, "But this grand experiment of yours and Danielle's —is it working out? Are we talking long term?"

"I'm not going anywhere."

Chris laughed.

"What's funny?"

"That's pretty much what you said when you were a ghost—you weren't going anywhere."

Walt shrugged and took another drink of coffee. He then asked, "So tell me, you and Heather, I mean…"

Chris stared at Walt. "Are you asking me if we're a couple?"

"Natural assumption, considering you are together a lot. And I know it's something your uncles are thinking about."

Chris laughed. "No. Not at all. I have to admit I like Heather, which surprises me. She grows on you—sort of like you, Walt."

"It's my charming personality."

Chris paused a moment and frowned. He then looked at Walt and asked, "Did you just say a moment ago that my uncles think Heather and I are a couple?"

"I got that idea."

Chris grinned. "That's kind of funny. I confess I sort of wanted to give them that impression."

"Why?"

Chris shrugged. "Keep them occupied. They're somewhat annoying and intrusive. But they are family."

"They are also the same men who took you to court to steal your inheritance," Walt reminded him.

"I understand that, but I can't see what it will hurt giving them a second chance. They were my father's brothers, and while I know he had issues with them, he still loved them. I'm sure by the time they're ready to leave, I'll know if they sincerely regret what they tried to do, or if they're simply trying to manipulate me for some reason."

"Good morning," Danielle greeted them when she came into the kitchen a moment later. "Chris, you're up early." She went to the coffee pot and poured herself a cup of coffee. Hunny immediately got up from where she had been lying under the table and went to greet Danielle, her tail wagging. Danielle set her cup on the counter and gave Hunny a welcoming pat.

"I thought I'd come over and help you with breakfast. I know Joanne's off, and it is my fault you have guests this week," Chris told her.

"And you also want breakfast," Walt added.

Chris chuckled. "That too."

Danielle walked to the table with her coffee and looked at Walt. "I already told Chris he was welcome to come over and have breakfast with his uncles while they're here."

Hunny followed Danielle and plopped down by Walt, resting her chin on his shoe. He looked down. *Good girl.* In response to Walt's silent message, she wagged her tail.

"So what do you want me to do?" Chris asked.

Standing next to the table, coffee cup in hand, Danielle flashed Chris a grin and said, "The dishes when we're done."

Before Chris could respond, Noah Bishop entered the kitchen. "Is that coffee I smell?"

Hunny started to get up to check out the new person, but Walt stopped her by conveying, *Just stay where you are.*

Hunny looked up at Walt. *I just want to see what he smells like and say hello.*

Walt silently responded with, *Let him see you first—let him come to you if he wants to. Remember what I told you; people are often intimidated by your appearance.*

With sad eyes Hunny conveyed, *It's not my fault.*

"Help yourself," Danielle said before taking a seat at the table. "I'll be starting breakfast in a few minutes. Will your wife be joining us this morning?"

"No. Like I said, she's not a breakfast person and prefers sleeping in."

"Noah, this is our neighbor Chris, Chris Johnson," Danielle said as Noah walked toward the table. He stopped abruptly when he spied the pit bull looking up at him.

Danielle, who was now looking at Chris, failed to see Noah staring at the dog. She continued with her introductions. "Chris, this is one of our guests, Noah Bishop."

"The dog is friendly," Walt interjected, noticing the man's reaction. Hunny began wagging her tail, and Noah visibly relaxed.

Chris stood briefly and shook Noah's hand while saying, "I met him and his wife briefly when they were taking a walk. Nice to see you again, Noah. And Walt is right, Hunny is friendly." Chris sat back down.

Reluctantly Noah petted the dog and was greeted with several sloppy kisses and more vigorous tail wagging.

Danielle motioned to the empty chair at the table for Noah to sit down. He accepted the invitation.

Noah turned his attention to Chris and asked, "So how long have you lived in Frederickport?"

"It's been two years now. I first came here like you—a guest at Marlow House for Christmas," Chris said with a grin.

"And you decided to stay? This is a charming little town, but I imagine it would be difficult to find a job," Noah noted.

"I was lucky, I managed to find a job with a nonprofit that opened up not long after I arrived."

Small talk continued, and when Danielle finished her coffee ten minutes later, she excused herself to go start breakfast. Both Chris and Walt offered to help, but she told them to remain seated, she had everything under control. Fact was, she really didn't want their help, but when it came to cleaning up after breakfast, she was prepared to accept their offer.

WALT SAT QUIETLY at the kitchen table, drinking his second cup of coffee, listening to Noah interrogate Chris—at least it sounded like an interrogation. The man could certainly ask the questions, yet he couldn't remember Noah being that inquisitive when they had first met.

Glancing over to the oven, Walt watched as Danielle removed a pan of freshly baked biscuits while sizzling bacon on the stove demanded her attention. He wanted to help, but he knew she preferred to do it herself, because when working alone in the kitchen, she typically moved quickly and decisively in her tasks, which meant if some well-intentioned person barged in to help, it could easily result in a collision and broken dishes—he had seen it happen.

However, it would be possible to stay out of her way and still help her, such as removing those biscuits from the oven or turning the bacon, without ever leaving the table. Suddenly a TV show popped into his head—*Bewitched*. He chuckled to himself over the thought. In that moment Walt felt like Samantha.

Walt remembered Danielle once comparing him to Samantha when he was changing the sheets on a bed. He had no idea what she was talking about at the time, yet later Danielle found the old reruns on a cable channel so he could watch the vintage television show. When watching *Bewitched*, he wondered why Samantha often didn't use her witchcraft, but instead did things the hard way. In that moment he had the answer to his question.

His mind no longer pondering old sitcoms, Walt turned his attention to Chris and Noah. Just as he tuned back in to their conversation, Marie appeared, sitting in the empty chair. Noah lurched as if surprised, but then continued with his conversation with Chris as if nothing had happened.

"For a moment there I thought that man could see me," Marie noted. Walt glanced at her but said nothing.

Ignoring Marie, Danielle said, "Chris, why don't you go check on your uncles? Let them know breakfast is about ready. When I came downstairs, I saw them going into the library."

Noah stood at the same time as Chris and said, "I'll go check on my wife, see if she's up yet."

"Let her know if she's changed her mind about having breakfast, we have plenty," Danielle told him as she removed slices of bacon from the pan.

"Thank you, I will."

"I'm going to take Hunny home first, and then I'll be right back," Chris told her.

After Chris and Noah left the kitchen, Walt said, "I have to agree with Marie. For a moment there I thought Noah saw her."

"Thought the man was about to jump out of his skin—but then nothing." Marie shrugged.

"Maybe he did see Marie," Danielle suggested.

"Are you serious?" Walt asked.

Walking to the table, she wiped her hands off on her apron. "I believe everyone has some psychic abilities; take, for example, how everyone could smell your cigars."

"So you're suggesting he may have caught a glimpse of Marie, like Heather used to see me before her abilities got stronger?" he asked.

Danielle nodded. "Exactly."

Marie glanced over to the door leading to the hallway. "If that's the case, I wonder what the poor man is thinking now."

Danielle shrugged.

Marie looked back to Danielle and asked, "What's that man's name again?"

"Noah, Noah Bishop," Danielle told her.

Marie pondered the name a moment and then shook her head. "No, that's not it."

"What's not it?" Walt asked.

"I don't recognize the name, but there is something familiar about that man. I can't quite place it, but definitely familiar."

TWENTY

Yellowed teeth absently chewed the unlit cigar, which hung crooked from the side of Loyd's mouth. He stared fascinated at the life-sized portrait. Pointing at the painting with his cane, he used his other hand to remove the cigar from his mouth and then said to his brother, "I don't get it. Why does she have a portrait of Marlow?"

Standing next to Loyd, Simon studied the second portrait. "I wonder who she's supposed to be."

Eva Thorndike stood in the corner of the library, watching. She had warned Chris not to give his uncles a second chance; no good would come of it. She had learned that lesson the hard way with her husband. Some people were simply born evil, and there was no redeeming them. Eva felt protective of Chris. It wasn't just that he had looks to rival Rudolph Valentino, but he was such an adorably sweet man. Much like Walt, she thought. Yet she wouldn't share that observation with either man.

When alive she had never harbored romantic feelings for Walt. She had always considered him a beloved brother—a younger brother. Her feelings toward Chris were not remotely sisterly. However, she wasn't foolish enough to imagine a future with him; after all, she was dead. And unlike Walt, her only doppelgänger she was aware of was a fictional character created by an illustrator. Just because she would never have a chance with Chris, like Walt was getting with Danielle, it didn't prevent Eva from watching over him.

"Good morning, Uncle Simon, Uncle Loyd. Are you ready for breakfast?" Chris asked as he walked into the library. He spied Eva on the sofa and flashed her a smile.

"Boy," Loyd said gruffly, pointing to the painting again with his cane, "why does she have a painting of Marlow?"

Walking to his uncles' side, Chris looked at the paintings and said, "I guess Danielle didn't give you a tour of the house when you arrived."

"She offered, we weren't interested, but she pointed out where the rooms were," Simon explained.

"If you had taken the tour, she would have explained that is Walt Marlow."

"We already know that," Loyd snapped. "We don't need a tour to see what's before our eyes. We've already met the man."

Chris chuckled. "No, Uncle Loyd. The man in the painting is not the Walt Marlow you met." *But actually he is*, Chris thought to himself.

"Are you speaking in riddles, boy?" Loyd asked.

"No. You see, this house was built by Frederick Marlow, who left it to his grandson, Walt Marlow. That's the man in the portrait. He was killed in 1925—in fact, he was murdered in this house."

"Then explain that man we met," Loyd demanded.

"He's a distant cousin, who was named after the Walt Marlow in the portrait. They bear an uncanny resemblance. Danielle believes one reason for the likeness—one of their great-grandparents along the line were double cousins of identical twins."

"What's the deal with the Walt Marlow we met and your friend Danielle? Are they fooling around?" Loyd asked.

Chris frowned. "I don't really think that's any of our business."

"Oh pshaw! Didn't you used to have your sights set on that girl?" Loyd asked.

Chris arched his brow at his eldest uncle. "Is that what your private investigator told you?"

"We were just worried about you. Your parents would never forgive us if we stood by and allowed someone to take advantage of you," Simon told him.

"With all due respect, I don't think it's anyone's business who I'm interested in," Chris said wearily. "In case you haven't noticed,

I'm a grown-up. And I've been handling my life most capably since the last time I saw you both. Danielle is a good friend. And yes, it's true that we dated briefly, but we're just friends now, and that's okay with both of us. As for Walt, I consider him a friend too. Now, why don't we all go in to breakfast. I imagine they're waiting for us."

"I'm sorry to have to say this, but I don't like your uncles," Eva told Chris.

BY THE TIME they arrived in the dining room, Loyd had returned his gnawed cigar to his pocket. Already sitting at the dining room table were Walt and Noah, along with Marie, yet not everyone could see her. Marie had taken a seat at the end of the table. Danielle had set cups of coffee, a bowl of fruit, a basket of biscuits, and honey on the table. She had gone back to the kitchen to retrieve the rest of the breakfast food.

The head of the table was vacant, but next to it sat Walt, with Noah sitting next to him, and the seats across the table were empty. Simon took the seat directly across from Noah. Chris assumed Loyd would take one of the seats next to his other uncle, but instead, he sat at the head of the table.

"That's Danielle's seat," Marie called out in protest, but Loyd couldn't hear her. She glanced at Walt, who shrugged in reply. Marie then looked to Chris, who acted if he was about to say something to his uncle, yet resisted the temptation.

When Danielle returned with the rest of the food, she set the plates on the table and sat down next to Noah, without saying anything to Loyd about where he was sitting.

"That's awful presumptuous of the man," Marie grumbled. "Considering his age, he really should know better."

"This food looks delicious," Noah said. "It's too bad my wife has to miss this."

"I don't think I've met your wife yet." Simon picked up a cup of coffee.

"I'm sure you will," Noah said while placing his napkin on his lap.

Conversation came to a halt as the platters of food made their way around the table and everyone—except for Marie—filled their breakfast plates. Noah was just pouring cream into his coffee when

Eva materialized and asked, "What have I missed?" For once she hadn't arrived in a hail of glitter.

"Eva, come, you can sit with me. The chair is already pulled out," Marie offered.

"Watch out, Noah!" Simon shouted. All heads turned to Noah, who had just overfilled his coffee with cream.

"Oh, I'm so sorry. I wasn't paying attention." Noah grabbed his napkin and tried mopping up the spill.

"It's okay. Accidents happen." Danielle passed him a couple of extra napkins.

"I think you startled him!" Marie told Eva.

"Don't be ridiculous. He can't see me," Eva said.

The two ghosts looked to Noah, who had just picked up a slice of bacon from his plate and was about to take a bite.

"I don't know about that," Marie said. Now curious, the ghost stood up and started walking toward Noah, taking the quickest route, straight down and through the table. She stopped in front of Noah, standing in the center of the table, the lower half of her body hidden under the tabletop. Marie leaned closer to Noah, their noses practically touching. He continued to eat.

"I told you he couldn't see you," Eva said.

Danielle, who sat next to Noah, cleared her throat, catching Marie's attention. Marie looked to Danielle and noted the young woman's stern expression.

Marie let out a sigh and said, "I'm sorry, Danielle, I was just curious, but I suppose I must have imagined his reaction." She returned to her seat, while all the time Noah continued to eat.

A moment later, Loyd looked at Walt and said, "I saw that portrait in the library. I thought it was you."

"It is an incredible likeness," Walt noted as he drizzled honey on his muffin.

"What I find fascinating, even your manner of dress reminds me of the man in the portrait. Tell me, do you always wear a hat?" Loyd asked.

"That's the oldest uncle," Marie told Eva.

"I could have guessed that. He looks old," Eva observed.

"What are you talking about, Uncle Loyd?" Chris asked.

"Mr. Marlow here was wearing a hat last night when he came into the restaurant. I haven't seen one of those hats for a good many years. My father used to wear one. You probably didn't notice his hat because he took it off before he sat down. That's also something else you never see these days." Loyd shook his head at the thought and then bit off a bite of biscuit, dropping crumbs on the tablecloth.

Chris frowned at his uncle, confused. "You never see people take off hats?"

"I'm talking about manners. Young men these days think nothing about sitting down to eat while leaving their baseball hats on, and half of those are on backwards!" Loyd grumbled.

Eva looked down the table at Chris and said, "Your uncle seems a bit grumpy."

Simon changed the direction of the conversation; he told Chris they would love to see his house, and then Loyd added he was interested in seeing the foundation office. When they were finally finished with breakfast, Noah excused himself to go upstairs while Chris went to help Danielle clear the dishes. Walt remained at the table with the uncles. But he wasn't the only one. Eva and Marie also stayed, eavesdropping on the conversation.

"Walt, I have a question I would like to ask you," Loyd said when he and his brother were alone at the table with him—and the two ghosts.

Walt eyed the uncle curiously. "Yes?"

"Is there some animosity between that girl who works for our nephew—Heather—and Danielle?" Loyd asked.

"Animosity?" Walt frowned.

Simon looked at his brother. "I understand what you're asking. I noticed it too."

"I'm sorry, I have no idea what you're talking about," Walt said.

"I understand our nephew used to date Danielle. Perhaps that was before you came here," Loyd suggested.

Walt studied Loyd curiously. "That's my understanding."

"We know why he's no longer seeing her, don't we?" Simon gave Walt a little wink.

"What am I missing here?" Walt asked.

"It's just clear to us that you and Miss Boatman are an item."

"We have been dating recently; that's no secret."

"I don't think Heather understands that," Simon said.

"Why would Heather mind if I'm seeing Danielle?"

Loyd shook his head. "It's not about you. No. But it is obvious

Heather has set her sights on our nephew, and she still sees Danielle as a threat—as her competition."

Simon nodded. "Which would explain her attitude last night."

Eva turned to Marie and asked, "What in the world are those two talking about?"

Marie shrugged. "I have no idea."

WHEN NOAH RETURNED to his room after breakfast, he found Zara standing by the window, looking outside, her arms folded across her chest.

"How was breakfast?" Zara asked without turning around, her back to Noah.

"It was really good. I wish you could have had some."

"Missing a good breakfast is the least of my regrets," she murmured.

Noah shut the bedroom door and locked it. "If Loyd is trying to make points with Chris, I'd think he'd make more of an effort to not be such a jerk."

Zara chuckled. "It's impossible for some people to change their stripes."

"I assume you got them together?"

"Yes. They were both in Loyd's bedroom. They'd already gone over things by the time I got there, and they had to cut the conversation short because they were afraid Chris was going to arrive at any moment."

"I don't imagine they want Chris to overhear what they have planned." Noah sat on the foot of the bed and readjusted one of his socks while leaving his shoes on.

"The plan has changed. Which I thought might happen. They're focusing on Heather now."

"I don't think I've met Heather yet."

"I showed you her house. She's the one I ran into when I was here before."

"After meeting Danielle, I didn't think the original plan was going to work. I think they may have a problem with Walt. Especially after what we found out."

"I could warn them, I suppose," she suggested with a laugh. "But what fun would that be?"

"Fun? You find any of this fun?"

Zara turned to face Noah. "Considering what happened—considering what those two narcissistic, greedy, evil old men are making me do, yes, I intend to find fun whenever possible."

Noah stared at Zara. "I'm sorry. This is all my fault."

She shook her head. "No. I got us into this."

"No. I shouldn't have told you in the first place. You would think I would have known better. After all, look what happened to my mother."

TWENTY-ONE

B arbara Jenkins drove her car down the street, humming along
to the Christmas carols blaring on her car radio, totally oblivious to her son's glares. Sixteen-year-old Tad Jenkins slumped back
in the passenger seat, his arms crossed stubbornly over his chest as
he pouted. When his mother failed to notice his silent tantrum, he
cleared his throat, only to be drowned out by "Jingle Bell Rock."
Frustrated at being ignored, he lurched forward and abruptly turned
off the radio.

"Why did you do that?" she asked, still steering the car down the
street.

"Do we have to listen to lame Christmas music?" he grumbled.

"Tad, why are you such a grinch?" she teased.

"I don't know why I had to come with you. All the guys were
going to the comic-book store. It's Christmas vacation. I don't know
why I can't do what I want; it's my vacation."

She glanced over at him and then looked back down the street.
"Yes, it is Christmas. Don't you want a Christmas tree?"

"I don't know why I had to go."

"Because, Tad," she began, her tone less friendly. She was
suddenly no longer interested in coaxing him from his sullen state.
"I can't get the Christmas tree down from that shelf in the storage
unit by myself, and your father had to work an extra shift. But if
Christmas is just too much of a bother for you, then I will be happy

to turn this car around, go back home, we can just forget Christmas this year, and you can go to the comic-book store with your friends."

Tad started to respond with a flip comment, but then noticed his mother's expression. He had pissed her off. Barbara Jenkins was normally laid-back and easygoing, but when she got mad—well, like his dad always said, you don't want to go there. Tad swallowed nervously, shifted uncomfortably in his seat, and mumbled, "No. That's okay. I'll help you."

"What did you say?" she shouted. "I didn't hear you!"

"I said I'll help you. I'm sorry," he said quickly.

Barbara took a deep cleansing breath, exhaled and smiled. Relaxing her tense muscles, she leaned back in the seat. When they arrived at their destination a few minutes later, the front office was locked up, with a note on the window saying they would be closed through Christmas. Since she, like other tenants of the storage complex, had the combination to the front gate, she let herself in and continued on to her unit.

She parked her car and handed the key to Tad, who hopped out and went to unlock the padlock and open the roll-up door to their unit. Just as Tad finished opening the door and his mother reached his side, it hit them. The unholy stench of death.

"Oh crap!" Tad groaned, holding his nose. "What's that?"

Waving her hand in front of her face, Barbara pulled up the collar of her shirt to cover her nose. "Something must have got in there and died. A cat maybe or possum. Smell's too bad to be just a rat."

"That's gross!" Tad whined.

Still holding the collar of her blouse over her nose, she waved at her son to go into the unit. "Go find it."

"I'm not going to touch it!" he protested.

"Just go look," she told him, "so we can tell your dad. He'll have to take care of it."

A few minutes later he came back outside and said, "The smell's not coming from our unit. It's coming from the one behind ours. Smells super nasty back there."

Barbara frowned and considered his words a moment. Finally, she said, "You stay here. I'm going to go look."

"Don't you believe me?" he asked when she entered the unit.

"Just stay here!"

A few minutes later Barbara hurried back outside to her son and asked, "Where's your cellphone?"

He pulled his phone out of his pocket and handed it to her. "You calling Dad?"

"No, the police."

He frowned at his mother as she punched numbers into the phone.

"Why are you calling the police?"

"Because I just realized what that smell is. It's not a dead animal. It's a dead person."

Tad was no longer anxious to go home and meet up with his friends at the comic-book store. He wanted to see if his mother was right. Was there a dead body in the storage unit behind theirs?

Twenty minutes later he and his mother stood outside the entrance of the smelly storage unit, watching. After the police had arrived, they had called the emergency number on the office window to gain access to the unit. They agreed with Tad's mother; the odor was highly suspicious.

On the plus side for Tad, he didn't have to lift the old Christmas tree off the shelf to take home. According to his mother, she was going to trash it. There was no way she was dragging that smell back to her house.

AFTER THE MANAGER opened the storage unit, he turned on the overhead light and stepped aside for the police officers. Officer Barnes entered first followed by his partner, Officer Clark. They took a quick visual inventory of the unit. A fishing boat took up most of the space, and by the thick coating of spiderwebs and dust, it didn't look as if it had seen water in years. On the far wall was a chest freezer.

"Is that thing plugged in?" Barnes asked the manager.

"I don't know." He shrugged. "There's electricity in these units, and some of our tenants keep freezers in here."

Officer Clark approached the freezer hesitantly, resisting the temptation to vomit. When he got about ten feet from the appliance, he pointed to its cord. "The thing's plugged in alright, but by the looks of that cord, some rat gnawed right through it."

"It's probably full of meat gone bad." The manager groaned.

"If that's the case, then this is your problem, not ours," Clark told him. "Go ahead and look."

The manager held his nose and walked to the freezer, expecting to find it filled with rotting meat that had thawed after the freezer had lost power. When he threw open the freezer lid, he didn't expect to find a decaying body—yet that was exactly what he found, just seconds before he puked.

———

BARBARA HAD SEEN ENOUGH. More police officers had arrived, along with someone from the coroner's office. She decided it would be best to get out of their way. After getting permission from one of the police officers to leave, she locked up her storage unit and drove with her son to Walmart to buy a new artificial Christmas tree. Meanwhile, a frazzled storage-unit manager sat in the front office, looking through records, trying to find the contact information for the person who had rented the unit with the dead body.

Finally, he found what he was looking for. "Here it is."

Barnes took the ledger sheet from the manager and glanced over the information. "What do you know about this tenant?"

"Not much, really. He's had that unit since before I started working here. I don't remember ever seeing him come in. But I do know he was always late on his payments. He usually ended up paying a late fee a couple of days before we were getting ready to lock up his unit. But then about six months ago, his payments started coming in like clockwork. Every month by the first we would get a money order from him. In fact, last month he prepaid for the year. Of course, now it makes sense. He obviously didn't want us to seize his unit since he had a body stashed there."

———

THIRTY MINUTES later Officers Barnes and Clark showed up at the address given to them by the manager of the storage complex. It was a small ranch-style house in a quiet residential neighborhood. A woman in her early fifties opened the door.

"Hello, Officers, is something wrong?" She peered over their shoulders, expecting to see some commotion outside.

"We're looking for Butch Peyton; we understand this is his address," Barnes said.

"Mr. Peyton doesn't live here anymore. I moved in five months ago."

"Do you happen to have his address?" Barnes asked.

"I don't have his address, but I know you can find him at Tranquil Gardens."

"Does he work there?" Clark asked.

"No, he's buried there. Mr. Peyton died this past spring."

"Do you know how he died?" Clark asked.

"I didn't know the man," she explained. "But I do know his sister, that's who owns this house. From what I understand, it belonged to their parents, it was left to both of them, and Mr. Peyton lived here until he died."

"Can you tell me where we can find his sister?"

IT DIDN'T TAKE long to find Butch Peyton's sister. She lived just down the street in another house she owned.

"I don't understand, why are you looking for my brother? He died over six months ago," Helena Peyton explained. She stood with the officers by her front door.

"Would it be possible for us to come in so we can ask you some questions?" Officer Clark asked. Ten minutes later the three sat at her kitchen table.

"What do you know about a storage unit your brother rented?" Clark asked.

"I know he used to have one for that old boat of his. But he got rid of it before he died."

"How did your brother die?" Clark asked.

Helena fiddled with one sleeve. "He had an allergic reaction."

Barnes cocked a brow. "What kind of allergic reaction?"

Helena shrugged. "He liked to drink tea—especially that herbal stuff that's supposed to be good for you. He had an allergic reaction to one of them. They aren't always that safe, you know, especially if you're on heavy medication, like my brother was."

"Do you know who has been paying for your brother's storage unit?" Clark asked.

"I assume he paid for it himself."

"No, I mean since he died."

She frowned. "He didn't have the storage unit when he died. Like I said, he only had it for his boat, and he got rid of that before he died."

"So you don't know anything about a storage unit?" Barnes asked.

"Just what I said, he used to have one. And when I went through his things, I didn't find any bills for a storage unit."

"Did you know he kept a freezer there?" Barnes asked.

"Yes. In fact, I gave it to him. He used to keep bait in it. Sometimes the fish he caught. But he started having medical issues a few years back and stopped taking the boat out. That's why he got rid of it. That and the fact he really couldn't afford to keep it."

"Do you know when he sold his boat?" Clark asked.

"He sold it about a month before he died."

"Do you know who he sold it to?"

"Officer, why are you asking me all these questions? My brother has been dead for months now. I don't know why you're asking me about a storage unit that he didn't even have at the time he died. What is going on?"

"Someone has been paying the rent on your brother's old storage unit."

"Well, I imagine if that is the case, it's whoever rented it after him."

"No, Ms. Peyton, the storage unit is still in your brother's name. In fact, his boat is still parked in the unit, along with his freezer. We checked the registration on the boat; it belongs to him."

"Is it possible that when my brother sold the boat, he let the new owner use the storage unit as long as they paid for it?"

"I suppose it's possible," Barnes conceded.

"I still don't get why you're investigating my brother's old storage unit. If the guy who bought the boat is paying the rent each month, why would anyone care? Is it because he failed to register the boat?"

"No. It's because a dead body was found in your brother's freezer."

TWENTY-TWO

C rouching, her butt in the air and tail wildly thumping against the inside walls of the crate, Hunny whimpered, barely able to contain herself as she waited for Chris to let her out. It wasn't that she disliked being in the crate, she just liked being with Chris better.

"How's my girl?" Chris greeted her as he knelt down to release his dog.

"You're not going to let it out, are you?" Loyd gasped. Loyd and Simon had just been given a tour of Chris's house, and the last room on the tour was his bedroom—which happened to be where he kept Hunny's crate.

"She's a sweetheart," Chris told them as he reached to unlatch the crate's door.

"Is that a pit bull?" Simon asked, taking a step back from the crate.

"Yes, she is, but don't worry, she's a lover."

Gripping his cane defensively, Loyd took a step back, prepared to whack the dog if she came too close. "Chris, please don't let her out."

Still crouching by the crate, Chris paused a moment and looked up at his uncles. "I have to let her out, because she's coming to work with me. But if it makes you feel any better, I'll put her on a leash."

Chris stood briefly, much to the consternation of Hunny, and grabbed the leash and collar off his dresser.

THE GHOST OF CHRISTMAS SECRETS

"You don't seriously take that dog to work with you, do you?" Loyd asked.

Once again kneeling by the crate, Chris opened the door and slipped the collar on the dog and then attached the leash. When the dog stepped out of the crate, Chris gave her the command to sit, to which she immediately complied.

Leash in hand, Chris stood and looked at his uncles, Hunny sitting obediently by his side. "Yes, I take her everywhere with me. When I go to Marlow House, I normally take her—both Walt and Danielle are fond of her."

"But a pit bull? They can turn on you at any time," Loyd said.

"It's how you raise them, Uncle Loyd."

"Why in the world would you even get a pit bull?" Simon asked. "If you wanted a companion, what's wrong with something like a chihuahua?"

"I initially bought her because I wanted a guard dog." Chris glanced down at Hunny and noted the way she looked up at him, with her head cocked, panting, her tongue hanging lopsided out of her mouth, flopping around with every pant, and her dopy expression. *Yeah, right, guard dog,* Chris thought. *A chihuahua might have made a more aggressive guard dog.*

"WE'VE GOT to get rid of that dog," Loyd told his brother as they drove from Chris's house to the Glandon Foundation Headquarters. Chris had offered to take them in his car, but the uncles had insisted on taking their rental car, as they had some Christmas shopping to do after visiting the foundation headquarters.

"I didn't count on him having a dog. And certainly not a pit bull!" Simon said.

"It would be nice if he was the one to get rid of it," Loyd suggested. "If it was his idea. If the dog suddenly disappears or is poisoned, it could draw suspicion."

"I don't see him voluntarily getting rid of it. Did you see how he babies it?"

"But maybe if he thought it was dangerous."

"You heard him, Loyd. He called it a sweetheart."

"That's what every dog owner says right before the family dog rips out their throat."

IF HEATHER HAD KNOWN it was bring-your-annoying-uncles-to-work day, she would have called in sick. To begin with, she thought it was stupid of Chris keeping poor Hunny on a leash just because the old codgers were afraid of the dog.

"What are you working on?"

Heather looked up from her keyboard. It was the older uncle, smiling at her in a creepy old man sort of way.

"I thought Chris was taking you on a tour?" she asked.

Loyd sat down in the empty chair next to her desk, using one arm of the chair to brace himself while using the cane to steady his descent. "Pshaw, I'm not going to walk all those stairs. I'll let Simon do that. I thought I would stay down here and keep you company."

Heather critically eyed the old man, finding him oddly friendly this afternoon, especially since he and his brother had made it perfectly clear the previous evening that they didn't feel she was qualified to work for their nephew.

"He did show me the kitchen. Looks like a kitchen you'd find in someone's house, not in an office."

Heather shrugged. "This used to be someone's home before Chris bought it."

"He even has a full wine rack in there. Does he always keep it fully stocked like that?"

"I suppose."

Loyd eyed her for a moment and then whispered, "Can I tell you a secret?"

"Uhh...yeah...I guess." Heather glanced toward the doorway leading to the hallway and thought Chris couldn't get back downstairs fast enough to suit her.

"My nephew has a little crush on you."

"Excuse me?"

"If you play your cards right, I think you might be calling me uncle in no time at all."

"What?" Heather frowned.

Loyd chuckled. "Come on now, you can't fool me. What young woman wouldn't see what a catch my nephew is? Handsome boy, richer than Croesus."

"If you're insinuating I'm after your nephew's money—we're not even dating!"

"Oh no! I'm not insinuating you're after Chris; I'm saying he's crazy about you!"

"No way." Her frown deepened.

"It's true. Before breakfast today, Loyd and I were in the library at Marlow House, looking at those portraits, when Chris came in and told us he thought he had feelings for you. Said you might be the one. Of course, the boy is gun-shy because of what happened between him and Danielle."

"He told you about him and Danielle?"

"Just that he was interested in her, thought she felt the same way, but she didn't. You see, the problem here, Chris is interested in you, but after getting burned by Danielle, he's not going to make the move. You're going to have to do it. If you're interested in my nephew, it's going to be up to you to chase him."

"Chase him?"

"It's the only way. And if he doesn't seem interested, don't give up. Because I know he's crazy about you; he told Simon and me so."

"So you're saying Chris is interested in me, but because of Danielle, he won't make the first move?"

Loyd nodded. "Exactly."

"And if I do show an interest in him—let's say show up with his favorite cookies—or buy him something special for Christmas—or start wearing provocative clothes around him, he will pretend he isn't interested?"

"Precisely. It's up to you to keep pursuing him—if, of course, it's what you want."

Heather stared at Loyd for a moment, a slow smile forming on her lips. She leaned toward him, patted his knee, and then whispered, "Thank you, Uncle Loyd; I will take your advice."

"I'M sorry if you're annoyed at me for what happened at breakfast," Marie said. "But, dear, for a minute there I seriously thought he saw something."

"Like I said earlier, maybe he did get a glimpse—which is why you shouldn't be pushing it unless you want the Bishops to start telling everyone Marlow House is haunted when they leave." Danielle sat in the parlor with Marie, Walt, and Eva. The Bishops had taken off about an hour after Chris left the house with his uncles.

"Didn't you always say a haunted house might be a good marketing strategy?" Walt teased.

"It's not so haunted since you joined my side," Danielle reminded him.

"What am I, chopped liver?" Marie asked.

"Not to mention we have been seeing Eva more these days," Walt reminded her. "Although I suspect she spends more time with our neighbor down the street."

"It's only because the view is so much better down there," Eva said with a wink.

"Should I be insulted?" Walt teased.

Eva flashed Walt a smile and then said, "If I did decide to settle in one place, I do believe I could pull off quite a spectacular haunt."

The next moment the doorbell rang.

"Do you think that's one of your guests?" Eva asked.

"I doubt it, they all have keys." Danielle walked over to the window and peeked outside. "It's Heather. I wonder why she isn't at work."

When Danielle opened the front door a few minutes later, Heather marched in without saying hello, pushing past Danielle. "We need to talk."

"Uhh...okay...is everything alright?" Danielle shut the door and watched as Heather anxiously paced the entry.

She abruptly stopped and turned to Danielle. "Is Eva or Marie here?"

"Umm...yeah, but how did you know?"

"I figured they would be here if they weren't with Chris—which they aren't. Those two spirits are the nosiest things, and I know they have been dying to check out Chris's wacky family."

"I wouldn't say dying exactly. After all, they're both already dead."

Heather flashed Danielle her signature *don't-be-stupid* glare and then without a hint of humor said, "Haha."

Danielle shrugged and said, "They're in the parlor with Walt."

Heather turned abruptly and marched to the parlor, Danielle trailing behind her. Once in the room, she looked at the two spirits and Walt and said, "Do you know Chris has a secret crush on me?"

Silence. They all stared at Heather.

"Oh yes. It's true. He's mad for me, but Danielle left him damaged, so I need to pursue him."

More silence. Danielle and Walt exchanged glances, as did Eva and Marie.

"Did you all know?"

Marie started to say something, but Heather cut her off.

"You didn't know, I didn't know, and do you know why that is?" Heather asked.

Danielle started to say something, but Heather cut her off too.

"It's because it isn't true!" Heather flounced to the sofa and flopped down, kicking off her shoes.

"What in the world are you talking about?" Walt asked.

Heather glanced around the room, making brief eye contact with each person—and each ghost. "For some reason, Chris's crazy uncle wants me to believe Chris has a secret thing for me, and he encouraged me to pursue him. I know the jerk doesn't like me, so what is he up to?"

Danielle walked to the sofa and sat down next to Heather. "Maybe you can fill in the pieces a bit. What exactly are you talking about?"

Heather let out a sigh and then recounted her conversation with Loyd at the Glandon Foundation Headquarters office twenty minutes earlier.

"I was in the library when they were looking at those portraits and Chris came in. I heard the entire conversation and, well—they never discussed you," Eva said.

Heather's smile widened. "Chris called me after he left his house to tell me he was on his way over to the office and bringing his uncles. He told me about breakfast here this morning and how both Marie and Eva had been here. I figured, if he had talked to his uncles this morning in the library, as dear old Uncle Loyd claimed, I was fairly certain one of you might have overheard the conversation. I didn't believe him for a minute—but he is an old dude, and I wasn't sure if maybe Chris said something about me, and he took it wrong."

"But you weren't mentioned at all," Eva said.

"Which means the old coot didn't misunderstand something Chris said—he made the entire thing up," Heather said.

"But why?" Walt asked.

"Could it be the uncle is simply playing matchmaker?" Marie asked.

"Which would prove he hates Chris," Heather said with a snort.

"That's kind of a harsh thing to say about yourself," Danielle said.

Heather turned to Danielle and rolled her eyes. "Oh, come on, we were both at Pearl Cove. Those old dudes thought I was some sort of freak. And they made it clear they didn't think I was qualified for my job. No, there is something else going on here, I just don't know what."

TWENTY-THREE

H eather picked up her cellphone and looked at the time. "I guess I should get going. Chris thinks I'm out picking up sandwiches from the deli. They're probably wondering what happened to me." In spite of saying she was leaving, Heather remained on the sofa, making no attempt to stand up.

"What are you going to do?" Danielle asked.

"When I can get Chris alone, I'll have to tell him what his crazy uncle Loyd said." Heather dropped her cellphone in her purse.

"I don't care for the man, but he seems more contrary than senile to me," Marie noted. "Which makes me wonder, what was the point of him fabricating such a story?"

"Personally, I think he was hoping I'd act on it and get my butt fired," Heather said. "You know, start coming on to Chris."

Danielle nodded. "I suspect you're right."

Heather looked to Danielle. "To be honest, there was a little part of me that was terrified the old coot was telling the truth."

"And having Chris interested in you would be so horrible?" Eva asked.

"What would be so horrible is realizing I had totally misread him," Heather said. "I may not be able to read people accurately when I first meet them. To be honest, when I first met Chris, I thought he was some freeloader who'd skated through life on his good looks."

"I remember when we first met, you accused me of stealing your cat," Danielle teased.

Heather rolled her eyes at Danielle and continued with her train of thought. "But after I get to know someone, after I'm around them a while, I'd like to think I'm a good judge of character."

"As I recall, you lived under the same roof with Chris, and you thought he'd murdered Peter Morris," Walt reminded her.

Narrowing her eyes, Heather glared at Walt and let out a grunt, reminding Danielle of an angry cartoon character with steam coming out of her ears. While there was no steam, Danielle figured if it had been possible, there would be.

"Okay, okay," Heather sputtered. "Sometimes I really suck at judging people. But if I had misread Chris in this instance, well, then I obviously sucked more than I thought."

"Don't get upset," Danielle said gently. "We were only teasing. And the truth is, we're all guilty of judging people unfairly—either we give them too much credit or not enough."

Heather stood up and dug a piece of paper out of her purse and handed it to Danielle. "Could you do me a favor and call in this order for the deli?"

Danielle glanced down at the paper before taking it. "No problem. I'll put it under your name."

"Thanks." Heather started for the door. Just as she reached it, she looked back and added, "Thanks. I'm glad I had someone to talk to."

"I wonder what Chris is going to say when you tell him," Eva mused. "I warned him not to give them a second chance."

Heather grinned. "Before I tell him, I think I'll have a little fun. Let him know how wonderful he is, while his uncles are standing there."

"When you say wonderful...exactly what do you mean?" Danielle asked.

Heather laughed. "I meant it in the true spirit of the word. I'll bat my eyes a bit, let him know I think he's hot." She giggled and left the room, giving everyone a final wave as she went.

"I almost think we should warn poor Chris," Walt said with a chuckle.

IT WAS LESS than a week until Christmas, and Adam couldn't get in to the holiday spirit. To him Christmas wasn't Christmas without his grandmother's homemade divinity and peanut brittle—or without his grandmother. He found it difficult to believe it had been over a year now—two Christmases, since Marie had been murdered.

Marie had never been the grandmother who baked homemade cookies. She didn't like to bake, or to cook in general. He suspected one reason she disliked cooking was because of all those years she had been married to his grandfather, and he had demanded three meals a day—breakfast, lunch and dinner, that he had expected his wife to make.

However, one thing Marie did enjoy making—occasionally—was candy. Specifically, divinity and peanut brittle, recipes passed down to her from her mother. Which was why Adam had decided several days earlier that if he was to get into the Christmas spirit, he needed to carry on with the family tradition and make Marie's divinity and peanut brittle. After all, he had her recipes.

What Adam hadn't realized—divinity was a bitch to make. He'd had no idea it was so difficult. After two failed batches, he finally went to the internet looking for helpful tips. While the peanut brittle turned out close to his grandmother's, the final batch of divinity, while edible, didn't resemble Marie's.

Now that he had all this homemade candy, he needed to disperse some Christmas cheer. The first stop was the Glandon Foundation Headquarters.

Adam entered the foundation office carrying a large Christmas tin. He found Chris sitting in the waiting area with two older men, Hunny sleeping by his side. The moment he entered, Hunny lifted her head and looked at Adam; her tail started to wag.

"Merry Christmas!" Adam greeted them. Hunny jumped up and ran to Adam, her tail still wagging. Adam reached down and scratched the back of Hunny's ears.

Chris introduced Adam to his uncles, referring to him as his good friend and Realtor. After introductions were made, Adam handed Chris the candy.

Tin now in hand, Chris asked, "What's this?"

"Homemade Christmas candy. Grandma's recipes."

Chris perked up. "Please tell me, her divinity?"

"Yeah, well, I gave it my best shot. Like six times. It's not bad, but not Grandma's."

"I thought you just said it was her recipe," Chris asked.

"Apparently, using the same recipe is no guarantee it will taste the same," Adam grumbled.

"I'd try some now, but we're waiting for Heather to come back with our lunch," Chris said as he set the tin on his desk.

The four men exchanged small talk for a few minutes when Loyd told Adam, "It's really nice to meet one of our nephew's friends."

"Chris has a lot of friends in Frederickport," Adam told them.

"You have no idea how proud we are of this boy," Loyd said, reaching over and patting Chris's knee. By Chris's expression he seemed surprised at his uncle's gesture.

"He's a tribute to our family," Simon said. "His parents would be so proud of him."

"We realize now how foolish we were, believing we were protecting Chris from himself by trying to manage his father's legacy. He's more than capable of handling it himself."

Before anyone could respond, Heather came barreling through the door into the waiting area, deli paper sacks in hand. She stopped short when she spied Adam. "Oh, I didn't bring you a sandwich."

"Probably because you didn't know I was going to be here," Adam teased.

Heather shrugged. "You want half of mine?"

Adam shook his head. "No, thanks. I already had lunch." He stood and glanced at his watch. "In fact, I need to get going. I have another stop to make. And, Heather, make sure Chris shares the candy with you; it's for you too." He pointed to the Christmas tin sitting on the desk.

A few minutes later, as Heather handed out the sandwiches and beverages, Chris walked Adam to the door. When they were out of earshot from the uncles, Adam asked, "Hey, Chris, can I ask you something?"

"Sure, what?"

"What your uncle just said in there, about trying to manage your estate. I thought they contested the will and tried to take it away from you completely."

Chris glanced briefly toward where his uncles were, and then looked back to Adam. "A little historical revisionism. You know how it is, some people do things they're later ashamed of, and it's easier for them to try tweaking the memory—to make it more palatable. Yeah, they did try to sue me for the entire estate, but now, well, now they are insisting I misunderstood. To be honest, I think they're just old and finally realized I'm the only family they have left. It's their way of mending fences."

After Chris said goodbye to Adam a few minutes later, he returned to his uncles and Heather. The three were already eating their sandwiches, and he found his lunch sitting on his desk, still encased in wax paper. He sat down and started to unwrap it.

"I hope you like your sandwich," Heather cooed from where she sat at her desk. "It's roast beef. I had them make it just like you like it."

Startled by Heather's tone, Chris looked up and found her staring at him. What he failed to see was his uncles staring at her.

"Is something wrong?" Chris asked.

"Oh no. I just want you to know what a wonderful employer I think you are."

Chris frowned. "Ummm…ah…okay…"

"And if you don't want me to go out with that electrician again, you just say the word, and I won't."

"Umm…why wouldn't I want you to go out with him?"

Heather smiled at Chris and fluttered her eyelashes. "I'm just saying you come first. If you want me here to do anything—and I mean anything—just ask."

ADAM'S next stop was Marlow House. Eva had already taken off by the time he arrived, yet his grandmother was still there.

"Ho ho ho! I come bringing Christmas cheer!" Adam said when Danielle opened the door and found him holding a holiday tin.

"That doesn't look like wine," Danielle said as she opened the door wider to let him in.

"I think I created a monster with you and that wine," Adam said as he walked into the house.

Just as Danielle closed the door, Walt stepped out of the parlor. He looked at the new arrival and said, "Hello, Adam."

What Adam didn't see was his grandmother's ghost standing next to Walt.

"Afternoon, Walt. I just dropped by to give Danielle some of my grandmother's Christmas candy."

"My Christmas candy?" Marie tittered.

"I'll let you two visit in private. I'm going to go upstairs and work a little on my new manuscript," Walt said before he headed toward the staircase.

"So that book wasn't a one-shot thing?" Adam asked when Walt was out of earshot.

"I don't think so. Let's go in the living room so we can enjoy the Christmas tree." Danielle snatched the tin from Adam and led the way, Marie trailing behind them.

By the time Danielle reached the living room, she had pried off the lid. She peeked inside. "Don't tell me this is your grandmother's divinity and peanut brittle."

Adam shrugged. "I tried. They were her recipes, but the divinity doesn't come close to hers. I suspect the recipe I found wasn't the one she used."

"You made my candy?" Marie cooed. "Oh, Adam, that's so sweet."

Danielle plopped down on the sofa with the Christmas tin, while Adam sat next to her. "Divinity is hard to make." She picked up a piece.

"Tell me about it," Adam groaned.

Danielle nibbled at the piece of candy. "It's good, but you're right, it doesn't taste like Marie's. She made killer divinity."

"Why, thank you, Danielle." Marie beamed.

Next, Danielle tried the peanut brittle. "That one was spot on!"

Adam smiled. "Yeah, the peanut brittle turned out pretty good."

Danielle offered Adam the tin to take a piece.

He shook his head. "No, I think I'm sugared out. I probably sampled two pounds of divinity trying to get it right."

Danielle chuckled.

Adam let out a sigh and leaned back in the sofa. "I really miss her, Danielle."

Danielle placed the lid back on the tin and looked at Adam. "Your grandmother?"

He nodded. "I can't believe this will be the second Christmas without her."

"Oh, Adam, I'm still here." Marie reached out to touch him, but her hand moved through his.

TWENTY-FOUR

"I don't need all this drama," Danielle whispered to Walt as they made their way up the staircase Wednesday evening.

"Now you don't want drama?" Walt asked with a chuckle. "Since you walked in my front door, it's been nonstop drama."

"That may be true. But I'm over it," Danielle said with a sigh. "I just want us to enjoy a nice quiet Christmas together."

"I wish I could take you on a dream hop—an escape from reality."

Danielle flashed Walt a soft smile. "That's okay, in spite of the drama, even the best dreams aren't as good as some realities. I'm rather grateful for my current reality, in spite of my griping."

"I understand what you're saying."

When they reached the top floor, they found Simon walking out of one of the upstairs bathrooms.

Simon greeted them with a smile and asked, "You two calling it a night?"

"Yes, how about you?" Walt asked.

"Yes, I already said goodnight to my brother and took a shower."

"Have a good evening," Danielle said.

"You too. And, Danielle, Walt…" Simon stopped in front of his bedroom door and turned to face them. "Danielle, thank you for welcoming us into your home. And both of you, thanks for being such a good friend to my nephew. He speaks highly of both of you. Loyd and I are so proud of him."

"Well, Chris is one of the good guys," Danielle said.

"Yes, he is. You have no idea how blessed my brother and I feel now that Chris is giving us this second chance. Especially when we realize this means as much to him as it does to us. Family is so important. Thank you again."

"Umm...yes...family is important," Danielle muttered.

She and Walt wished Simon another good night and then started down the hallway toward their rooms. When the two reached her bedroom door, Danielle glanced down the hall. Simon continued to stand by his doorway, his eyes watching them. She flashed him a smile and then looked to Walt and wished him a goodnight.

Once in her bedroom, she locked the door and then removed the baby monitor from the dresser drawer, set it up, and turned it on. Hastily she undressed and then tossed her clothes in the hamper. Before heading upstairs, she slipped on her robe, intending to take a shower in the new attic bathroom. Danielle walked to her closet and opened the doors. Pushing aside her hanging clothes, she slid open the back panel and started up the hidden staircase to Walt's room.

"What took you so long?" Walt greeted her when she entered the room.

"I had to take my clothes off."

Walt arched his brows. "I could have helped you with that."

Danielle chuckled and swatted him away. "I'm going to take a shower."

"Go ahead. I took mine earlier. Would you like me to pour you a brandy?"

"Oh, yes, that would be nice." Danielle started for the bathroom and paused when Walt called her name. She turned to him.

"What do you think all that *I'm so proud of my nephew* was really about back there?" Walt asked.

"So it wasn't just me; it didn't sound sincere to you?"

Walt shook his head. "No. It sounded scripted."

ON THURSDAY MORNING Danielle kissed Walt before heading back down to her bedroom. After dressing, she applied her makeup and combed her hair. She then unhooked the baby monitor and shoved it back in the dresser. Danielle paused a moment and looked down at the closed drawer.

"Okay, this is getting dumb," she said aloud. "I think we need to come out of the closet." She giggled at her choice of words and added, "Well, so to speak."

The next moment she opened her bedroom door and glanced down the hall—first to her left, which led to the other two guest rooms—one currently occupied by the Bishops and the other bedroom empty—and to the staircase leading to the attic. She then looked straight ahead down the section of the hallway leading to the stairs to the first floor and to the room she had given Simon. No one was in sight.

Danielle was about to shut the door when she realized she had left her cellphone sitting on the table next to the door, just inside her room. She paused, turned back to her room, and snatched her cellphone off the table. When she turned back to the hallway, closing the door behind her, she saw Zara standing in front of Simon's bedroom door, her back to Danielle.

The moment Danielle closed her door, Zara turned abruptly in her direction and stared at Danielle with wide eyes. Zara blinked several times and then stammered, "Good morning, Danielle. I was just heading downstairs, thought I would take a little walk on the beach."

"Umm...have a nice walk. Will you be joining us for breakfast?" Danielle asked.

"No, thank you, I'm not a breakfast person."

The door to Simon's room started to open.

Zara glanced to the opening door and said hastily, "Have a nice day," before taking off in a sprint and heading down the hallway to the stairs leading to the first floor.

———

"I THOUGHT her husband said she wasn't a morning person?" Walt asked as he poured Danielle a cup of coffee. The two stood alone in the kitchen.

Danielle shrugged. "Maybe he just meant she wasn't a breakfast person. Either way, I swear she was coming out of Simon's bedroom."

"I can't imagine why she would be in his room. I find the idea of those two having a tryst preposterous. Not to mention, I don't believe they've even met yet."

Danielle cringed. "That idea didn't even cross my mind."

"You did say you thought she was sneaking out of his room. When a woman sneaks out of a man's room so early in the morning, that's a logical conclusion to jump to."

"Speaking from personal experience?" Danielle teased.

Walt grinned. "Only with you love."

Danielle picked up her cup and took a sip. "All I know, when I looked out in the hall, no one was around. And the next minute, there was Zara, standing in front of Simon's door. She said she was on her way downstairs, which would mean she would have walked right by me. But I know she didn't."

"She obviously stopped at the bathroom on the way downstairs. When you looked out the door the first time, that's where she must have been."

Danielle shook her head. "If that was the case, then she had to have run from the bathroom door to Simon's door to get there in the short time I looked away."

"You did say she raced down the stairs, didn't you?" he reminded her.

A knock came at the kitchen door. Just as Walt and Danielle looked that way, Lily came walking in the house, waving her key. She wore tight-fitting blue jeans, knee-high boots, and an extra-long bulky red sweater. Gold snowflake earrings dangled from her ears, while her hair was tied back in a green bow.

"The door was locked. I had to use my key," Lily explained.

"Morning, Lily, you look Christmassy," Danielle greeted her.

"Thanks. I feel Christmassy." By the time Lily reached the counter, Walt had already poured her a cup of coffee.

"Thanks, Walt." Lily picked up the cup. "Although I do miss your old flair."

The next moment the coffee pot floated up off its burner and into the air. "You mean like this?" Walt asked.

"Stop that!" Danielle scolded, reaching for the airborne pot.

Lily giggled and sipped her coffee.

Walt took the pot from Danielle's hand. "Careful, you could have burned yourself grabbing it like that." The next moment he dropped a quick kiss on Danielle's lips.

Lily's eyes widened. "You just kissed her!"

Walt set the pot back on its burner. "You'll have to get used to it."

ZARA WAS SITTING QUIETLY on the edge of Loyd's bed when Simon walked into the room.

"Took you long enough," Zara said. "Danielle about caught me coming out of your room. Just how would I have been able to explain that? You could have waited a few minutes before leaving your room. That would have been an awkward conversation if Danielle had us both trapped in the hallway at the same time!"

"It would be a lot easier if Danielle had us on the same floor," Simon said.

"Easier for whom? I can't climb those stairs," Loyd grumbled.

"It's always about you, isn't it, Loyd?" Zara muttered to herself.

"By the way, I did what you suggested. Last night I ran into Walt and Danielle before going to bed, and thanked them for being such good friends of Chris's. But I do worry this entire thing is too complicated."

"Pshaw. Everything is falling into place. Heather jumped faster than I expected. I was right again. She's more perfect for this than Danielle."

"SHOULD I WAVE A WHITE FLAG?" Heather teased Chris when she walked into the office on Thursday morning.

"I still wish you'd let me say something to my uncle," Chris grumbled.

"Don't you dare. He's up to something," Heather warned.

"I agree with Heather," Eva said when she materialized a moment later.

Heather pointed to Eva and said, "See, even poor Eva is worried about what your uncles are up to; she's so upset she forgot to glitter!"

Eva let out a dramatic sigh and flopped down on the sofa, crossing one leg over the opposing knee, sending the long skirt of her gown fluttering. "That's not the reason for the absence of glitter.

It was no longer obtaining the desired effect. I need to find a new entrance."

"What was your desired effect?" Heather asked as she took a seat at her desk.

"It certainly wasn't to annoy—and apparently glitter is not particularly popular." Eva waved one hand—a flurry of snowflakes fell from the ceiling, vanishing before hitting the floor.

"Hmm…nice touch. Also fitting for the season," Heather noted.

Eva nodded at her and smiled. "Thank you."

"If you ladies are done discussing glitter and snowflakes, can we get back to my uncles?"

"When are they leaving?" Eva asked.

"Apparently not soon enough," Chris grumbled. "I just wish I knew what Loyd was up to."

"I told you what I thought," Heather said. "He doesn't like me, and he figures if I start coming on to you, you'll get annoyed and fire me."

"What are you talking about? You annoy me constantly, and I haven't fired you yet," Chris smirked.

"True. But your uncle doesn't know that," Heather reminded him.

Eva waved her hand dismissively and said, "Wait a minute. I don't understand. After all, you did invite Heather to dinner with you the first night your uncles were in town. Why would they assume Heather making advances at you would turn you off? She is an attractive woman…in her own way."

Heather frowned at Eva. "Umm…thanks…I think."

Chris shrugged. "I don't know. Which is why Heather's theory doesn't make a lot of sense to me."

The next moment Chris's cellphone rang, and he answered the call.

When he got off the phone, he said, "That was Uncle Simon, they want to take me out to lunch." He turned to Heather and asked, "You want to go with us?"

"I would rather stab myself in the eye with a fork."

"I take that as a no?"

TWENTY-FIVE

C hris had suggested Pier Café for lunch. His uncles were already sitting at a booth when he arrived.

"That waitress has purple hair," Loyd told Chris when he sat down at their table.

"Yeah, well, that is Carla. She's also had pink hair and green hair...and, well...she's a regular rainbow." Chris shrugged, picked up a menu, and started looking through it.

"I believe a confession is in order," Simon announced.

Chris set his menu on the table and looked at Simon. "Confession?"

"You know we hired an investigator to see how you were doing. I know it wasn't right, but to be honest, I can't truthfully say I wouldn't do it again. We only want what's best for you," Simon told him.

"Yeah, that's what you keep saying," Chris said wearily.

"According to the investigator, you've made Danielle Boatman the executor of your will."

Chris's eyes widened. "Wow. I guess you got your money's worth."

"We just want to make sure she's worthy of the faith you've put in her. After all, we don't know anything about her."

"Didn't your investigator tell you all you needed to know?" Chris smirked.

"That's not what I mean," Simon said.

"All you need to know, Danielle is someone I trust with my life. I know she would never discuss my business with anyone. She isn't after my money. Like I said, I trust her."

"Alright, if you honestly believe that, then that is good enough for us." Simon reached across the table and patted Chris's hand.

"We just want you to be safe, son," Loyd told him. "A young man in your position needs to take precautions. You can't always trust people."

"I can trust Danielle," Chris repeated.

"It's not just the people you get close to we worry about. It's people who force themselves into your life. You have a lovely office, but I do wonder how safe it is. I noticed it has an alarm system. I assume it has security cameras?" Simon asked.

"Funny you should mention that. I recently purchased some security cameras," Chris told him.

"I'm glad to hear you're taking your security seriously. Are the cameras monitored by a security company?"

"At the moment they aren't even up," Chris told them. "I plan to have them installed after Christmas."

Simon nodded. "Just as long as you take the necessary steps to secure your office."

"What you don't realize, Chris," Loyd told him, "we loved our little brother dearly. I know you lost your parents, but we lost something too. We lost our baby brother. You're all that's left of him."

"Even though I'm adopted?" Chris asked, his face devoid of expression.

"You were their son," Loyd told him.

STANDING on the end of the pier, Noah by her side, Zara looked out to sea. It reminded her of a painter's canvas—a painter using one color—gray. A little white had been added to brighten the gray, and in other areas black to darken the clouds. Yet there were no shades of blue or true white on the canvas.

Noah shivered, pulling his jacket closer around him.

Zara looked to him and said, "We should go back. You're going to freeze."

"I'm fine," he said with a shiver.

Zara laughed. "Yeah, right."

"Maybe I should go to the police," he suggested.

"Seriously? And what are you going to tell them?"

"Okay, not the police, but Chris—even Danielle."

"Not yet, Noah. Not until we have more details for them."

"I just hate this waiting game."

"I understand." Zara glanced to the diner briefly. "Maybe you aren't freezing your butt off, but we should probably head back before they come out of the diner and see us."

"They just went in; they aren't going to be out for a while. But now that you mention it, there are places on my body that I can't feel anymore, so maybe we should head back. I'd kill for a cup of hot tea. Or better yet, one of those brandies Walt likes."

"Okay, let's head back before we run into someone we don't want to."

Together Zara and Noah started down the pier toward the diner and street. They were about ten feet from the diner when Noah whispered, "Speak of the devil."

Walking in their direction were two police officers. Noah guessed the older gray-haired one was in his fifties, while the younger, dark-haired officer looked to be in his late thirties. Both officers looked their way, and by their scrutiny Noah suspected the pair was trying to figure out if he was a tourist or a local they should recognize.

Just as they passed by the two men, Noah said, "Good afternoon."

"Afternoon," they both returned.

CHRIS SPIED Joe Morelli and Brian Henderson the moment they walked into the diner. As they passed by their table, Chris said hello. Both men stopped.

"Afternoon, Chris," Brian said, glancing over at the two older men.

"Joe, Brian, I would like you to meet my uncles," Chris began, introducing the officers to Loyd and Simon. The men exchanged brief pleasantries before Joe and Brian continued on to an empty table on the other side of the dining room.

"Are they good friends of yours?" Loyd asked when the two officers were out of earshot.

"Good friends? I wouldn't call Joe and Brian good friends. Not even sure I would consider them friends. Acquaintances."

"They seemed friendly enough," Simon said.

Chris shrugged. "This is a small town."

"Are they aware of your true identity?" Loyd asked.

"Yes."

"I suppose that's smart," Loyd said. "It's always helpful to have the local police in your pocket."

Chris frowned. "In my pocket is not the way I would describe my relationship with Joe and Brian."

Loyd laughed. "Come on now, Chris, surely you've learned by now a young man of your position is wise to have a close relationship with local law enforcement. It's vital they understand your best interest is their best interest."

"Not sure Joe and Brian would see it that way," Chris said under his breath.

AFTER LUNCH, Chris left the diner first, leaving his uncles, who told him they wanted to sit a few minutes and enjoy the view. After Chris was gone, Loyd stood up.

"I'll be right back," he told his brother. He walked across the diner to the table with the two police officers.

"Excuse me," Loyd said, standing by their table. "Could I speak to you gentlemen for a minute?"

"Certainly," Brian said, scooting over to make room for him. "Sit down."

Once Loyd was seated, he asked, "Are you familiar with Heather Donovan, the woman who works for my nephew?"

With a snort Brian said, "Yeah."

Loyd arched his brow. "Is there something you know about her?"

Brian shrugged. "She's just a little—different."

"What is it you wanted to know?" Joe asked.

"I'm just a little concerned about my nephew. Please don't say anything to him about me talking to you. We've made some horrible mistakes regarding Chris after his parents died. All we want to do is make it all right and have him back in our lives. We're old men, and we don't have much time left. We just want to spend that time with our nephew."

"What are you concerned about?" Joe asked.

"This Heather Donovan, we think she's manipulating our nephew—that she's trying to weave herself into his life. Is there any way you might be able to check into her past? Something is not right with her. I can just feel it."

JOE AND BRIAN returned to the police station after lunch. They went straight to the chief's office, where they found him behind his desk, sorting through his mail.

MacDonald looked up when they walked in the office. "How was lunch?"

"It was okay. But we had an odd encounter," Brian said as he took a seat in front of the desk.

"Yeah? You said you were going to Pier Café. Carla always makes it interesting." MacDonald snickered.

Joe took the seat next to Brian and said, "Chris was there with his uncles."

"Ahh…" The chief dropped the envelope he was about to open on his desk and leaned back in the chair. "Danielle told me they were here. Did you meet them?"

"Oh yes, we had an interesting conversation." Brian then went on to elaborate, telling the chief of their private exchange with Chris's uncle Loyd.

MacDonald chuckled. "I suppose I can understand how a quirky person like Heather might set off red flags to someone like the Glandon brothers. I imagine people from their station are always suspect of us little people trying to take advantage."

"I read a little about them after we found out who Chris is," Joe said. "They have their own money, but nothing like Chris's estate. I have to admit, the man did seem sincere, in spite of what I've read about them."

"I always found it odd that Chris hired Heather," Brian said.

The chief shrugged. "She needed a job. He was just helping her out."

"True. But they deal with a lot of money, and I can see how that might be tempting for someone like Heather, who has been struggling financially. I can understand why his uncle is concerned," Brian said.

"Yes, it is understandable. But what you forget is we already know about Heather's character—quirkiness aside," the chief reminded them.

Joe frowned. "What do you mean?"

"If you'll remember, not only did she save Danielle and Lily from that fire, she gave the stolen emerald her grandfather had to Danielle, when she could have kept it without anyone knowing. And then later, she returned the missing jewels to the Eva Aphrodite."

"That was weird in itself," Brian snarked. "She paid to have someone put valuable gems on a sunken boat. Who does that? I say Heather is paddling with one oar. I don't blame Chris's uncles for being concerned. The fact he actually hired her makes me question his judgment."

"That's not our call to make—nor is it Chris's uncles," MacDonald reminded him.

"I understand what you're saying." Brian nodded. "Anyway, I need to remember what I read about the uncles. They did try to cheat him out of his inheritance."

"I suspect that much money can make even good people do things they later regret," Joe suggested.

"Which is why you both need to be a little less judgmental when it comes to Heather. Yeah, she may be a little quirky—" the chief began.

"She can also be bitchy," Brian said under his breath.

"But two times when she was tested—when she could have kept something of value that would have improved her situation, she resisted the temptation. I suspect when Chris was looking for someone to hire for the foundation, that was the one trait he found most critical."

Brian let out a sigh. "I suppose."

The chief turned his attention back to his desk. He picked up a photograph of a woman and handed it to them. "Have a look at this."

Brian took the photo and studied it. He then handed it to Joe.

"Who is it?" Joe asked.

"It came in today's mail. Does she look familiar to either one of you?" the chief asked.

They both shook their heads no. Joe tossed the photo back on the desk and asked his question again.

"A missing woman from Southern California. I received it in today's mail. It's not from law enforcement, but from the missing woman's roommate, a Corky Summers. The woman went missing over six months ago. Summers isn't happy with the efforts—or should I say the lack of effort—in trying to find her."

"What about her family?" Joe asked.

MacDonald picked up the roommate's letter from his desk and tossed it to Joe. "According to the letter, the missing woman doesn't have any family. She spent her youth in the foster care system, which is why no one from her family is on the local police to find her. She's self-employed as a photographer, so there was no employer reporting her not showing up for work."

"Maybe she just moved?" Brian suggested.

"That seems to be what the local police think. But according to Summers, if she moved, she did so without taking her cameras with her—or any of her personal belongings."

"Why does Summers think she might be here?" Brian asked.

"We're not the only police department she reached out to."

"Why were we on the list?" Brian asked. "Did she just send it out randomly to any police department?"

MacDonald shook his head. "According to Summer's letter, the missing woman was obsessed in some sort of internet search. She had borrowed Summer's computer a few times. But she never confided in the roommate what she was looking for. Summers believes she was searching for her birth family. After she went missing, and the police were no help, the roommate started checking out some of the sites on her computer that her missing roommate had visited. Apparently, Frederickport websites came up numerous times."

Brian picked up the photograph and studied it for a minute. Finally, he tossed it back on the desk and said, "She doesn't look familiar to me."

"If she is here, then it would seem to mean she left without telling her roommate where she was going, and maybe, for whatever reason, she doesn't want her roommate to know," Joe suggested. "After all, she is an adult, free to go wherever she wants without telling her roommate."

The chief nodded. "That's apparently what her local police department seems to believe."

TWENTY-SIX

Taquitos from Beach Taco sounded good. But what she really wanted was nachos. Nachos from Beach Taco were a killer—piled with beans, grated cheddar cheese, chili peppers, diced tomatoes and onions, and topped with salsa, homemade guacamole and their spicy sour cream concoction. Heather's stomach growled. She was practically salivating at the thought. Unfortunately, even the smallest nacho order was too much for her, and Heather usually split them with Chris. But he had gone to lunch with his uncles, and while she might get Eva to join her for lunch to keep her company, the ghost wouldn't be sharing her food. Plus, nachos weren't terrific as leftovers. She had tried that once, and the tortilla chips ended up soggy and soft.

She wondered when Chris would return so she could go to lunch. Heather glanced at the clock and then at Eva, who sat on Chris's office chair, staring toward the entry.

"You know, you didn't have to stay with me. You could have gone with Chris," Heather reminded her.

Eva looked at Heather and shrugged. "I got the feeling Chris didn't want me tagging along. I suppose I could have gone without him knowing, but that seems deceitful."

"So it is true, just because I can see a ghost doesn't mean I will always see one if it's there."

In response Eva vanished. The next moment she reappeared. "I never left."

"Ahh...so it is true."

Eva shook her head. "Not necessarily."

Heather frowned. "What do you mean?

"You should know by now our powers—so to speak—are often unique to our situation. Walt, for example, was fully capable of making himself invisible to someone like Danielle, as well as his ability to move objects, but harnessing those powers meant he was limited in range. I know of some spirits who can control who can see them—even making themselves visible to people who typically can't see spirits."

"Ahh...like Darlene Gusarov."

Eva nodded. "Exactly. And some spirits are incapable of making themselves invisible to someone like you. Of course, that doesn't mean they can't harness that particular skill with practice."

Heather sat up straight in the chair and looked to the entry. "I think I heard something," she whispered. "They're back."

Hunny, who had been sleeping in the corner, jumped up and ran to Chris, who had just walked in the front door, his uncles trailing behind him. While Chris had left the diner first, his uncles had arrived back to the office minutes after he pulled up.

Before leaning down to greet his dog, Chris tossed an envelope on a nearby table. "I stopped at the post office after lunch, picked up some stamps."

"That's what took you so long. I'm starving." Heather snatched her purse from under her desk and stood up.

"You could have come with us," Chris reminded her.

"I like my eyes."

"You could have closed up and left to get something to eat," Chris added.

"I wanted to keep Eva company," Heather said with a grin.

After Heather left the office, Loyd looked down at Chris's dog and said, "I thought the dog's name was Hunny."

Chris glanced down at his pit bull, who now sat by his side, tail wagging.

"It is Hunny," Chris told him.

"I thought Heather just called her Eva?" Simon asked.

Chris looked innocently to Simon. "She did?"

"And what did she mean she liked her eyes?" Loyd asked.

Chris shrugged. "I think it's in reference to not wanting to stab them with a fork."

"What in tarnation does that mean?" Loyd snapped.

Chris chuckled. "Nothing. Just an inside joke."

"Inside joke? Not a very funny one," Loyd grumbled.

"So what are you two planning for the rest of the afternoon?" Chris asked. "I have a few things here I have to wrap up. In fact, I was surprised to see you pull up when I got back. I assumed you were out exploring."

"I'd like that tour you offered earlier," Loyd said. "I'm feeling pretty chipper today. I think I can handle those stairs." To emphasize his point, he whacked his cane against the floor several times.

"Sure, I'd love to give you a tour," Chris said. "Now?"

"If you don't mind. Not sure if I'll feel this good later."

Chris turned to the doorway, Loyd following him, but then paused and looked back at Simon, who had just sat down. "You want to come with us, Uncle Simon?"

"No. You two go. I've already been up there. I think I would like to rest."

"I'll stay down here too," Eva called out.

Chris flashed Eva a smile and then looked down at Hunny. "You stay down here until I come back."

"Hunny, dear," Eva said, translating for Chris, as Hunny wasn't really sure what Chris was telling him, "you stay with me until Chris returns."

Hunny looked from Eva to Chris and then let out a little grunt before walking to Chris's desk and lying down under it.

"I'm impressed; she seems to listen to you," Simon murmured.

"I had a little help," Chris said with a chuckle before continuing on his way upstairs with Loyd.

After Chris and Loyd left the room, Simon stood up and eyed Hunny nervously. "I wish he would have taken you upstairs."

"If you and your brother would simply go back to where you came from, you wouldn't have to deal with Hunny," Eva smirked.

Eva watched Simon as he walked to Chris's file drawer and opened it. "Oh, you nosy thing you! Just wait until I tell Chris."

She watched as Simon hastily rifled through the files. After a few moments he pulled out a piece of paper, set it on the desk, and then snapped a picture of it with his phone. In an instant Eva changed positions and was now sitting on the edge of the desk, looking down at the document. After taking the picture, Simon returned it to its place in the file cabinet and then removed another document.

"What are you up to?" Eva wondered aloud.

She watched as Simon hastily removed one document after another from the file drawer, snapping a photo of each one. He did this five times and then quickly shut the drawer—all the documents returned to their original files.

She watched as he looked at his phone. He appeared to be doing that texting thing. She then heard a swishing sound coming from his phone. Simon smiled, congratulated himself on the good work, and then tucked the phone back in his pocket.

"I NEED to speak to you about your uncles," Eva told Chris after Loyd and Simon left the office.

"Eva, I know you don't like them. But it is Christmas, and they are family, and—"

"Simon rifled through your file drawer and took pictures of some of the documents."

Chris stared at Eva. "He didn't."

She nodded. "He did."

"What documents?"

"Open the drawer, and I'll show you which ones."

Chris frowned at Eva, but he went to the file drawer and opened it. She stood by his side, looking into the drawer as he shuffled through the files, trying to find the documents that had interested Simon.

Eva pointed to the corner of one piece of paper sticking out of a file. "Wait, let me see that one."

Chris removed the document and showed it to Eva. She nodded. "That was one of them."

"Why would he be interested in that?" Chris muttered.

"I have no idea why he took a picture of it. I just know that's one of them. I counted. He took pictures of five different pages from that drawer."

"Okay, let's see if we can find the other four."

LILY DUNKED her chocolate chip cookie in her glass of milk before taking a bite. She sat with Danielle at Marlow House's kitchen table, discussing their plans for Christmas.

"How's your mom handling it, you not spending Christmas with them this year?" Danielle asked.

Lily shrugged and dunked the last bite of her cookie. "I reminded her we spent last Christmas with them. And I told her I want to spend Christmas in our own house. I wanted my own tree."

"Does this mean you aren't having Christmas dinner here?" Danielle asked.

"Are you kidding? I'm not about to miss the feast you put out."

Danielle grabbed herself a cookie. "I'm surprised Ian's parents aren't coming for Christmas. After all, both their kids live here."

"Please, they were here for Thanksgiving; isn't that enough?" Danielle chuckled.

Lily picked up a napkin and wiped her hands. She crumpled it up and tossed it on the table. "You know what Kelly asked me?"

"What?"

"She wanted to know if it was true, were you really dating Walt Marlow."

Danielle smiled. "So it's out there now." She took a bite of her cookie.

Lily nodded and leaned back in her chair. "Yep. I reminded her how helpful you've been since his accident. And, well, he's been in Frederickport for over nine months; it's not like he's a stranger. I told her, considering everything, I wasn't surprised that he eventually asked you out."

"What did she say to that?"

"She wanted to know if he still had amnesia."

Danielle let out a sigh.

"You do seem happy, Danielle, and so does Walt. But—it is so freaking weird. I still can't get used to actually seeing him. I mean, other than in a dream hop."

"It doesn't seem that strange to me anymore. It did at first. But not anymore."

"So what now? I always suspected you had feelings for Walt, but now that you have a real chance with him, are you going to take it? Or is this going to be like you and Chris?"

Before Danielle could respond to Lily's question, Chris's uncles walked into the kitchen from the hallway.

"Afternoon, Danielle," Simon greeted her.

Danielle stood up from the table and faced the men. "Did you have a nice lunch with Chris?"

"We did. And I remembered you telling us about those home-made cookies, wondering if we could have some," Simon asked.

"Certainly."

Simon and Loyd looked over to the table and noticed the redhead looking their way.

"Oh, Simon, Loyd, I'd like you to meet my friend Lily. Lily and her husband live across the street."

"Nice to meet you, Lily. I assume you know our nephew?" Loyd asked.

"Certainly. Chris is a good friend of mine. I used to live at Marlow House when he stayed here."

"Really?" Loyd asked.

Danielle brought out more cookies and offered the men something to drink. After they took a seat at the table with Lily, the landline began to ring.

"If you will all excuse me, I'm going to take that in the parlor," Danielle said before rushing out of the room.

"She could have answered the call in here," Simon said.

Lily shrugged and grabbed another cookie. "The only calls she gets on the landline are for B and B business, that's probably why she's taking it in the parlor."

"So you used to live here?" Loyd asked.

"Yes. Dani's my best friend. I helped her open the B and B and planned to go back to California, where I lived. But I had some medical issues, and Dani took care of me. I met my husband here, and, well, the rest is history, as they say."

"Seems like Danielle is a trusted friend for many," Loyd said.

Lily nodded. "Yes, she is."

"Although not everyone feels that way," Simon noted.

Lily frowned at Simon. "Excuse me?"

Simon shrugged. "I was just thinking of that girl who works with Chris. She seems to have an issue with your friend."

"Heather?"

"I think it's just a little jealousy," Loyd suggested.

"Why do you think she has a problem with Dani?" Lily asked.

"I'm sure you're aware our nephew dated your friend for a brief time," Loyd reminded her.

"Sure. So?"

"Let's just put it this way, Heather is anxious to take your friend's place in our nephew's life, if you know what I mean," Simon said.

TWENTY-SEVEN

W rapped snugly in Ian's Pendleton jacket, Lily stood behind her house on Friday morning and watched as Sadie raced down the beach for the tennis ball. The golden retriever had barely snatched the ball from the sand when she changed direction and headed back to Ian, who was prepared to grab the ball and throw it again. This went on for another fifteen minutes, and while Ian claimed Sadie needed a rest, Lily suspected it was her husband who needed a time-out.

"You want to walk over to Dani's with me?" Lily asked when Ian and Sadie made their way back to her. Sadie's tongue hung out the side of her mouth as she panted.

Ian tossed the tennis ball up into the air and caught it. "Sure."

Instead of going back into their house, they walked around to the front of the property and to the sidewalk, Sadie trailing beside them. They stood on the sidewalk a moment, about to cross the street, when a man parked in front of Marlow House pulled his car out into the road and turned around in front of them. Instead of crossing the street, they waited for the man to drive on.

"That must be one of the people staying with Dani."

"Obviously not an uncle," Ian said.

"No. Dani said it's a couple here on their honeymoon."

After he drove away, they crossed over to Marlow House.

"I CAN'T BELIEVE tomorrow is Christmas Eve," Ian told Walt. The two sat in Marlow House's library, enjoying a cup of coffee and a cinnamon roll while Sadie napped at Walt's feet.

"What are you getting Lily for Christmas?" Walt asked.

"I don't know yet."

Walt laughed. "You know, it is Christmas Eve tomorrow."

"Didn't I just say that?"

They both laughed.

"Do you mind if I join you?" Loyd asked from the open doorway.

"Certainly not, come in. Have you met Ian?" Walt asked. He and Ian looked Loyd's way and watched as the elderly man made his way into the room, cane in hand. Sadie lifted her head and started to stand up, but Ian told her to stay. Reluctantly the dog obeyed, resting her chin back on her front paws.

"Yes, Danielle introduced us earlier. He and his wife are hosting the Christmas Eve open house they've graciously invited my brother and me to." Loyd sat down in one of the empty chairs.

The men chatted for another twenty minutes, discussing nothing more personal than the weather and what Danielle might be serving for Christmas dinner, when Ian excused himself to go home, leaving Walt alone in the library with Loyd.

"I thought you would be visiting with Chris today?" Walt asked after Ian and Sadie left.

"Simon went over to see him, but I'm waiting for a delivery."

"Delivery? Something for Christmas?" Walt asked.

Loyd shook his head. "No, just something pertaining to one of our business interests. It seems that even when you get to be my age, it's still impossible to get away for a holiday and not be interrupted by some meddlesome paperwork. But it is the end of the year, and you know taxes and all that."

"Both Danielle and I plan to be here most of the morning, so if you need to go somewhere, I'm sure one of us can accept your delivery."

"Thank you for your offer, but I need to go through the papers as soon as they arrive, and get them back to my accountant."

Walt nodded. "I understand."

Loyd eyed Walt curiously and then said, "You and my nephew seem to get along fairly well, considering everything."

Walt met Loyd's inquisitive gaze. "I suspect you mean the fact I'm now dating Danielle?"

Loyd nodded. "It must be a little awkward, living under the same roof as the woman you're dating."

"Awkward?"

Loyd shrugged. "It's been a lifetime since I was in your shoes—a young bachelor courting a woman—but I can't imagine living under the same roof as my late wife when I first started seeing her. Mighty awkward."

Walt chose not to respond. He just smiled and sipped his coffee.

"I suppose it's more awkward for my nephew, working with a woman who obviously has her sights set on him."

"I assume you're referring to Heather Donovan?" Walt asked.

"Hiring someone you feel sorry for is never a good idea. And now…well…I just hope my nephew knows what he's doing. I worry about him. And it's also a shame, the woman's attitude toward Danielle. Danielle seems like such a nice woman."

"You do know Heather is a neighbor, and Danielle considers her a friend," Walt asked.

Loyd shrugged. "All I know is what I've heard her say behind Danielle's back since I've been here. That woman is obviously jealous of Miss Boatman."

IAN HAD HEADED BACK HOME with Sadie, but Lily remained at Marlow House. She sat in the kitchen with Danielle, picking through the Christmas tin of candy Adam had brought over. She picked up a piece of peanut brittle and sniffed it. "Adam actually made this?"

Danielle, who had just finished cleaning up after breakfast, wiped her hands on a dishtowel and tossed it on the counter. She walked to the table.

"It was his tribute to Marie, I think." Danielle sat down.

Lily nibbled the peanut brittle and smiled. "Hey, this is pretty good. It tastes like Marie's."

Danielle nodded. "I thought so."

After Lily tried the peanut brittle, she picked up a piece of divinity. "So how come he gave you candy and didn't bring us any?"

Danielle shrugged. "I'm special."

Lily took a bite of the divinity and then wrinkled her nose. "No, that doesn't taste like Marie's." Instead of finishing the piece, Lily set it on a napkin and then closed the tin.

"He gave it a good try."

Lily set the closed tin on the table.

"Adam really misses Marie. I felt sorry for him when he brought the candy over. I thought he was going to cry."

"I imagine he does. Even when Adam wasn't my favorite person, I gave him credit for taking care of his grandmother," Lily said. "He's not close to the rest of his family. Which, after meeting them, is totally understandable."

"He took his grandmother's recipes and tried to recreate a memory. But divinity isn't easy to make—I know, I've tried. Even though Adam had his grandmother's recipe, the candy didn't turn out right."

"Why don't you make it for him? As a Christmas gift. I bet he would love that," Lily suggested.

"Didn't you just hear me say I've tried making divinity before, and mine didn't turn out much better than Adam's—and he has Marie's recipe."

Lily laughed. "True. But you have Marie."

"What do you mean?"

"Get Marie to help you make the candy. Maybe she can't do anything physically, but she can walk you through it, share whatever tricks she had. I bet you could do it with her help."

Danielle smiled at the thought. "Wow, I didn't even consider that."

"See, one Christmas gift taken care of." Lily smiled.

"Considering tomorrow is Christmas Eve, not sure I can squeeze in divinity making, but it is a good idea."

"Have you finished your shopping?" Lily asked.

"Pretty much."

"Hello, ladies," Walt said as he walked into the kitchen and to the table.

"Hey, Walt," Lily greeted him.

Walt stopped behind Danielle's chair, placing his hands along the edge of its backrest. He smiled at Lily. "Hello, Lily." He looked

THE GHOST OF CHRISTMAS SECRETS

down at Danielle, who tilted her head back in the chair and looked up at him and smiled. He leaned over and gave her a quick kiss.

Lily's eyes widened. "I still don't know if I can get used to that."

Danielle laughed and tilted her head back upright and looked at Lily. "Why?"

Lily responded with a shrug.

Walt took a seat and told Danielle, "I was just talking to Loyd, and he's got this idea in his head Heather has some resentment toward you."

"He said the same thing to me!" Lily said. "I was telling Dani about it earlier."

"He's up to something." Danielle glanced to the doorway leading to the hallway.

"Why is he here anyway? I saw Simon leaving right when I got here," Lily asked. "I figured he would go with him."

"According to Loyd, he's waiting for some sort of postal delivery," Walt said.

"Good luck this time of year," Lily muttered.

"He mentioned it to me too," Danielle said. "His accountant is overnighting something to him; that's why he's hanging around the house, waiting for it."

"What are your other guests like?" Lily asked.

Danielle shrugged. "They seem nice enough, but I haven't really talked to them much. She doesn't come down for breakfast, and when they are up, they usually take off, I assume sightseeing. They left right before you and Ian came over."

"I saw him drive off, but she wasn't with him," Lily said.

Danielle frowned at Lily. "I'm sure I saw them both leaving."

"I didn't think there was anyone in the car with him, but I could be wrong."

"Maybe she decided not to go," Danielle suggested.

LOYD MADE his way into the living room so he could have a view of the street. Motion from the front window caught his attention. He stood up, but then sat back down again when he saw it was just Noah Bishop returning to the house. A moment later he heard the front door open and close, and then the sound of Noah walking down the hallway.

He started to pick up a magazine off the coffee table when he noticed the postman coming up the walk. Scrambling to his feet, Loyd made his way to the entry hall before the mailman rang the bell. A moment later he hastily opened the front door and quickly snatched the envelope from the mailman. After signing for the delivery, he slammed the door shut without further fanfare. Several minutes later he was alone in his room, opening the envelope.

He removed a handkerchief from his pocket and used it to slip the sheet of paper from the envelope, careful not to get his fingerprints on it. He set it on his bed and examined it. A smile curled on his lips. He grabbed his phone from the dresser and dialed his brother.

When Simon answered his phone, Loyd said, "It's here—and it's perfect. He did an excellent job. Of course, now we need to take care of him like we did Peyton."

"Careful what you say on the phone," Simon warned.

"Fine, but then come get me so we can go somewhere and talk. Somewhere where we won't be overheard," Loyd said.

"Where do you suggest?" Simon asked.

"Down to that beach parking lot. We can stay in the car."

When Loyd ended the call, he tossed the phone on the bed and headed to the bathroom.

Several minutes later Zara slipped into Loyd's room unnoticed. She could hear him in the bathroom—the water was running.

"Okay, just what did that mailman bring you?" Zara asked as she approached the bed and spied the recently opened eleven-by-fourteen-inch cardboard envelope sitting on the bed, along with a document.

Standing over it, she began to read. "Good forgery," she muttered. "So nice of Chris to put you back in his will. Of course, that means he has to die for you to inherit." Narrowing her eyes, she looked from the forged document to the closed bedroom door and back to the bed. A moment later she heard the door to the bathroom open. As quietly as she had slipped into his room, she slipped out.

TWENTY-EIGHT

Lily stood up from the kitchen table and groaned. "I think I'm on sugar overload. First Adam's candy and then your cookies." She rubbed her stomach and cringed.

"Want me to make you a sandwich? I find if I eat a little protein, it helps balance my blood sugar after too many sweets," Danielle offered.

Lily shook her head and moaned. "No. I think I'd rather go home and puke."

"I guess this means you don't want to go to the police station with us. We're taking them some cookies."

Lily put out her hand as if to make Danielle stop talking. "Please don't say that word again!"

"You mean cookie?" Danielle grinned.

"Ugh…" Lily rubbed her stomach again.

"Lily, if you plan to get sick, perhaps you should go outside," Walt teased.

"I get no sympathy from you two."

"I did offer to make you a sandwich," Danielle reminded her.

"Yeah, well, it was my fault. I didn't see anyone shoving those cookies in my mouth but me." She looked to Danielle. "It would probably be a good idea to take some down to the station. Less for me to eat."

Walt stood up and looked to Danielle. "You want to go now?"

"Sure."

"I'll go get my jacket."

Danielle nodded. "Okay."

Walt gave her a quick kiss, told Lily goodbye, and left the room.

Lily stood in the kitchen and watched him leave. After he disappeared down the hall, she shook her head and sat back down. "I still can't get over that."

"Why? I mean seriously, why?"

Lily studied Danielle a moment before answering. "I don't remember you and Lucas being particularly—well, affectionate. And then you dated Joe for a brief time—and then Chris. I don't know, you always seemed reserved. Aside from a New Year's kiss—which really doesn't count—I don't think I ever saw you kiss either one of them."

Danielle smiled at Lily. "They weren't Walt."

BRIAN HENDERSON WALKED into the break room, eating a chocolate cookie. Joe Morelli, who was just finishing his lunch, looked up and frowned.

"Is that one of Danielle's chocolate drop cookies?" Joe asked.

Brian nodded and sat down at the table with Joe while shoving the remaining cookie in his mouth.

"Where'd you get it?"

Brian licked a smidge of chocolate off his thumb and nodded toward the door. "Danielle just came in with Marlow. She left a big box of cookies at the front desk, and they were headed to the chief's office with another box."

"She's here with Marlow?" Joe asked.

"You're the one who told me they were dating now. I'm not surprised. They always seem to be together anyway."

Joe shook his head. "I just don't get those two. It's like he's a different person."

Brian shrugged. "Maybe he is."

"What's that supposed to mean?"

"He does have amnesia. From all accounts he hasn't regained his memory. So I suppose, in some ways, it's like he was reborn—a blank slate," Brian suggested.

"It's weird," Joe grumbled.

"Don't let Kelly hear you say that. She might think you still have feelings for Danielle," Brian teased.

"Kelly thinks it's weird too."

"I have to admit the entire thing is somewhat bizarre. Especially considering how much he looks like the original Walt Marlow," Brian conceded.

"I remember when I first met Danielle. She was investigating his death. The guy had been dead for almost ninety years, but she was determined to prove he was murdered and hadn't committed suicide. Looking back, I think I was taken in by a pretty face, and I didn't stop and consider the entire thing—her interest—was odd."

Brian shrugged. "Some people love a good mystery. And she had just moved in to the house. A lot of people are into local history. Look at Frederickport's historical society. Also proof that sometimes people get a little carried away, especially considering the shenanigans they tried pulling on Danielle."

"I suppose. But you have to admit, so many odd things have happened at Marlow House. For example, remember that letter Marlow wrote—the original Walt Marlow?" Joe asked.

Brian shook his head. "I don't know what you're talking about."

"Back when those gold coins disappeared from the bank, and those people were staying at Marlow House and they tried to steal the Missing Thorndike. The guy was a cousin of the bank manager."

"Yeah, I remember. What about it?" Brian asked.

"Someone locked the woman in the bathroom and left a note telling what they were up to. At the time we thought Chris wrote the letter."

Furrowing his brow, Brian considered what Joe was saying. "I forgot all about that. The handwriting in the note matched the handwriting of Walt Marlow—the letters Marie Nichols had given Danielle."

"Just an example of some of the weird crap that's gone on in that house."

Brian stared blankly past Joe, thinking about how months earlier he had discovered the eerie similarity between the signatures of the original Walt Marlow—the one murdered in the attic of Marlow House—and the current Walt Marlow, the man who used to call himself Clint Marlow. He wondered—how would the handwriting in general compare between the two Marlows?

"ARE YOU SERIOUS?" Danielle asked the chief. She and Walt sat with him in his office with the door closed. "Chris's uncle Loyd asked Brian and Joe to investigate Heather?"

"Yes. But I suppose I can understand," the chief said.

"Understand? His uncle is a jerk!" Danielle snapped.

"Come on, Danielle. Think about it," the chief said. "Chris is a very wealthy man, and Heather does come off—well, a little quirky. He's just concerned about his nephew."

"Danielle's right." Walt spoke up. "Although I wouldn't use the term *jerk. Maniacal* might be more apt. For whatever reason, Loyd Glandon is attempting to sow the seeds of suspicion regarding Heather. The question is, why?"

"I disagree. He's just worried about his nephew," MacDonald argued.

"No, Chief." Walt shook his head. "Loyd Glandon has repeated conversations he supposedly has had with Heather and Chris— which I know have been fabricated. And it's not because Heather has contradicted Loyd, it's because there have been witnesses to the conversations that he was not aware of."

"Witnesses? What witnesses?" the chief asked.

"Marie and Eva," Walt explained.

"Marie—as in Marie Nichols? And Eva as in—"

"Yes, Eva Thorndike. Ghosts," Walt finished for him.

"There you go throwing around that *ghost* word," Danielle teased.

Ignoring Danielle's comment, the chief looked at Walt and said, "Why would the uncles be making up stories?"

"Danielle discussed it with Chris this morning," Walt said.

"Chris has been coming over for breakfast, since his uncles are staying with us," Danielle explained. "Heather seems to think they just want Chris to fire her because they don't like her. But Chris is starting to wonder if his uncles—especially Loyd—are just getting senile. He figures if their end goal really is to just get her fired, it's a strange way to go about it. But if they did ask Joe and Brian to check into her background, maybe this really is just about getting her fired. Maybe they're hoping something horrible will come up that'll force Chris to get rid of her."

"It just proves sometimes family can be a major pain," the chief grumbled.

"I might agree in Chris's case. But for me—especially this time of year—I miss my family. Even Cheryl, who could be a major pain." Danielle glanced up to the ceiling and added, "Sorry, Cheryl."

Walt shifted the direction of the conversation a few minutes later by asking, "Are the boys excited for Christmas?"

"What do you think? They're kids." MacDonald laughed. "It's been nice having my in-laws here this week, spending time with the boys while I have to work. I feel guilty when they're off for Christmas break and I can't be home with them, like their mother would have been."

"Maybe you should get remarried?" Danielle suggested.

MacDonald laughed. "I tell you what, when you get married, I'll start looking for a wife."

Walt chuckled.

Danielle grinned. "Deal." Giggling, she stood up to seal the deal with a handshake when she glanced down and spied something on the chief's desk that caught her attention.

"What's this?" She picked up a large photograph.

The chief glanced at what was in her hand. "A missing person."

Still holding the photograph, she stared at it and sat back down on her chair. "She's not missing. She's staying at Marlow House."

The chief stood up. "Are you serious?"

Danielle nodded and showed the photo to Walt.

"It looks like Zara," Walt noted.

"Did you say Zara?" the chief asked, now frantically looking for the letter that had accompanied the photograph.

"Yeah. Zara Bishop. Her and her husband are staying at Marlow House through Christmas. So what's the deal?" Danielle asked.

Now holding the letter he had been looking for, MacDonald quickly reread its contents. He shook his head. "According to this, her name is Zara, but not Zara Bishop, and she's not married. Her name is Zara Leighton and she went missing the end of May."

"Who sent you this?" Walt asked.

"It came from Leighton's roommate, Corky Summers. Summers was frustrated that the local police weren't taking her case seriously, so she decided to do her own investigation. Apparently, Ms.

Leighton had used Summer's computer to do some research, and one location she was looking at was Frederickport."

"What was she researching?" Walt asked.

"Summers didn't know. But she suspected she was searching for her family. According to Summers, Leighton had been raised in foster care."

"Or maybe she was looking for honeymoon spots?" Danielle suggested.

"Are you saying Zara is on her honeymoon?" the chief asked.

"She didn't say they were on their honeymoon exactly, but when she made her reservation, she made a comment about them being newlyweds. I have to assume it's the same woman, they look just alike, and they have the same first name. Zara isn't exactly a common name. Maybe she isn't missing—her roommate just doesn't know where she went."

Walt looked at the chief. "I have to agree with her. The woman staying at Marlow House is probably the same one in the photograph, for the reasons Danielle mentioned. The Zara we've met seems quite content to be with her husband, so perhaps she simply does not want her roommate to know where she is—or that she got married."

"But why did she leave all her belongings behind?" the chief asked.

Danielle shrugged. "Maybe she intended to come back for them later."

"Odd that she'd leave her cameras. Summers claims Leighton is a professional freelance photographer."

"I've no idea. But she must have had her reasons," Danielle said.

"If this woman doesn't want her roommate to know where she is, I wonder if she knows Summers is looking for her. I should probably go over to Marlow House and talk with her. Let her know her roommate is looking for her—that she has been sending out those flyers to various police stations. She can decide what she wants to do about it."

"I think that would be a good idea," Danielle agreed. "Can I read the letter the roommate sent you?"

"Sure." The chief leaned over his desk and handed Danielle the sheet of paper.

"Hmm…" Danielle muttered as she read the letter.

"What?" Walt asked.

"The description fits—right height, body type. Says here she has a feather tattoo on the back of her neck. I don't recall seeing that, but I really didn't look. The name really clinches it." Danielle glanced to Walt and smiled. "Of course, if our Zara doesn't have a feather tattoo, we'll know it's another same-name doppelgänger."

TWENTY-NINE

I t was the third—maybe fourth—time Noah had reread the page. The novel had been on his must-read list for some time. It was by his favorite science fiction author, but concentrating was an impossible task considering all that was going on. Reclining on the bed, he looked up to Zara, who stood at the bedroom window, looking down at the street.

"Simon just pulled up," Zara told him without turning around.

"Is he coming in?" Noah asked, still stretched out on the bed, his head resting on several pillows piled against the headboard.

Zara didn't answer immediately. Instead she silently watched to see what Simon was doing. Finally, she shook her head. "No. It looks like he's picking up Loyd."

"Those two are a pair," Noah grumbled. He closed the book and tossed it next to him on the bed.

"Yes, I was right. Loyd's getting in the car."

"You think they took it with them?" Noah asked.

Still gazing out the window, Zara shook her head.

"I don't know."

"Maybe it's time," Noah suggested.

"If we could get ahold of that document, then you could take a picture of it. It would give us something to show Chris rather than just telling him our crazy story."

"Then let's do it now," Noah said, getting up from the bed. "Let's see if it's in his room."

"What if the room is locked?" Zara asked.

"We won't know unless we try."

Zara followed Noah to the door. The moment he opened it, Zara cried, "Close the door! That cat's out there!"

Noah shut the door and turned to Zara. "Are you going to let a cat keep you locked up in here?"

Zara shook her head emphatically. "I can't deal with that cat right now."

"Just don't look at him. Think of something else; keep your mind off it. You can do it," Noah urged.

Zara closed her eyes for a few moments—concentrating—and then she opened them again and nodded. "Okay, I can do this."

Noah opened the door and peeked out into the hallway. Max sat by Danielle's closed bedroom door, his golden eyes looking Noah's way as his tail swished back and forth behind him.

"Okay, he's by Danielle's door. Just don't look at him. Pretend he's not there."

"Easy for you to say," Zara grumbled. Hesitantly she followed Noah out of the bedroom, leaving the door ajar. Together they moved quickly down the hallway and past the black cat. Max didn't follow them. Instead, he remained by Danielle's room, watching the pair.

When they reached Loyd's room a few minutes later, they found it unlocked.

"Yes!" Zara exclaimed when Noah opened the bedroom door. Together they started looking through the room, with Noah opening dresser drawers and Loyd's suitcase while Zara looked around the room and in the closet and bathroom.

"I don't think it's here," Noah finally said.

"Dang. I should have realized that when we found the door unlocked. He's certainly not going to leave that around for someone to see," Zara grumbled. "Especially if Chris happened to come into his room."

"Oh crap!"

Zara turned to Noah; he stood at the bedroom window, looking outside. "What is it?"

"It's a police car; it just parked in front of the house. And it looks like Walt and Danielle just pulled in behind it."

"You get out of here; I'll stay. If they're bringing some cop in the house, I don't need to be in the entry when he walks in. If Danielle asks where I am, say I took a walk."

With a nod, Noah hastily left the room, closing the door behind him. He made it to the living room sofa by the time he heard the front door opening. Looking around frantically, Noah spied a magazine on the coffee table and picked it up. Opening it, he pretended to read.

A few minutes later he heard Danielle say, "Hello, Noah." She walked in the living room with Walt and a man Noah had never seen before.

Noah looked up from the magazine and smiled. "Afternoon, Danielle, Walt."

"Umm...Noah, I would like you to meet a friend of ours, Police Chief MacDonald. Chief, this is one of our guests, Noah Bishop."

Noah closed the magazine and tossed it back on the coffee table before he stood up and shook the chief's hand in greeting.

"Actually, Mr. Bishop, I'm here to speak to your wife," the chief explained.

"Zara? Why do you want to talk to her?"

"Is she in her room?" the chief asked.

Walt stood silently by Danielle, listening, when he heard a meow. He turned around and spied Max sitting in the doorway, watching.

Noah shook his head. "No, she went for a walk. I don't expect her back for a couple of hours. What is this about?"

Walt frowned at Max. *Who doesn't like you?*

"A couple of hours? That's quite a walk," the chief said.

Noah shrugged. "She wanted to do some Christmas shopping and decided to walk down to the shops."

Walt glanced from Max to Noah, back to the cat. *Maybe she's allergic.*

The chief glanced at his watch. "I suppose I can come back later when she returns."

"What is this about?" Noah asked. "Why would the police be interested in my wife?"

Don't take it personally, Walt silently conveyed to the cat.

"Mr. Bishop, how long have you and your wife been married?" the chief asked.

"Not long, why?"

"What's your wife's maiden name?" the chief asked.

"Maiden name?" Noah frowned.

"Or the surname she used before you two were married," the chief clarified.

"Ummm...Smith. Why?"

"How long have you known your wife?" the chief asked.

"I met her in middle school. What is this about? Why do you want to talk to my wife?"

"A missing person's report came across my desk, with a photograph of the woman, and according to Danielle, she looks just like your wife."

Noah stared at the chief a moment and then let out a sigh and sat back down on the sofa. "That's what this is about? Some woman in a photograph resembles my wife? That's all it is, a resemblance. I can assure you my wife is not a missing person."

"Are you sure your wife's last name didn't used to be Leighton?" the chief asked.

"I think I know my wife's maiden name."

"The reason I ask, the missing woman is named Zara...Zara Leighton," the chief told him.

Noah stared at the chief a moment and then said, "That is an interesting coincidence; they have the same first name. I suppose I can see why you wondered if it was her. But, no, it is not the same woman."

"Okay. But I'll need to come back later and talk with your wife," the chief said.

"Chief MacDonald, my wife is a private person. She also doesn't feel comfortable around strangers. I can assure you this missing woman is not her. But if you would like Danielle to talk to her when she returns later, I'm sure she won't mind. But quite frankly, I know my wife, sir, and she would not be comfortable talking with you. Zara is dealing with some issues, and she does not need the additional stress of an unnecessary interrogation from a perfect stranger."

"What kind of issues?"

Noah stared at the chief for a moment before answering. "None that need concern the local police, but if you must know, she is a bit phobic. I'm sure Danielle can attest to that. She doesn't like shaking hands or unnecessary physical contact. She prefers small groups, and while she's friendly after she gets to know someone, she would have difficulty with the type of interrogation you're suggesting. Chief MacDonald, we are here on our vacation. I'm sorry this woman is missing, but it has nothing to do with us."

Max, he just said his wife is phobic—it means she's afraid of things. Maybe she's afraid of cats, Walt suggested.

Danielle glanced to the chief. "This probably is some bizarre coincidence. I can talk to Zara when she gets back. And I'm sure she'll verify what her husband just told you. Noah's right, this is their vacation, and it's not really fair to put her through this."

The chief looked at Danielle for a moment, considering her suggestion. Finally, he nodded and said, "I suppose that will work. Like you said, it's probably just a bizarre coincidence."

Ten minutes later Danielle stood outside by the police car with MacDonald.

"So you really believe it's just a coincidence?" the chief asked.

"I don't know what to believe. But I do know Zara doesn't seem comfortable around strangers. She never comes downstairs when Chris's uncles are around. She claims she isn't a breakfast person, but maybe she just doesn't like being around that many people at one time. But she hasn't seemed to have a problem talking to Walt or myself." She then added with a laugh, "As long as I don't try shaking her hand."

"I do wonder—is she here of her own free will?" the chief asked. "Is Noah controlling her somehow?"

Danielle shrugged. "I haven't noticed anything like that. He'll leave her here and go out without her—and I know she's taken walks on the beach without him. And she's in town by herself now. So it's not like they're always together. But I'll talk to her."

"It's always possible she is this missing person, but not because she's been held against her will, but because she wants to disappear," the chief suggested.

WHEN DANIELLE RETURNED to the house a few minutes later, she was greeted by Walt.

"I think Noah lied about Zara walking to town," he told her.

"Why do you say that?" Danielle asked.

"Because after you went outside with the chief, Noah went to the kitchen to get some cookies, and I headed upstairs. When I went by their room, the door was ajar. Zara was in there. I saw her. She was standing by the window, looking outside. I don't think she saw me."

Danielle glanced toward the kitchen. "So he lied?"

"Either that or she came back when we were in the living room, and she went upstairs without us seeing her. There is another thing," Walt said.

"What?"

"Max is convinced Zara hates him. His feelings are hurt."

"Hates him? Did she do something to him?"

"Other than ignore him—refuse to look at him, no."

"That's good. I thought maybe she did something to my sweet cat. Like kicked him or something."

Walt arched his brow. "Sweet cat?"

"He is sweet," she said defensively.

"Tell that to the poor rodents he terrorizes."

"YOU'RE GOING to have to talk to Danielle," Noah said after he returned to their bedroom.

"Talk to her about what?"

Noah recounted the conversation he'd had with the chief.

With a sigh she took a seat at the foot of the bed. "I wondered why you guys were taking so long."

"I thought you might have overheard our conversation from the hallway." Noah sat down on a chair next to the bed.

Zara shook her head. "Not with that cat out there. I looked out, saw him walking toward the living room."

"The cat is the least of our problems."

Zara studied Noah for a moment. "Did you really tell them we met in middle school?"

"It's the truth, isn't it?"

Zara chuckled. "What were you, twelve? You were so angry."

"I had a reason to be angry," he said. "They killed my mother."

"And for all intents and purposes, my mother killed herself. When we were kids, I used to wonder which was worse."

187

"Did it really matter?"

Zara pulled her feet up on the bed and wrapped her arms around her bent legs. "I suppose not in the big picture. We both ended up in the same place."

"You were the first person I ever trusted," he said. "But now…"

Zara shook her head. "Don't go there, Noah."

THIRTY

B ella persistently batted at the coffee cup, sending it closer and closer to the desk's edge. Hunny stood nearby, watching the calico cat, anticipating the inevitable. Oblivious to her cat's antics and the potential minor disaster, Heather gave the man on the telephone her lunch order. The crash came at the precise moment the call ended.

Heather jumped up and spied the shattered ceramic cup, its contents spilling on the floor. "Bella!"

The unrepentant cat sat on the edge of the desk, looking down at what she had done, her tail swishing back and forth. Hunny retreated to her dog bed, hiding her head in its cushion.

"You little heathen!" Heather shouted, grabbing the cat from the desk and tossing it away from the broken mess.

Chris, who had been standing in the entry talking to his uncles, peeked his head into the room and asked, "Did Bella kill another cup?"

"She does this to torment me," Heather grumbled as she got down on her hands and knees to clean up the mess.

Chris laughed and then turned his attention back to his uncles.

"Why do you let her bring that cat to work?" Simon asked.

"Why not? I bring Hunny."

"Not quite the same thing, son," Loyd said. "I think that girl takes advantage of you."

"You don't like Heather much, do you?" Chris asked.

Loyd shrugged. "I just don't want to see someone take advantage of your good nature. You're a lot like your mother, you know. Always trying to save someone."

"Like an orphan kid?" Chris asked.

Loyd reached out and patted Chris's arm. "I understand why you think that way."

"Think what way?" Chris asked.

"That we don't see you as a real Glandon. It's understandable you believe that, considering what we tried to do, and how it looked. But in our misguided attempt to protect you, we allowed ourselves to listen to our attorneys when we went to court. They lost sight of what our real intention was—they just wanted to win—and we were too close to the situation to realize what was really happening."

Chris glanced briefly over to the doorway leading to where Heather was working. "You don't need to worry about Heather. She's alright."

"Can I make one suggestion?" Simon asked.

"What's that?" Chris asked.

"You said you have a meeting with your Realtor this afternoon, the one who brought you that candy."

"Umm…yes, what about it?"

"You told us he wasn't just your Realtor but a good friend. I suspect he's someone you might discuss business with—maybe even bounce ideas off?" Simon asked.

Chris shrugged. "Sometimes."

"Then get a second opinion. We don't expect you to take our advice, especially considering everything. But talk to your friend, tell him some of the things we've noticed since we've been here. Maybe you'll be surprised. Perhaps he's noticed the same things we have and just didn't want to say anything. You've no idea how many times we had to fire someone, and then later close confidants would tell us they were glad we let the employee go, and then they would go on to tell us what they had witnessed the employee do. I always wondered why they didn't just say something earlier. But they typically won't, not unless you ask them. Just ask him."

Chris was spared responding to his uncle's suggestion when Heather walked into the room the next moment.

"I'm going to go pick up my lunch," she announced.

Chris glanced at his watch. "And I need to head over to

190

Adam's."

DANIELLE SAT ALONE at the kitchen table, jotting down on a pad of paper what she intended to prepare for Christmas dinner. Lily and Ian were hosting a Christmas Eve gathering, which would mean all she would need to do was bring some of the cookies she had already made. Lily had invited Chris's uncles, along with the Bishops, but Danielle already knew Mr. Bishop had declined. According to him, he and his wife were planning something else for tomorrow night.

"Danielle, Noah said you wanted to talk to me," Zara said from the open doorway.

"Hello, Zara. Yes, I'd like to talk to you. Can you come sit with me?" Danielle leaned over to the next chair and pulled it out for her.

Zara smiled at the gesture. She walked into the kitchen and sat down in the chair.

"Noah told me about the police chief stopping by this afternoon. It's a crazy coincidence, this woman that you say looks just like me, has the same first name, but it isn't me. Honest."

Danielle glanced back to the doorway leading to the hallway and then back to Zara. 'Where is Noah?"

"He's up in our room taking a nap. Why?"

Danielle leaned forward and started to touch Zara's hand but stopped when Zara lurched back, obviously terrified at the prospect. Danielle quickly changed course and pulled back into her own chair, folding her hands on her lap. Zara visibly relaxed as Danielle retreated.

"I just want you to know you are safe here. If you need any help, I'm here for you."

Zara smiled at Danielle. "Oh, you think maybe I'm this other Zara, and Noah is somehow threatening me? Maybe he kidnapped me and is keeping me hostage?"

"I'm just saying if you need help, all you have to do is tell me."

"I'm fine, Danielle. It's really sweet of you, but I'm not in danger. I'm not a missing person. And Noah is the kindest man I know. He is the last person in the world who would ever hurt or threaten me."

Danielle studied Zara for a moment and then smiled. "I hope you understand, I had to ask."

Zara nodded. "Yes I do. I just don't want to deal with some police interrogation. I'd rather enjoy my Christmas holiday."

"No problem, I'll tell the chief it isn't you," Danielle conceded. "It was just so weird…seriously, maybe you have a twin sister out there that you don't know about."

"I seriously doubt that. But I do feel bad this woman is missing. What her family must be going through." Zara shook her head at the thought.

"According to the information, she doesn't have any family," Danielle explained.

"Really? Well, that's sad. Everyone should have family. If her family isn't looking for her, who is?"

"I don't think the chief mentioned this to your husband, but the missing person's notice didn't come from another police department, it came from the missing woman's roommate."

Zara arched her brow. "Her roommate?"

Danielle nodded. "When the other Zara disappeared, she didn't take anything with her, not even her cameras. She's a freelance photographer. The roommate didn't feel the police were putting much effort into finding her, so she sent out the flyers."

"Do you have any idea why she sent one here?" Zara asked.

"Apparently the roommate decided to do her own sleuthing. The missing woman had used her computer, so she started looking into her search history. A number of websites she had visited were from Frederickport."

Zara smiled. "Really? My, that is resourceful of the roommate."

"Yes, and if you had been the missing woman, we could say it was pretty good detective work."

Zara stood up. "Yes, we could. Thanks again for taking care of this and talking to your police chief for me."

"Sure, no problem." Danielle smiled.

"Thank you, Danielle. That makes me feel much better." Zara stood up and flashed Danielle a smile and then headed to the doorway leading to the hallway.

Danielle turned in her chair, preparing to ask Zara a final question. But she froze when she noticed something on the back of Zara's neck—a tattoo—a feather tattoo.

THIRTY-ONE

D anielle found Walt in the parlor with Max. The pair sat
together on the sofa, and by the looks of the two, they were in
the midst of a conversation. She stood in the doorway and watched
them. It fascinated her how he could still communicate with most
cats and dogs. Neither knew she was standing there. After a moment
Walt looked up and noticed her in the doorway. He smiled.

"It's her," Danielle said as she walked into the room and shut the
door behind her.

"She admitted being the missing person?" Walt asked.

Danielle walked to the sofa and picked up Max. He meowed.
She sat next to Walt and settled Max on her lap. He began to purr.
"No, just the opposite. She swore it wasn't her, just some bizarre
coincidence."

"Then why do you think it's her?" he asked.

"Because having the same name as a missing woman who looks
identical to her might be a wild coincidence—but to have the same
tattoo, I think not."

"She has a feather tattoo on the back of her neck?" Walt asked.

Danielle nodded. "She does."

Walt leaned back in the sofa, silently considering what Danielle
was telling him. He could hear Max's loud purr. The cat was clearly
enjoying Danielle's attention as she gently stroked his back.

Finally, Walt said, "She doesn't want to be found. She must have her reasons."

Danielle sighed and leaned back in the sofa. She propped her feet up on the coffee table. Max remained on her lap. "Plus, that notice of her disappearance didn't come from law enforcement. It came from a woman who claimed to be her roommate."

Walt looked down at the cat curled up on Danielle's lap. "Max and I were just discussing her."

"You mentioned she seemed to have an issue with him."

"He claims she's always telling him to go away."

"How does he know that's what she's saying?" Danielle teased. "Cats are notorious for misunderstanding what us living humans are telling them. Just the other day I told Max to stay off my bed, and he hopped right on it."

Walt laughed. "I suspect that was more a case of Max ignoring what you were saying, as opposed to not understanding."

"I think you're right." Danielle leaned down and kissed the top of Max's head.

"What are you going to tell the chief?" Walt asked.

"Just what we know. I don't imagine he's obligated to do anything, since that wasn't an official missing person's bulletin. But I would like to know more about the people staying under my roof."

Walt considered Danielle's words for a moment before suggesting, "I think you should take them some milk and cookies."

DANIELLE STOOD at the door to Noah and Zara's room, holding a serving tray with a plate of cookies and two glasses of cold milk. Juggling the tray in one hand, she knocked on the door. A moment later, the door opened a few inches, and Noah peeked out into the hallway.

"I come bringing a peace offering," Danielle said brightly.

Noah opened the door wider and eyed the tray in Danielle's hands.

"Cookies?" He smiled.

Danielle handed Noah the tray. "I'm sorry for any stress I caused you and your wife." She looked past Noah and spied Zara standing by the window, watching her. "I wasn't sure how I could make it up to you, but I figure cookies always help me."

THE GHOST OF CHRISTMAS SECRETS

Noah's smile broadened as he accepted the tray. "Your cookies are difficult to resist."

"I hope you enjoy them. I wasn't sure if you both liked milk with your cookies."

"I certainly do. Thank you," Zara said.

"You can just leave the tray outside your room when you're done," Danielle said before leaving.

Danielle went to her bedroom and shut the door, leaving it open a few inches. Walt was already inside, sitting on the edge of her bed. Together they waited. Fifteen minutes later she heard the Bishops' door open and close. She peeked outside and spied the tray sitting on the floor outside their door. The glasses and plate were empty.

Danielle slipped out of her room and picked up the tray. She headed downstairs with Walt following along beside her. Once they got in the kitchen, Danielle set the tray on the counter.

Just as she started to pick up one of the glasses, it flew up, away from her hand, and Walt yelled, "Don't touch it!"

"I was just going to put it in the sack," Danielle explained, pointing to the sack she had set on the counter earlier.

"And get your fingerprints on it?" The glass hovered above the counter. "You were meticulous cleaning both of those glasses before filling them with milk, wiping them down, and setting them on the tray, free of any prints. And now you plan to get your prints all over them, maybe smudge theirs?"

"I guess I didn't think." With a sigh, she reached for the paper bag and opened it. Holding it wide open, she watched as the airborne glass floated over to the sack and gently dropped into it. A moment later, the second glass lifted from the tray and joined the first glass. Carefully, she folded closed the top of the paper bag and then looked at Walt. "Thank you."

"You're welcome." Walt smiled.

"YOU WANT me to run the fingerprints on these glasses?" the chief asked incredulously. He stood behind his desk, the paper sack with the glasses in hand.

"You can do it, can't you?" Walt asked.

"Yes, but—"

"I know it's her. She has the feather tattoo on the back of her neck. But she insisted it isn't her. I just want to know who these people are who are staying with us. I understand she might just want to disappear, and she has that right, but I need to know who they are—who he is—should we be concerned? They are staying in our house. Please, Chief."

MacDonald considered the request a moment. Finally, he said, "Okay. I'll do it. Give me a couple of hours, and I'll see what I can find out."

WHILE WAITING for the results of the fingerprints, Walt took Danielle to Lucy's Diner to have some coffee and pie. When they walked into the restaurant, they found Adam Nichols alone at a table. He asked them to join him, and they accepted.

"Chris's uncle Simon stopped by my office earlier today. He told me he was just curious to see what housing prices are in Frederickport," Adam told them after the waitress took their order and left the table.

"You don't sound like you believe his reason for stopping by," Danielle said.

Adam shrugged. "I think it was a PR ploy on his part."

"What's a PR ploy?" Walt asked.

Adam looked at Walt. "You know, PR, public relations. He did a lot of talking about how proud he is of Chris—thanked me for being such a good friend. Talked about his regrets in contesting their brother's will, and how grateful he was that Chris had forgiven them. Although, I'm not sure Chris has really forgiven them." Adam picked up his coffee and took a sip.

"Did he mention Heather?" Walt asked.

Adam frowned a moment and then set his cup back on its saucer. "Actually he did. Talked about how he felt she was manipulating him—trying to take advantage of him. I didn't really take it seriously. Heather is a little different, and to someone like him, she probably seems like an alien."

"Both uncles have been doing a lot of trash-talking about her," Danielle grumbled.

"What's stranger, they've told Heather how much Chris likes her, and encouraged her to pursue a personal relationship with him," Walt told him.

Adam frowned. "That doesn't make sense. I can't see them doing that."

"Heather thinks they did that so she would act inappropriately toward Chris, in hopes he'll fire her," Danielle explained.

Adam laughed. "Don't they know she already acts inappropriately toward him? I've heard her tell him to shut up more than once."

Walt chuckled. "True. But the uncles don't know that."

"I saw Chris after his uncle stopped by. I almost said something to him about it, but I decided not to. He seemed a little stressed out over their visit," Adam said.

WHEN WALT and Danielle returned to the police station, they found the chief at his desk, just getting ready to call Danielle to tell her he had the results.

"Good, you're here," the chief said as he hung up his phone. They walked into the office, and he nodded to the door, motioning for them to close it.

"So what did you find out?" Danielle asked as she took a seat facing the desk. Walt sat down in the chair next to her.

"I learned your Zara doesn't like milk," the chief said, leaning back in his chair.

"What do you mean?" Danielle frowned.

"There was only one set of prints on those glasses," the chief explained. "Another thing, your guest is not Noah Bishop, he's Noah Church."

"He's using a fake name?" Danielle asked.

"Apparently so."

"Church...Bishop? He has a theme going there," Walt muttered.

The chief picked up a printout and skimmed over it. "His name is Noah Church, and he has no priors. Not even a parking ticket I could find. By the way, how did he pay for his room? I would assume a credit card."

"No, not a credit card. He paid with a gift card."

"He gave it to you over the phone when he made the reservation?" the chief asked.

"No. Zara made the reservation and asked if they could pay

with a gift card when they arrived. Said it was a gift from her husband's parents. Normally I require a down payment when they make a reservation, but considering the late date of the reservation and the fact I had other vacancies, I didn't make a point of taking a down payment."

"She said it was a gift from Noah's parents?" the chief asked.

Danielle nodded. "Yes."

"That would be a little tricky, Noah Church was orphaned when he was twelve. Grew up in foster care. And he happens to live in the same town as Zara Leighton."

"I guess I'm not surprised. I knew it was her," Danielle said.

"What does Noah Church do for a living?" Walt asked.

"He's a high school teacher. Well liked from all accounts. If he and Zara have decided to disappear together, his school doesn't know about it. They believe he's returning after Christmas break. One more thing. He's not married. At least, not that they are aware of. Which could support the story they're newlyweds. Maybe his work just doesn't know yet that he got married."

"None of this makes any sense," Danielle murmured.

"Maybe Zara is only missing from her roommate's perspective," the chief suggested.

"You're saying Zara had problems with the roommate and just left," Walt asked.

"It happens. We have no idea what type of relationship the roommate had with Zara. By her letter it sounds like they were good friends, and she is worried about her. But we don't know her, and Zara, while she has lied to both of us, she's made it perfectly clear she doesn't want to be found by her roommate," the chief reminded them.

"How do we really know the person who sent you that letter was ever Zara's roommate, or if it is really a woman?" Walt asked.

"I don't doubt that part," the chief explained. "When I first received the flyer, before Danielle ever saw it, I called the police station working on the case. The detective I spoke to said he knew the roommate had sent out those letters, but he didn't feel Zara was a missing person. She has a history of just taking off and disappearing for weeks at a time, and there was no indication of foul play. Her car was never found. They assume she just took off."

"Would you be opposed to me calling the roommate?" Danielle asked.

"Do you think that would be fair to Zara if she wants to just disappear?" Walt asked.

"I'm not going to tell her Zara is here. I'm just going to say I happened to see her flyer, and I was curious about her and wondered why she thought Zara might be heading to Frederickport."

"You can try, but I doubt you'll learn anything," the chief said.

THIRTY-TWO

Not long after Danielle and Walt's elopement, Danielle had checked with the city to see if she would be able to build a garage where the carriage house had once stood. After they told her it would be possible, she had hired a builder to construct a two-car garage. While she had used Bill Jones for remodeling the attic, she felt she needed a licensed general contractor more familiar with new construction to build the garage.

They had it completed within three months. While Walt routinely parked his Packard in the garage, Danielle often forgot to turn down the alley and inevitably ended up parking alongside the house, as she had become used to doing since moving into Marlow House.

She pulled up along the side of the house after returning from the police station. As soon as she turned off the engine, she glanced up in her rearview mirror and spied Lily coming her way.

"Where have you been?" Lily asked when Danielle got out of the car. "I called, but you didn't answer."

"I'm sorry, Lily, I turned off my phone."

"I hate when you do that," Lily grumbled and then looked to Walt, who was walking around the car toward them. "Hi, Walt."

"Lily, what's so urgent?" Walt asked.

"Well," Lily said with a sigh, taking a moment to look him up and down, "I could use some of your magical powers."

Walt arched his brow. "Magical powers?"

"Sure. I have to get the house clean for the open house tomorrow. Maybe you can stop over and do that thing you do." Lily grinned.

"Walt is not going over and cleaning your house," Danielle said.

Lily wrinkled her nose. "You're so selfish. It's not like he has to actually touch anything."

Walt laughed.

"I suppose that's a no." She sighed dramatically and then turned back to Danielle. "Actually, the real reason I'm here, I wanted a head count. Chris said his uncles are coming with him, but I haven't heard for sure about the Bishops."

"According to Noah, they have something else planned."

"I suppose it's not a big deal if they decide to change their minds and come." Lily grinned. "I have to admit I'm excited. This is our first real party at our house since we got married."

"Is there anything else you want us to bring?" Danielle asked.

Lily shook her head. "I can't think of anything."

After Lily left a few minutes later, Walt and Danielle walked into the house. Danielle tossed her purse on the counter while Walt closed the door behind him.

"I'm going to call her," Danielle abruptly announced.

"The roommate?" Walt asked.

"Yes. Ever since we left the chief's office, it has been bugging me. I need to know more. Who are these people staying under our roof, and why is Zara hiding from her roommate? But I think I'm going to make the call from my bedroom so I can lock the door and one of them doesn't walk in on me when I'm on the phone.

DANIELLE SAT at her dressing table in her bedroom and opened her purse. She removed the copy of the letter the chief had received regarding the missing woman and reread it. After a few minutes of contemplation, she retrieved her cellphone and then tossed her purse on the floor.

A moment later she dialed the roommate's number.

"Hello," came a woman's voice.

"Hello, is this Corky Summers?" Danielle asked.

"Yes, it is. Who is this?"

"You don't know me, but I'm calling about the missing person bulletin you sent to the Frederickport police station."

"What do you want?" Corky demanded.

"I...umm...I was under the impression you were looking for Zara Leighton and—"

"What do you know about her? Do you know what happened?"

"No. I was just curious why you happened to send one of your fliers to Frederickport."

"Do you have any information on Zara?" the woman demanded.

"No, but if I happen to see her—"

"You won't."

"Excuse me?"

"I told them, and they wouldn't listen to me. No one would listen."

Danielle frowned at the phone. It sounded like the person was crying. "Are you okay?"

"No! I am not okay. My friend is dead. Someone murdered her and no one cares. I'm sick of you reporters calling me. If you would have done your job and actually run a real story on her when she vanished, maybe she wouldn't be dead now. Unless you know something to help find her killer, don't call me again!" The line when dead.

Danielle stared blankly at the phone in her hand. Setting it on the vanity, she tried to comprehend what Corky had just told her when she heard footsteps overhead. She glanced up to the ceiling. Walt was in his room. Danielle stood up and headed for her closet.

"HEY, WALT," Danielle said as she peeked into his room from the secret passage.

He sat at his desk, working on the computer. He glanced over to Danielle and smiled. "Did you talk to her roommate?"

"That's why I'm up here. My laptop's in the parlor, and I really don't want to use it down there. Can I borrow your computer for a minute?"

"Sure. What's going on?" Walt stood up and moved out of the way so Danielle could sit down at his desk.

"Zara Leighton is dead."

"Excuse me?"

"Yeah, that's what I said too." Danielle sat down in front of Walt's computer. "I talked to the roommate—Corky Summers. For some reason she thought I was a reporter, and she got pretty upset, told me to stop calling her. The only thing I got out of her was that Zara was dead. She hung up on me."

"Why does she think she's dead?" Walt asked.

"I have no clue. That's why I want to use your computer and see if I can find anything about her online."

Walt stood behind Danielle and watched her fingers quickly dance over the keyboard as she searched for information. After a moment he walked over to a wingback chair and sat down, waiting for Danielle to complete her search.

Five minutes later Danielle muttered, "She's dead alright."

Walt stood up and walked to the desk. Standing behind Danielle, he placed his hands on her shoulders and looked down at the computer monitor. "What did you find?"

"A news article, posted today," Danielle explained, her attention still focused on what she had pulled up on the monitor. "According to the article, her body was found a couple of days ago, in a freezer in a storage unit in Fullerton, California. But they just made the identification this morning. Obviously her poor roommate just found out. No wonder she was so upset."

"Do they know how long she's been dead?" Walt asked.

Danielle shook her head. "Not really. According to the article, she was stored in a freezer. I imagine that would make it more difficult to determine the exact time of death if the body was frozen for who knows how long. At least it was frozen until the freezer stopped working after a rat or something decided to chew through the cord. And then the body started to thaw and—"

"The smell." Walt cringed.

Danielle nodded. "Exactly."

"Whose freezer was it?"

"That's what makes it such a mystery. The guy who rented the storage unit died around the same time Zara went missing. According to the article, the roommate reported her missing the first of June, but she hadn't actually seen Zara for a couple of weeks. She assumed she was on some photo assignment, but when she went into her room for something and found her cameras still there, along with her suitcase, she began to worry."

"Why didn't the chief know her body was found? I thought he called the police station after he received the report," he asked.

"Because they just positively identified her body this morning. Until then, they didn't know who it was."

"If Zara Leighton—the missing person—is who they found in the freezer—just who is Zara Bishop, who looks just like her, has the same name and tattoo, and who is married to a man who is using an alias? Plus, the fact he lived in the same town as the missing woman."

Danielle stood up abruptly. "I think I know."

"You do?"

"Yes. And I'm going to find out if I'm right." Danielle started toward the secret passage.

"Should I come with you?" Walt asked.

Danielle paused and looked back at Walt. "Hmm, yeah, it might be a good idea. I might need some of your—magical powers—as Lily calls them."

"I'll meet you by their room." Walt headed for the door leading to the stairwell to the second floor, while Danielle took the hidden stairs to her room. A few minutes later she met Walt in front of the Bishops' door. Or was it the Churches'?

Danielle knocked on the door. There was no reply. She knocked again. The door opened just a few inches.

"Yes?" Noah peeked out.

"We need to speak to you and Zara," Danielle told him. Walt stood at her side.

"This isn't a good time. Zara is taking a nap."

"I'm afraid Zara is going to have to wake up," Danielle snapped.

"Please, Danielle, this really is not a good time," Noah said.

"You can either let me in, or wait for the police chief to arrive, because if you don't let Walt and me in your room, that's who I am calling, Noah *Church*."

Noah stared at Danielle through the small opening for a moment and then reluctantly opened the door.

Zara stood by the window, her attention on Walt and Danielle.

Danielle walked into the room, her eyes meeting Zara's. "Do you always take your naps standing by the window?"

"What do you want?" Zara asked.

Danielle glanced back to Walt, who stood just inside the room, the door still ajar. "Walt, you'd better shut the door all the way. I don't think we want anyone else to hear this."

With a nod Walt shut the door, and Danielle turned to face Zara.

THIRTY-THREE

A combination of evergreen, fresh-brewed coffee, and homemade biscuits about to come out of the oven filled the air. It was Christmas Eve. Over her leggings and long-sleeved sweater, Danielle wore her vintage Christmas apron, its appliqué Santa yellowed with age, as she lined several wicker baskets with clean linen napkins for the biscuits.

"Something smells good," Simon said when he entered the kitchen.

"Breakfast is about ready," Danielle told him. "Please go on into the dining room. Coffee's on the table."

Simon took Danielle's advice and was surprised to find not just Chris sitting at the table with Loyd and Walt, but Lily and Ian from across the street.

"Merry Christmas Eve," Lily said cheerfully. "Dani invited us over. I think she felt sorry for me because I'm going to be busy all day getting ready for tonight's party."

"I just want to make sure you're properly fed," Danielle said as she brought two baskets of biscuits to the table. "Because if you're hungry, I'm afraid you might eat up all the appetizers you're making before I have a chance to eat them."

"Entirely possible." Lily laughed and snatched a biscuit.

"Where's Mr. Bishop?" Loyd asked, glancing around the table.

"He and his wife left last night," Danielle said as she took a seat at the table.

"You mean they checked out?" Simon asked.

"Yes. They had some family emergency and had to check out early." Danielle shook out her cloth napkin and placed it on her lap.

Simon chuckled. "I never did meet his wife."

"I never even saw her," Lily added.

"She was shy," Danielle said as she plucked a biscuit from the basket.

"What does everyone have planned today?" Ian asked. "I think I know what Lily has planned for me."

"Yes, I have a list of appetizers for you to make." Lily giggled. "He's a better cook than me anyway."

"I have to go back to the office until three. And Heather's not happy about working today," Chris told them.

"What's wrong with Heather? She doesn't usually mind working," Danielle asked.

Chris shook his head. "I don't know what her problem is lately. She's been acting strange. Kinda bitchy."

"Well, it is Heather," Lily said with a chuckle.

"No, I mean like she's seriously annoyed with me," Chris said.

"I suppose I can understand her feelings. It is Christmas Eve," Lily said.

"I know, but I have to finish stuffing some envelopes for a fundraiser that we have to get mailed out this afternoon. She's mad that I didn't hire someone to stuff them. She keeps reminding me I can afford to pay someone to do those things. I pointed out I had hired someone to do it—her. She didn't find that amusing."

"She is your employee; doesn't she expect to work?" Loyd asked.

"I'm not doing anything today. Why don't I come over and help? That way she can leave early," Danielle suggested.

Chris shook his head. "You don't have to do that."

"No, I want to. Anyway, I don't have to do anything until Lily and Ian's party tonight." Danielle flashed Lily a grin.

"That would be great. Can you come over about two?"

"Sure. Why don't you just let Heather go home when I get there?" Danielle asked.

"That would make her happy." Chris smiled.

Danielle looked at Walt. "You want to come help?"

Walt shook his head. "Sorry, this afternoon I promised to take Evan and Eddie Christmas shopping for their dad."

"Cutting it a little close to the wire, aren't you?" Ian asked with a laugh.

"You have to do a little shopping on Christmas Eve if you want an old-fashioned Christmas," Walt insisted.

"Walt, before you take the boys shopping, any chance you can stop by my house and take Hunny out?"

"You aren't taking her to the office today?" Walt asked.

Chris shook his head. "No, I have too much to do, and I don't want the hassle. As it is, I told Heather she could leave Bella at the office tonight."

"Bella? Isn't that her cat?" Simon asked.

"Yes. I guess Bella has been attacking her Christmas tree. She just figured she'd leave the cat at the office until she takes her tree down."

"That girl certainly has nerve," Loyd grumbled.

"So what are you both doing this afternoon?" Chris asked his uncles.

"We're going to finish up some Christmas shopping," Loyd told him.

"WHAT ARE YOU SMILING ABOUT?" Simon asked his brother after Loyd dragged him into his room later that morning.

"Today's the day." Loyd was practically giddy.

Simon shook his head. "It's too soon."

"Too soon? It's perfect! Were you paying attention at breakfast? Danielle and Heather will be at Chris's office at the same time. And we don't have to deal with that blasted dog. It couldn't be any more ideal if we had planned it ourselves."

Simon sat down on the foot of Loyd's bed and nodded. "You're right. Providing there are no surprises, no one just dropping in, we could actually do this today."

"We are going to do this today. And I don't think anyone is going to be dropping in. It's Christmas Eve, and everyone who might just drop in is tied up, and the rest of their friends expect to see them at the party tonight. There is no reason to drop by."

"This will put a damper on the party." Simon snickered.

THE GHOST OF CHRISTMAS SECRETS

"But it will brighten my Christmas." Loyd laughed.

LOYD GLANCED AT HIS WATCH. Danielle hadn't left the house yet, and he was certain Walt was still upstairs in the attic. A soft knock came at the bedroom door. It was Simon. Loyd let his brother into his room and then locked the door.

"I did it. You were right, the stupid woman keeps a key to her front door under a rock," Simon told him.

"No one saw you?" Loyd asked.

Simon shook his head. "No. I was careful. I was in and out of there in a matter of minutes."

"Good thing she had already left for work," Loyd said. "We might as well get everything else ready."

"You'd better do it; your hands are steadier than mine."

"Where is everything?" Simon asked.

Loyd pointed to the dresser. "In the bottom drawer."

With his cane, Loyd tottered over to one of the chairs and sat down as he watched his brother. Simon opened the bottom dresser drawer and removed a bottle of wine and a small plastic bag with a vial of liquid inside. He set them both on the dresser. From the drawer he pulled out a pair of latex gloves and slipped them on. He then removed a clean cloth from the drawer and wiped down the wine bottle.

"You're certain there's one of these in Chris's wine rack?" Simon asked.

"There were three yesterday, and while one may be gone now, I don't think they drank all three."

From the drawer Simon pulled out a corkscrew and used it to open the bottle. He then removed the vial from the plastic bag and unscrewed its lid. Loyd watched as Simon poured the liquid into the wine and then recorked the bottle.

Loyd pointed to the closet. "The gift bag for the wine is in there."

DANIELLE ARRIVED at Chris's office a few minutes before two in the afternoon on Christmas Eve. Heather left the office a short time after Danielle's arrival. Ten minutes later, Loyd and Simon showed up, gift bag in hand.

"Uncle Loyd, Uncle Simon, what are you doing here?" Chris asked when he opened the door to let them in.

"We've come to help," Simon announced.

"Help? That's sweet of you, but Danielle and I have this covered." Chris led his uncles into the office, where they found Danielle sitting at Heather's desk, a stack of envelopes waiting to be stuffed on her left and a poinsettia plant on her right.

"What are you two doing here?" Danielle asked.

"We felt sorry for you both having to work on Christmas Eve," Simon explained.

"What's in the bag?" Danielle asked.

"We brought you a bottle of wine," Simon said as he lifted the bag to show her, yet he did not remove the bottle.

"Wine? That sounds good," Chris said.

"Then let's have some," Simon suggested.

"It does sound good," Danielle agreed.

"You two relax; and I'll take it in the kitchen and open it," Simon offered.

"The wine corkscrew is in the top drawer to the right of the sink," Chris called out as Simon headed for the door.

A few minutes later Simon returned with a tray carrying four glasses of wine, and handed one to each of them.

Danielle picked up her glass. "This will make stuffing envelopes more enjoyable."

Loyd lifted his glass. "I would like to make a toast, to my nephew for sharing Christmas with us, and to Danielle for opening her home to us."

Just as they were all about to take a drink, what sounded like glass breaking caught their attention. Both Loyd and Simon looked toward the doorway leading to the hallway. The next moment Heather's cat, Bella, came racing into the room while making an unholy shrieking sound. Like an animal possessed, she ran around in circles numerous times, running under the uncles' chairs, knocking Loyd's cane on the floor, and then flew back out through the doorway and disappeared.

"What in tarnation?" Loyd shouted, still holding his full glass of wine.

Danielle laughed and set her now empty glass on the desktop. "That cat acts crazy sometimes!"

"It's a good thing I left Hunny at home," Chris said, setting his glass on the desk. Like Danielle's, it was empty.

Loyd and Simon exchanged glances and then looked back to Chris and Danielle.

"Oh my, I drank that kind of fast." Danielle giggled. "Bad me."

"I didn't do bad myself. Want another glass?" Chris asked.

Before Danielle could answer, Chris grabbed hold of his forehead and closed his eyes.

"I don't feel right," Chris said, doubling over.

Danielle reached toward Chris. In doing so she tipped her empty wineglass over. She tried to stand up, but her knees buckled under her and she fell to the floor.

Simon and Loyd did not move. They simply stared.

"Oh my heavens, that was too easy," Loyd said before breaking into a laugh.

"It's not done yet. Let's do what we have to do."

Simon removed two pairs of latex gloves from his coat pocket and handed his brother a pair. They both put them on. Loyd removed an envelope from his coat pocket and slipped out the document it held. He walked to Chris, who was slumped over his desk.

"It won't be long now, boy," Loyd told Chris. "It paralyzes you first. Even if the paramedics showed up now, there's nothing they can do for you." He shoved the document under Chris's right hand. "I need your fingerprints. Then I need some from Danielle." He laughed.

Meanwhile, Simon was busy pouring wine from one of Chris's wine bottles down the sink and replacing it with what was left of the tainted wine. After he did that, he washed the four glasses that he had filled earlier. Taking two glasses out of the cupboard that he had seen Heather place there the day before, he added a few drops of tainted wine to each glass and swished it around before setting the glasses by Danielle and Chris.

"Don't forget their fingerprints," Loyd reminded him. "You need their fingerprints on those glasses."

Ten minutes later the two men surveyed the scene one final time, making sure they had thought of everything, before hastily leaving out the front door without locking it.

THIRTY-FOUR

W hen Simon and Loyd returned to Marlow House, they were
surprised to find Walt sitting in the living room reading
a book.

"I thought you were going Christmas shopping?" Loyd asked.

Walt looked up and closed his book, setting it on his lap.
"Change of plans. What about you, did you go Christmas
shopping?"

"We did a little." Loyd smiled.

Walt tossed his book on the coffee table and picked up the TV
remote. "*It's a Wonderful Life* is starting in a couple of minutes; would
you like to watch it with me?"

"This early?" Loyd asked, glancing at his watch.

Walt shrugged. "They've been running Christmas movies
all day."

Simon glanced at his brother and then looked back to Walt. "I
love that movie."

THE THREE MEN had been quietly watching *It's a Wonderful Life* for
about thirty minutes when Walt's cellphone rang. When he got off
the phone, he stood up abruptly and turned off the television. "That

was the police chief. There's something wrong at the foundation headquarters."

"You mean Chris's office?" Loyd asked.

Walt nodded. "He wouldn't say what was wrong, just that I was to go right over there." Without another word, Walt ran from the room, leaving Loyd and Simon sitting on the sofa together.

"You really need to work on that smile," Simon told his brother.

"What are you talking about?"

"That infernal grin. I swear you looked like you were smirking when Marlow said there was something wrong. I thought you were going to break into laughter at any minute."

"You're exaggerating."

"I'm serious, Loyd. Now pull it together, and get your sad face on, because in a few minutes we're going to have to put on the performance of our life."

"I can't help it." Loyd smiled broadly. "It was just too easy. I kept thinking of the expression *lambs to slaughter*. Such a helpful accommodating pair. It was as if they were reading my mind and doing exactly what I told them to do."

"Yes, we were lucky, but it isn't over yet."

"The important part is."

"You do realize we could have really been screwed if Marlow had decided to stop at the foundation office after his plans changed."

Loyd shrugged. "Yes, but that didn't happen, did it?"

"No, but it could have. We're in the end stretch, and we can't afford to screw this up now."

"You worry too much."

TWENTY MINUTES later Simon drove the rental car up the street to the Glandon Foundation Headquarters, his brother sitting in the passenger seat. There were cop cars parked everywhere, several with their strobe lights flashing. Simon and Loyd stayed in the car a moment and watched. What looked like two bodies were being removed from the building on stretchers and loaded into a van from the coroner's office.

"Ahh, how sad, there goes our dear nephew," Loyd smirked.

"I said put on your sad face," Simon snapped.

Loyd chuckled and opened his car door. As he got out of the vehicle, he spied Walt Marlow sitting in the passenger seat of one of the squad cars, its door open, and his head bent over as if crying. An officer stood nearby, patting his shoulder. "Showtime," Loyd muttered.

POLICE CHIEF MACDONALD stood by the sidewalk outside the Glandon Foundation Headquarters and watched as the two older men hurried toward him.

"Where is our nephew?" Loyd shouted, shaking his cane at the chief. Simon attempted to walk around the chief and up the walkway, but MacDonald stopped him.

"Sorry, you can't go up there. It's a crime scene," MacDonald said.

"What do you mean? What happened? Where is Chris?" Simon demanded.

"I'm very sorry to have to tell you this, but your nephew is dead. Heather found Chris and Danielle Boatman both dead in the office about thirty minutes ago. Danielle was on the floor, and Chris was slumped over his desk."

"Heather found them?" Loyd asked. "Chris said Heather wasn't going to be here this afternoon. She was leaving at two after Danielle got here."

"Apparently, Heather forgot something and came back and found them."

"Heather killed them. I know she did!" Loyd shouted.

"Loyd, please," Simon hushed.

"If you wouldn't mind, I'd like you both to come down to the station. I don't really want to do interviews here. But I need to speak to everyone who saw either Chris or Danielle today."

"WHAT WERE YOU DOING BACK THERE?" Simon asked when he climbed in the rental car with Loyd.

"How perfect is this? Heather finds them. We couldn't have planned it any better!" Loyd laughed.

"Just stop with the improvising, would you? That's not how we planned it. You can't be accusing Heather. Not yet."

"Why not?"

"For one thing, we don't know they were murdered yet, do we? MacDonald just said they found them dead, not that they were murdered."

"He said they were dead. How else would they get that way?" Loyd asked.

"I don't know, maybe Chris had a heart attack and Danielle tripped and broke her neck running for help. Stop offering information. At this point the only thing we're supposed to know is that they're dead!"

SIMON AND LOYD sat quietly together at the table in the interrogation room. Each time Loyd would start to say something, his brother would nudge his ankle with one shoed foot and glance over at the two-way mirror. After about ten minutes Brian Henderson entered the office, carrying a manila folder.

"Sorry to keep you waiting, gentlemen," Brian said as he tossed his folder on the table and sat down across from them.

"You're that officer our nephew introduced us to at the diner," Loyd noted.

Brian nodded. "Yes, my name is Brian Henderson. I'm very sorry for your loss. I wasn't close to Chris, but I understand he was your nephew."

"Thank you, we appreciate that," Simon said. "But I know this must be difficult for you too. I understand Danielle Boatman was one of your friends."

Brian shrugged. "Not really. To be honest, she was kind of a pain in the ass, but don't repeat me. I mean, I'm sorry she's dead, sorry when anyone dies, but it's not like it's going to mess up my Christmas."

Loyd let out a snort, followed by a kick to his shin by his brother, reminding him to suppress the grin that was currently itching to turn up the corners of his mouth. Loyd then asked, "Did you ever look into Heather Donovan like we asked?"

Brian arched his brow. "Heather Donovan?"

"My brother is just upset," Simon told him. "Ever since he

heard Chris was dead, he's been convinced this wasn't just a tragic accident. What happened, Officer, was there a gas leak? Carbon monoxide poisoning?"

"You are correct on one thing; it was poisoning, but not an accident. According to the coroner, someone poisoned the wine Danielle and Chris consumed."

Simon slumped back in the chair and shook his head.

"I need to ask you a few questions. First, when was the last time you saw your nephew?" Brian asked.

"At breakfast this morning," Loyd said. "The Bartleys from across the street and Walt Marlow were also there."

"And Danielle? When was the last time you saw her?" Brian asked.

"The same time," Simon told him.

"What did you do after breakfast?" Brian asked.

"We stayed at the house for a while, went out later, took a drive, did a little Christmas shopping, but we didn't buy anything," Simon said. "We've been trying to find the perfect gift for our nephew, but he is—was—difficult to shop for." Simon looked down at the table for a moment and closed his eyes while using his fingertips to wipe away invisible tears.

"You showed up at the foundation offices this afternoon while they were loading up the bodies. How did you happen to come then?"

Simon looked back up at Brian. "We had been at Marlow House, watching a Christmas movie with Walt, when he got a call that something was wrong at Chris's office. So we went right over."

"You mentioned Heather Donovan. You obviously think she is responsible for this. Can you tell me why?"

"Like I told you when I met you in the diner, there is something not right with that woman. And we could see how she took advantage of our nephew—took advantage of his generous nature. She had no business in that job, but he felt sorry for her," Loyd told him.

"But it wasn't just that," Simon explained. "Yesterday we heard them fighting. She was angry. And this morning at breakfast, Chris mentioned how strangely she has been acting lately—like she had some sort of grudge against him. You can ask Lily and Ian Bartley —or Walt Marlow, they were all there when Chris told us. In fact, that's why Danielle agreed to go down to the office, so Heather could leave earlier since it was Christmas Eve."

"Do you know why they were arguing?" Brian asked.

Loyd started to say something but closed his mouth when Simon nudged his foot again.

"I'm pretty sure it was about us," Simon said wearily.

"You? How so?" Brian asked.

"We walked in on the argument. They were in the kitchen and didn't see us come in. Heather was yelling at Chris, saying he was a fool to ever trust us, that she had been there for him, and that if he needed a backup, it should be her and not us. The moment they saw us, Heather stopped talking and stormed out of the room. We didn't know what they were talking about, not until this morning after breakfast."

"What were they talking about?" Brian asked.

"Chris decided to add a codicil to his will, naming my brother and me to replace Danielle should she not—well, if something happened to her." Simon rubbed his forehead with the back of his hand and shook his head. "It was only a gesture on Chris's part, his way of showing us he had forgiven us for what we had done. We never expected to outlive Danielle; we are old men. We were just touched he wanted to do it."

"He may not have even gotten around to doing it," Loyd added. "He just told us his intentions this morning."

"Actually…" Brian opened the manila folder and pulled out a document, sliding it across the table to the brothers. "This is a copy of what we found in Chris's file drawer. Naturally we wanted to know who inherited. Apparently he had both Danielle and Heather sign it yesterday. Heather swears she never saw the document before."

Loyd picked it up and stared at it a moment. "He really did it…"

Simon reached over and patted his brother's arm. He then looked at Brian and asked, "What now?"

"We got a search warrant for Heather Donovan's house. They found an empty glass vial in her bathroom cabinet that has traces of the same poison found in the wine. Of course, she insists she didn't do it."

Loyd slammed his fist on the table. "I knew it! I told Chris he shouldn't trust that woman!"

Brian's cellphone buzzed. He paused a moment and looked at it. He glanced up to the uncles and said, "They're bringing in Heather for more questioning, and they need to use this room. Would you like to wait in the adjoining office with me and hear what she has to say?"

Loyd perked up. "We can do that?"

Brian shrugged. "It's a little unorthodox, but considering the circumstances, I don't see a problem. If it was my nephew who had been so brutally murdered, I would want to listen."

"Yes, yes, I would like to do that," Loyd said as he pushed the document back across the table to Brian.

Brian returned the document to the file and started to stand up and then paused a moment. He sat back down and said, "I have a quick question for you. Do either of you know a woman by the name of Zara Leighton?"

Loyd stared blankly at Brian, as did his brother.

Simon blinked several times and then stammered, "I don't think so, why?"

"They found her body in a storage unit the other day in Southern California and just recently made a positive identification."

"What does this have to do with our nephew?" Loyd asked.

Brian closed the folder and looked up into Loyd's face. "One of the other guests at Marlow House, a Noah Church, although I believe he was using the name Noah Bishop for some reason, was a friend of the dead woman."

"You said her name was Zara?" Loyd frowned. "That's the name of his wife."

Brian smiled and shook his head. "No, he isn't married."

"Then who was the woman with him?" Loyd asked.

Brian shrugged. "I'm not sure what you mean. According to Walt Marlow, Noah Church didn't have anyone with him."

"No, he had a wife with him," Loyd insisted.

Brian frowned. "Did you see her?"

"No, but…" Loyd mumbled.

"Excuse me, but what does any of that have to do with our nephew?" Simon demanded.

"The man who rented the storage unit where they found her body was your gardener. Also, according to Noah Church, he's your nephew's biological brother. In fact, they're running DNA tests now."

THIRTY-FIVE

A s the two elderly men followed Brian out of the interrogation room, they passed Heather Donovan and the police chief. Heather, who had dressed for Christmas—with candy-cane-patterned leggings, a red striped oversized sweater, and green ribbons woven through her braids—looked like an angry elf when she passed them, sending both men a drop-dead glare.

Brian took Simon and Loyd to the adjoining office and said, "If you'll wait in here, I'll be right back."

The two men entered the small room and immediately walked to the large picture window on the far wall. Looking through the two-way mirror, they watched as Heather sat quietly at the table while the chief sat across from her, shuffling through papers in the folder before him. Even if Heather and the chief had been talking —which they weren't yet—the Glandon brothers would not have been able to hear what was being said, as Brian had not yet turned on the speakers.

"They found her body," Loyd whispered to his brother.

"Be careful what you say in here," Simon warned.

"Good luck with the DNA results, not going to do much good for him now."

"I said be quiet," Simon hissed.

The office door opened and Brian re-entered, this time with Joe Morelli by his side. After a brief introduction, the four men moved to the window, and Brian turned on the speakers just as the chief handed Heather a piece of paper.

"Do you recognize this?" the chief asked.

Heather looked at the document and shook her head. "I told that other officer. I've never seen it before."

The chief pointed to a section on the document. "Isn't that your signature?"

Heather shrugged. "It looks like mine, but I've never seen that before."

"Are you saying that's not your signature?"

"I said it looks like mine. But I didn't sign it."

The chief returned the document to the envelope. "We found this in Chris's file drawer with copies of his will."

Heather shrugged again. "I don't know. I didn't put it there. Like I said, I've never seen that before."

"According to the date, you signed this yesterday."

Heather shook her head. "I didn't. Someone obviously forged my signature."

"She's lying," Loyd grumbled.

"Can you tell me what you and Chris argued about yesterday?"

Heather shrugged. "We didn't argue. No more than normal. I was a little annoyed he wanted me to stuff envelopes on Christmas Eve. But he got Danielle to help him do that, so I was okay."

"She doesn't seem to be broken up about Chris's and Danielle's deaths," Loyd snorted.

"How did you get along with Chris's uncles?" the chief asked.

"Okay, I guess. At first I didn't think they liked me, but then they told me Chris had a thing for me and encouraged me to pursue him."

"She's lying!" Loyd snapped.

Simon let out a deep breath and glanced briefly at his brother from the corner of his eye.

"Did you want to pursue Chris romantically?" the chief asked.

"Oh gawd no!" Heather laughed. "Chris? Not really my type."

"Not even for all his money?" MacDonald asked.

"Money isn't everything, Chief."

Simon frowned and glanced at his brother again. *She really doesn't seem very upset*, he thought. *Not about the deaths or about being questioned as a suspect.*

The chief removed a photograph from his folder and slid it

across the table to Heather. "This is a picture of a small glass container they found under your bathroom sink. It has traces of the same poison found in the wine that killed Danielle and Chris."

Heather shrugged, but she didn't seem overly concerned. "I've never seen it before."

"Do you know how it ended up in your house?"

"My guess, the real killer broke into my house and planted it there."

A knock came at the door, and the chief paused a moment, looking from the door back to Heather. He stood up. "That's about all for now, Heather. You can go."

"What do you mean they're letting her go?" Simon blurted.

"That woman killed our nephew!" Loyd protested.

Neither Joe nor Brian responded; instead they kept watching what was going on in the interrogation room.

With a grumble, Loyd turned his attention back to the window and watched as an attractive woman entered and Heather exited. The chief shook the woman's hand and asked her to sit down. Simon was about to ask who she was when he was given the answer.

"Thank you for coming down here, Ms. Carmichael. I understand you were Chris's attorney?"

"I was one of them," Melony said as she sat primly at the table, her hands folded on the desktop.

"Can you look at this document, please, and let me know if you've seen it before." The chief removed the document he had shown Heather minutes earlier and slid it to Melony.

She picked it up and shook her head. "This isn't one of mine. I didn't prepare it." She set it down on the table and smiled. "Of course, that doesn't mean anything regarding its legitimacy. Chris was capable of preparing something like this without my help, and he had other attorneys."

"So you're saying this is a valid, fully executable legal document?" the chief asked.

"Yes—"

Loyd couldn't help it, he smiled.

"—it would have been, had Chris not come in this morning and had me prepare another one for him."

"What other one?" Loyd blurted.

"You saw Chris this morning?"

Melony nodded. "Yes. Last night he found out one of the guests staying at Marlow House was actually his older biological brother. The brother has spent years looking for Chris."

Silently Loyd and Simon hung on every word, each man holding his breath.

"This morning I prepared a new codicil, that would supersede the one you just showed me—assuming the one you showed me is even valid. Chris left his entire estate—not just executor privileges and management of his estate—to his only brother. Billions."

"And that newest codicil is valid?"

"Yes. I didn't just have it properly signed, I had it notarized, which isn't required in Oregon, but it does speed up the probate process. Plus, it's been filed with the court."

"No!" Loyd shouted before he started pounding on the window.

In the next room, both the chief and Melony stopped talking and looked toward the two-way mirror.

Simon grabbed hold of Loyd's wrist, twisting it. "Pull it together," he hissed. He looked over to the two officers, who were now staring at them.

"You have to understand, my brother and I are upset that Heather Donovan isn't being held for the murder of our nephew. I'm afraid it's just been too much for my brother."

Brian smiled at Simon and nodded. "Yes, I understand this is a stressful time for you both."

"Unfortunately," Joe added, "we don't have sufficient evidence to hold Heather for their murder."

Simon glanced back to the window and noticed the interrogation room was now empty. Both the chief and the attorney had left.

Simon patted his brother's right shoulder and said, "I think we should go now."

"Before you leave, I believe the chief wants to see you both one more time in the interrogation room," Joe said.

"Is that really necessary?" Loyd asked. "I don't feel very well; I just want to go home."

"I'm afraid it is," Brian said, opening the door and motioning in the direction of the interrogation room.

After the Glandon brothers were led back to the room, Brian told them the chief would be in shortly. The two men took a seat at the table and waited.

Loyd glanced up to the two-way mirror and leaned close to his brother and whispered, "We're going to get that codicil overturned in favor of ours."

"Shut up," Simon hissed. "We'll discuss this later."

"I didn't come all this way to give up now," Loyd grumbled under his breath.

"I said shut up," Simon snapped, his eyes darting nervously to the two-way mirror.

The next moment the chief walked into the interrogation room. He carried what looked to be a computer tablet. "Thank you for staying, gentlemen."

"Why haven't you arrested Heather Donovan for our nephew's murder?" Simon demanded.

The chief shrugged and took a seat at the table. "I don't think Heather killed anyone. Anyway, I consider her a friend."

"A friend?" Loyd snapped. "Is that what happens around here, friends of the police chief get away with murder?"

"Like I said, I don't believe she killed anyone."

"I don't know what more proof you need. I heard you say they found some of the poison used to kill our nephew in her house!" Loyd shouted.

The chief shrugged again. "As Heather pointed out, the real killer could have broken into her house and planted the evidence."

"She lied about signing that document!" Loyd argued.

"Maybe she didn't sign it," the chief suggested. "Just like Chris didn't have a new codicil that supposedly was drawn up today."

Simon frowned. "What are you saying?"

The chief rested his elbows on the table and leaned forward. "Melony Carmichael, you saw me talking to her in this room a few minutes earlier. She is an attorney, by the way. But she didn't see Chris this morning at her office. She made it all up."

"Are you saying Chris didn't leave everything to his brother?" Loyd asked, a smile forming on his lips.

MacDonald shook his head. "Not a penny

"Why would she lie about that?" Simon asked. Unlike his brother, he was not smiling.

"It was a favor for a mutual friend," MacDonald explained. "Not particularly professional, but I figured in this instance I would make an exception."

"A favor for whom? Why?" Simon demanded.

"I suppose you can see for yourself," the chief said as he pulled his cellphone out of his pocket and sent a text message. Several moments later the door opened and in walked a very alive Chris Glandon and Danielle Boatman, followed by an angry Walt Marlow.

Audible gasps emanated from the uncles, with Loyd lurching back in his chair and grabbing his chest as if he was about to have a heart attack.

"Oh my god, you are alive!" Simon cried out. "I'm so relieved!"

"You're really alive," Loyd sputtered, barely choking out, "Yes, we're so relieved."

Danielle stood near the doorway next to Walt, his arm wrapped protectively around her shoulders, but Chris angrily approached the table, towering over his uncles. He leaned down, resting his hands along the table's edge as he looked Loyd in the eyes.

"Uh…umm…thank God you're alive," Loyd stammered.

"*'It won't be long now, boy. It paralyzes you first. Even if the paramedics showed up now, there's nothing they can do for you,'*" Chris hissed, recounting the chilling words Loyd had said when he believed Chris had been dying.

Walt heard the words Chris whispered to his uncle, and while he had told himself a man his age had no business inflicting physical violence against an older man, he was unable to restrain himself. The next moment both Loyd and Simon toppled backwards in their chairs, as if someone had sucker punched their jaws. No real damage was done, yet Walt felt slightly better for the effort.

In the adjacent room Joe and Brian watched through the two-way mirror.

"What in the world just happened?" Joe asked. "Their chairs just flew backwards."

A slow smile crept over Brian's face as he silently watched the chief help both men to their feet while officially putting them under arrest.

"To be honest, I sort of wondered if something like this would happen," Brian muttered, his gaze now shifting to Walt Marlow, who hovered protectively by Danielle's side.

THIRTY-SIX

"This is all a mistake," Simon insisted after the chief helped him back in his chair.

"Someone hit me," Loyd whined. "I want to see my attorney! I want to press charges." He started to stand up.

"Please sit down, Mr. Glandon," the chief ordered, gently pushing him back in his chair.

"We're going to leave now," Chris announced, turning to the door.

"Wait! Chris!" Simon called out. "It's all a misunderstanding. You can't believe we'd try to hurt you."

Chris didn't turn around again, but walked out of the office with Walt and Danielle.

"This is all a mistake. I want to see our attorney," Loyd insisted.

"I'm not sure why we're being arrested," Simon said. "You said attempted murder, but what proof do you have that we did anything to try to harm our nephew and Miss Boatman?"

"I want to see my attorney before you ask me another question!" Loyd blustered.

"They're bringing in a phone so you can call your attorney before we take you down to lockup."

"Lockup? Surely you don't expect us to spend the night in jail? It's Christmas Eve," Loyd protested.

"This is outrageous," Simon snapped.

225

"While we wait for them to bring us the phone, I'd like you to watch something." The chief turned on the tablet. He arranged it so both men could watch. A video came on the screen.

"What are we looking at?" Simon asked.

"Chris put up a few cameras in his office—even in the kitchen area. This afternoon was captured for posterity—along with sound." MacDonald started the video, and to the Glandon brothers' horror, the afternoon at the foundation office replayed on the tablet. It proved to have excellent audio, capturing the chilling words Loyd had whispered to Chris.

"WELL, THIS WAS AN INTERESTING CHRISTMAS EVE," Joe said as he and Brian watched through the two-way mirror.

"You probably need to get home to get ready for your brother-in-law's open house," Brian said.

"Haha. He isn't my brother-in-law."

"Yet."

Joe glanced over to Brian. "You think they're still having it?"

"According to Danielle, they are. When they left, Danielle said she wouldn't let Chris's uncles ruin the rest of Christmas."

Joe shook his head. "Does Lily even know what went on here?"

"If she doesn't, I imagine Danielle will tell her when they get home."

Joe glanced at his watch. "Let's get those jokers the phone so we can take them off the chief's hands and get them booked. I imagine he wants to get home to his boys."

"I imagine you want to get home to Kelly."

Joe let out a snort. "I'm not sure about that. She was pretty pissed at me when I had to come in today at the last minute."

"I'M NOT sure you should have slugged them," Danielle told Walt as he held open the passenger door of the Packard so she could get in. Chris had already gotten into the back seat. "After all, they are kind of old."

"I'm glad he did it," Chris grumbled. "I wish I'd done it myself."

"Happy to oblige, Chris." Walt closed the car door and then

headed for the driver's seat. When he got into the Packard, he added, "I would have happily killed them, but I didn't want to risk their spirits sticking around."

"No, I agree with you there," Chris said, leaning forward, resting his arms on the back of the front seat. "I'll just be satisfied that those two SOBs will be spending the rest of their miserable lives locked up behind bars. Eva was right, I shouldn't have let them back into my life."

"It might be better this way," Danielle suggested.

"Better?" Walt choked out. "You could have been killed."

"But I wasn't. And if they weren't staying in our house where we could keep an eye on them, then who knows, it is entirely possible they might have tried something else and been successful."

When they got home, Lily and Ian were waiting in the living room of Marlow House with Heather, Marie and Eva.

"We let ourselves in," Lily announced when the three walked into the living room.

"I see." Danielle tossed her purse on an empty chair.

"What happened today? I'm right in the middle of wrapping brie cheese in pastry when I get a call from Walt, telling me you and Chris are okay, but to stay home and don't say anything to anyone until you can explain," Lily asked.

Danielle perked up. "Oh, you're having brie cheese in pastry tonight?"

Lily met the comment with a glare and then continued. "Heather tells me she was framed for your murder, but you are alive, and I have to wait until you get home to explain. And then the chief calls and says the uncles have been arrested and you guys are on your way home and will explain everything. What happened?"

Danielle let out a sigh and took a seat. She began by telling about Zara Bishop.

THIRTY-SEVEN

DECEMBER 23

W alt and Danielle stood in front of the Bishops' bedroom. Danielle knocked on the door. There was no reply. She knocked again. The door opened a few inches.

"Yes?" Noah peeked out.

"We need to speak to you and Zara," Danielle said, Walt standing at her side.

"This isn't a good time. Zara is taking a nap."

"I'm afraid Zara is going to have to wake up."

"Please, Danielle, this really is not a good time," Noah said.

"You can either let me in, or wait for the police chief to arrive, because if you don't let Walt and me in your room, that's who I am calling, Noah *Church*."

Noah stared at Danielle through the small opening for a moment and then reluctantly opened the door.

Zara stood by the window, her eyes on Walt and Danielle.

Danielle walked into the room, her eyes meeting Zara's. "Do you always take your naps standing by the window?"

"What do you want?" Zara asked.

Danielle glanced back to Walt, who stood just inside the room, the door still ajar. "Walt, you'd better shut the door all the way. I don't think we want anyone else to hear this."

With a nod Walt shut the door, and Danielle turned to face Zara.

"What do you want?" Zara repeated, clearly agitated.

"I'm sorry you ended up in a freezer. But why are you here?" Danielle asked.

Zara frowned at her. "I don't know what you're talking about."

Danielle lurched forward and grabbed Zara's right hand—but her hand moved through Zara's like it was air.

Zara gasped and stumbled backwards, her eyes wide. "How did you know?"

Danielle stared at the woman. "I was right. You are a ghost. You had us all fooled."

Zara looked over to Noah and sighed. "Okay, Noah, it's time."

"Perhaps we might go somewhere more private," Noah suggested. "I don't want to chance Loyd or Simon hearing us."

"I don't think that will be a problem," Danielle said.

Zara looked Danielle in the eyes. "It could be if they overhear our discussion. You see, they're the ones who murdered me, and they're planning to kill you next."

Fifteen minutes later Walt, Danielle, Zara and Noah were up in Walt's attic apartment's sitting area.

"First, I would like to formally introduce myself," Noah said. "My name is Noah Church, and I'm Chris Glandon's biological brother."

Danielle stared dumbfounded at Noah. "His brother? Are you sure?"

"I can see the resemblance," Walt observed. "Marie thought he looked familiar; I think that's why."

Noah nodded. "I'm ten years older than Chris. Our father died in a car accident right before Chris was born. Like Chris—like our mother—I can see spirits."

"How do you know Chris can?" Danielle asked.

Noah laughed. "He could see Zara, couldn't he?"

Danielle frowned. "Yeah, but...so you didn't know until you got here?"

"I think we need to start at the beginning, but first, what did you mean when you told Zara you were sorry she ended up in a freezer?"

"Because her body was found in a freezer in a storage yard. They just made the identification."

"So it was a freezer," Zara muttered.

"You didn't know?" Danielle asked.

"She was confused after it happened," Noah explained. "But as I said, we should probably start at the beginning."

"Noah and I were in foster care together," Zara told them. "My mother was a drug addict, always looking for her next fix. She died of an overdose when I was eight. But until that time I had been in and out of foster care for a couple of years. She would clean herself up, get me back, then fall into her old habits, until she overdosed and there was no coming back. If she had any family, they never came forward. It was just me and her, until there was just me. And then there was Noah."

"After Mom died and I went into foster care, Zara and I became close friends. Zara was the first and only person who I ever told about my—well—how I could see ghosts. You see, my mother had the gift, and after my father died, she could see him—of course I could see him too, and well, when our neighbors realized my mother was claiming to see her dead husband—and her older son seemed to be buying into her delusion, they called social services."

"I can't even imagine how that went," Danielle muttered.

"Not good. They put me and Chris in foster care and locked Mom up. She had a breakdown. My father came to me and said goodbye, said his sticking around was hurting our family, and promised me that once he moved on, they would let Mom come home again."

"But she didn't come home again, did she?" Danielle asked.

Noah shook his head. "No. She committed suicide. I think she just wanted to be with Dad, and quite honestly, considering her mental state back then, had they let her go, she might have killed Chris and me before committing suicide. I realize that now."

"Wow," Danielle muttered, slumping back in the sofa.

"And you just stayed in foster care?" Walt asked.

"According to our records, there was mental illness in the family —Mom and me, since I had been foolish enough to claim I had seen my father too. No one was anxious to take that on. At the time, I thought I was helping Mom, trying to show them she wasn't crazy."

"So you stayed in the system?" Danielle said.

"Yes. When they put us in foster care, they separated Chris and me. I never knew what happened to him until Zara started researching."

"You see," Zara interrupted, "I knew I didn't have anyone out there, but I knew Noah did. I wanted him to have his brother. Because, well…"

"Because Zara had been like my sister," Noah interjected. "And she didn't want me to be alone when she was gone."

"Gone?" Danielle asked, looking from Noah to Zara.

"I was diagnosed with ALS," Zara explained. "I didn't tell anyone, not even Noah. I wasn't afraid to die—but I was terrified of the disease. I suppose in some ways I should be thankful that the Glandon brothers killed me. It was virtually painless."

"Don't even say that!" Noah snapped. "You weren't ready to go. They had no right!"

Zara smiled softly at Noah. "I know. I would never have done what your mother did. I understand life is precious." She looked from Noah to Danielle. "But I didn't want Noah to be alone when I left. I wanted him to have his brother. So I started looking. That became…well, my new bucket list. I finally tracked down who had adopted him, but I couldn't find him. I suspected he might be in Frederickport, but I wasn't sure. So I went to his uncles for help."

"Zara led them to believe she was his long-lost sister," Noah explained. "She knew things that supported her claim, things she had learned about the adoption."

"You say they killed you, why?" Danielle asked.

"They saw me as competition. I didn't realize that at the time. What I didn't know, they were planning to insert themselves back into Chris's life. They certainly didn't want a long-lost sibling mucking up their scheme."

"They drugged her, and when she woke up, she was in a small confined place."

"The freezer," Danielle muttered.

"I didn't know where I was," Zara said. "It felt like a coffin; it was dark and hard and cold. I tried to yell for help, but I was so sleepy. And the next thing I know, I'm standing next to a boat, and Loyd and Simon are there. I try to get them to listen to me, but they can't see or hear me. I was confused. I followed them back to their house."

"She was there for months, not understanding what had happened to her," Noah explained.

"I still wanted to find Chris. I kept begging the uncles to help me. Of course they couldn't hear or see me. I still hadn't grasped that I had died. It's hard to explain—I knew, yet I didn't."

Walt nodded. "I understand exactly what you mean."

Zara flashed Walt a smile and then continued. "One day, when I was trying to figure out how to find Chris, I started thinking about Frederickport, and suddenly I was here, standing on the pier. It's weird, I didn't even find that strange. I eventually returned to the Glandons and, by that time, figured out I was dead—that they had killed me. I also knew they intended to kill Chris. So I went to find Noah. I knew he would be able to see me."

"We couldn't just go to the police," Noah explained. "They would think I was crazy."

"And I didn't know where my body was."

"Zara kept tabs on Loyd and Simon, listening to them plot and scheme. When they made plans to come for Christmas, we realized we'd need to come too. But we didn't know if Chris was like me and my mother."

"I decided to come back to Frederickport one more time before I came with Noah. But I got lost and ended up in a cemetery in Silverton. I met another ghost, Ramone Cavalier, and I asked him how to get here. He told me about all of you, how you could see people like us. He's a friend of those ghosts who I've seen hanging around—Eva and Marie."

Danielle smiled. "So Marie was right. You did see them."

Zara nodded. "I never told Ramone why I was coming here. In fact, I don't think I ever told him my name. Once he mentioned a spirit friend who knew the people who lived at Marlow House—where the Glandons were planning to stay—I was careful what I told him. I didn't want him to tell his friends."

"If you knew about us, why didn't you save yourself some time and just tell us everything?" Danielle asked.

"I wanted to," Noah said. "But Zara reminded me we really didn't have anything on the uncles to have them arrested. We didn't even know where her body was. The best we could do was warn you of their intentions. She wanted to figure out what they had planned before we went to you."

"But now I think I know what they're planning," Zara said.

"You said they want to murder Danielle? Why?" Walt asked.

"Loyd went through one of the file cabinets at Chris's offices. He got copies of Danielle's, Heather's and Chris's signatures, along with the codicil to Chris's will that makes Danielle executor and beneficiary of Chris's estate. He then sent it to a man he hired who forged a new codicil. It doesn't remove Danielle, but adds Simon and Loyd in case something happens to her. Their intention is to poison both Chris and Danielle and then frame Heather, claiming she killed them because of jealousy. Of course the police will conveniently find the new codicil in Chris's file cabinet, and it will be signed by Heather and Danielle. Heather will deny signing the codicil and Danielle will be dead, so she won't be able to say anything. Heather will go to prison for killing Chris and Danielle, and the uncles will finally get control of the Glandon Foundation. And trust me, their idea of philanthropy is not what Chris envisions."

"When do they plan to kill us?" Danielle asked.

"I don't like the way you say that—so calmly," Walt seethed. "I could easily strangle them both right now."

"Walt, we need to catch them," Danielle said, "so they go to prison."

"Danielle's right," Zara agreed. "They plan to poison you. Loyd says poison is a woman's murder weapon. They drugged me, and I suspect they put me in that freezer so people might think I committed suicide if my body was ever found. But that is only speculation."

"From what Zara has pieced together, they're trying to figure out how to get you, Heather and Chris all over at the foundation office at the same time. Once there, they intend to find some way to get Heather to leave early and go home. After she leaves, they're going to suggest you all have a Christmas toast, their way of thanking Danielle for letting them stay here."

"Some thank-you," Walt grumbled.

"Well, gee, I think we should help them out," Danielle said.

"What is that supposed to mean?" Walt asked.

"I think I need to go see Chris."

"The only reason I'm agreeing to this and not just shooting those two—" Walt began.

"I know, Walt," Danielle interrupted. "You don't want their ghosts sticking around Marlow House after you kill them."

"Exactly!"

THIRTY-EIGHT

Sleepily opening his eyes, Max stared at the shiny gold ball. It swayed back and forth ever so gently, catching the reflection of the Christmas tree lights. Reaching out one paw, he batted it lightly, sending it swinging in the branches.

"Max! What did I tell you about that!" Walt said sternly.

The cat looked up to the man towering over him.

"If you want to nap under the tree, leave the ornaments alone. That was the deal, remember?"

The cat yawned, showing off his sharp little teeth. He drew in his paw, tucking it under his chin, and closed his eyes.

"You need to come out of there anyway. I need your help."

Max didn't budge.

"Danielle is in danger."

Max opened his eyes and practically flew out from under the tree. Landing by Walt's feet, he looked up and meowed.

Walt smiled and leaned down, petting the cat. "I figured that would get your attention."

A woman behind Walt caught the cat's eye. Max hissed and began backing up ever so cautiously. Walt glanced over his shoulder to see what was there. It was Zara.

"Ahh, Max, I can explain," Walt said. "Zara has been avoiding you not because she hates cats, but because she's been trying to tune you out so you wouldn't know."

"Hello, Max," Zara said gently, bending down closer to Max's line of vision. The two stared at each other in silence for a few moments. Finally, Max understood.

"What's going on here?" Marie asked when she appeared the next moment. "I've been sensing rumblings—so has Eva. She went to check on Chris. Is something happening that we should know about?" Marie paused a moment and then looked from Max to Zara. "Wait a minute, she's talking to him!"

CHRIS HAD JUST GOTTEN HOME, and all he wanted to do was take a shower and change his clothes. He grabbed a beer from the refrigerator and was just getting ready to head down the hallway when Eva arrived in a flurry of snowflakes.

"I'm here!" she announced.

"Uhh...I see..." Chris wearily started down the hallway.

"Is something wrong here? I sense it."

"I need a shower really bad, does that count?"

"I'm serious, Chris, something is wrong!"

The doorbell rang, stopping Chris in his tracks. Reluctantly he turned around and started toward his front door, Eva at his heels. When he opened the door, he found Walt and Danielle on his front porch, and standing behind them were the Bishops.

"Heather and the chief should be here pretty soon," Danielle announced as she marched into the house with her entourage.

Chris frowned. "Uhh, Danielle, I don't know what this is about, but I was just getting ready to jump in the shower."

"It is annoying when people just drop in unexpected, isn't it?" Walt said on his way into the house.

Standing in the hallway, a beer in hand, Chris looked from Danielle to Walt in confusion. The Bishops stood quietly just inside the doorway, as if waiting for someone to tell them where to go.

Danielle spied Eva. "Hello, Eva. Marie told me you were on your way over here."

Chris frowned, looking curiously from Danielle to the Bishops. "Uhh, Danielle...did you forget you have someone with you?" He then nodded from the Bishops to Eva.

"No, I didn't. Because Noah and Zara can see ghosts. In fact, Zara is a ghost, which is why we're here," Danielle explained. "And,

Chris, I am really sorry to just blurt this out, but Noah's last name is not really Bishop, it's Church. He's your biological brother. And Zara, she was never his wife, but she is dead because your uncles killed her, and they intend to kill you and me. That's why I'm here."

Ten minutes later Heather arrived, and five minutes after that, the chief showed up.

———

THEY SAT HUDDLED in Chris's living room, a flame slowly burning in the nearby fireplace. Danielle explained what Zara had told her. Had the chief been able to see and hear ghosts, Danielle would have left it to Zara to tell her own story. Chris continually looked over to Noah; countless questions—none relating to what Danielle was talking about—filled his head.

"Marie and Max are at the house, keeping an eye on Loyd and Simon. If they leave or start over here, either Max or Marie will warn us," Danielle explained.

"I knew they were up to something," Heather grumbled. "Those old coots were going to frame me for murder!"

"I can't believe they would do this," Chris muttered. He then shook his head and said, "No. That's not true. I can believe it. I don't know what I was thinking going along with them coming here." He looked to Eva. "I should have listened to you."

"So what now?" Heather asked.

"I think we should let the uncles kill us," Danielle said.

"That's accommodating of you." Heather snickered.

"Exactly. That's what we need to do, be accommodating," Danielle said. "Zara told me how they see this thing going down. Right now, they're waiting for the right opportunity. I say let's give them the opportunity."

"And what happens when you have to drink the poison?" Walt asked.

"Obviously we're not going to drink it. But we can pretend to."

"Not sure how you intend to carry that out. Chances are, they will be watching your every move," the chief said. "This sounds dangerous."

"We just need a diversion when the time comes for us to drink the wine. Something to make them look away for a minute so we can dump our drinks and make them think we drank it."

"Like what?" the chief asked.

"Bella!" Heather suggested. "If she ran through at the right time, knocked over a few things, that would distract them, and you would have time to dump your wine."

"How are you going to get your cat to do that at the right time?" the chief asked.

"Either Marie or I can help with that," Eva suggested.

"Eva just said she and Marie could help with that," Danielle told the chief.

"This is going to take some serious acting skills from you and Chris." Walt looked at Danielle. "I know you've become adept at fabricating believable stories when you have to, because of your gift, but this is different. You and Chris will be alone with two killers, and I'm not sure you can pull it off."

"They won't be alone," the chief said.

"And I can help," Eva offered. "I'll be their acting coach and walk them through this. I'll be with them every step of the way."

Danielle took Walt's hand in hers and looked him in the eyes. "We have to do this."

Walt nodded. "I know."

"I need to call Adam," Chris said.

"Adam? What do you need from Adam?" Danielle asked.

"I bought some of those surveillance cameras a while back, but I never had them installed. I'm going to see if Adam can hook them up for me tonight," Chris said. "They're the same kind he uses. He's the one who recommended them to me."

DANIELLE ARRIVED at Chris's office a few minutes before two in the afternoon on Christmas Eve. She found Heather and Chris waiting for her in the office area.

"I put a stack of envelopes on my desk, but I didn't bother finding anything to stuff them with," Heather explained. "I figure they'll kill you first."

Chris cringed. "Did you have to say it like that?"

Heather rolled her eyes at Chris and turned back to Danielle. "I put the poinsettia plant on the desk. I figure it would be a good place to dump the poisoned wine."

"I just hope that's how they still intend to kill us," Chris said. "I don't need a change of game plans and have them show up with guns."

"Oh brother, Joe and Brian are upstairs listening in," Heather reminded him.

"Remember, Noah overheard them saying poisoning was a woman's method of murder, and if they're trying to frame Heather, I don't think they're bringing guns." Danielle said that more for Joe and Brian's benefit. The two officers were currently upstairs, monitoring the potential crime scene. Danielle didn't think they would understand their prime informant was a ghost.

Heather's cellphone buzzed. She looked down at it. "That's the chief. He wants me to leave now. The two homicidal maniacs are parked down the street."

"Can you call them something else?" Danielle groaned.

"Sorry." Heather quickly kissed Danielle's cheek and then Chris's. "You two be careful. I really do not want to have to find a new job."

Seven minutes later Marie and Eva appeared.

"They're coming up the walk," Eva announced.

"Evil little men," Marie grumbled. "Using a Christmas gift bag to conceal their murder weapon!"

"Uncle Loyd, Uncle Simon, what are you doing here?" Chris asked when he opened the door to let them in.

"We've come to help," Simon announced.

"Help? That's sweet of you, but Danielle and I have this covered." Chris led his uncles into the office, where they found Danielle sitting at Heather's desk, a stack of envelopes waiting to be stuffed on her left and a poinsettia plant on her right.

"What are you two doing here?" Danielle asked.

"We felt sorry for you both having to work on Christmas Eve," Simon explained.

"Evil, evil man," Marie hissed.

"What's in the bag?" Danielle asked.

"We brought you a bottle of wine," Simon said as he lifted the bag to show her.

"Wine? That sounds good," Chris said.

"Then let's have some," Simon suggested.

"It does sound good," Danielle agreed.

"You two relax, and I'll take it in the kitchen and open it," Simon offered.

"The wine corkscrew is in the top drawer to the right of the sink," Chris called out as Simon headed for the door.

A few minutes later Simon returned with a tray carrying four glasses of wine, and handed one to each of them.

Danielle picked up her glass. "This will make stuffing envelopes more enjoyable."

"Bella, get ready," Marie told the calico cat from the other room.

Loyd lifted his glass. "I would like to make a toast, to my nephew for sharing Christmas with us, and to Danielle for opening her home to us."

"Now!" Marie called out.

"Go, Bella!" Eva shouted.

Just as they were all about to take a drink, what sounded like glass breaking caught their attention. Both Loyd and Simon looked toward the doorway leading to the hallway. The next moment Bella came racing into the room while making an unholy shrieking sound. Like an animal possessed, she ran around in circles numerous times, running under the uncles' chairs, knocking Loyd's cane on the floor, and then flew back out through the doorway and disappeared.

During the commotion, Danielle and Chris quickly dumped the contents of their wineglasses into the poinsettia plant and then pretended to be drinking, careful not to touch the glasses to their lips.

"What in tarnation?" Loyd shouted, still holding his full glass of wine.

Danielle laughed and set her now empty glass on the desktop. "That cat acts crazy sometimes!"

"It's a good thing I left Hunny at home," Chris said, setting his empty glass on the desk.

Loyd and Simon exchanged glances and then looked back to Chris and Danielle.

"Oh my, I drank that kind of fast." Danielle giggled. "Bad me."

"I didn't do bad myself. Want another glass?" Chris asked.

"Grab your forehead, Chris, and close your eyes," Eva coached. After Zara told them what type of poison the uncles intended to use, they had looked it up online to discover how quickly it would act.

Chris grabbed hold of his forehead and closed his eyes. "I don't feel right."

"Collapse on the desk," Eva told him. Chris doubled over.

"Danielle, reach for Chris," Eva coached. "Yes! Now clumsily tip over your glass. Okay, stand up, let your knees buckle. Yes, what a beautiful dying scene! You are such a natural!"

"Are you sure they aren't really dead?" Marie asked.

"They did wonderfully, didn't they?" Eva said proudly. "Now the difficult part is staying perfectly still. Fortunately, you don't have to fake death yet. They expect it to take a while."

Simon and Loyd did not move. They simply stared.

"Oh my heavens, that was too easy," Loyd said before breaking into a laugh.

"Oh, you are a horrid, horrid man!" Marie hissed.

"It's not done yet. Let's do what we have to do," Simon said.

"Times like this I wish I had Walt's powers," Eva grumbled.

THIRTY-NINE

"Why didn't you tell me what was going on?" Lily asked. Danielle had just finished explaining what had happened since discovering the truth about Zara. She sat on the arm of the sofa next to Walt. "We were here for breakfast this morning, and you never said a thing."

"I didn't want you to worry, Lily, and frankly, I figured this way you would just act naturally, which is really what we needed you to do."

"So all of that about Heather being upset with you was made up?" Ian asked Chris.

"Oh, I'm always mad at Chris for one thing or another," Heather teased.

"I wasn't going to have her stuff envelopes on Christmas Eve. I'm not that jerky of a boss."

Heather flashed Chris a smile and said, "If I want to be totally honest, Chris isn't a jerky boss at all. I love working for the foundation—working for Chris—and where else can I bring my cat to work?"

"That cat came in pretty handy, if you ask me!" Danielle said. "In fact, Bella's getting some catnip from Santa!"

"Is Noah really your brother?" Ian asked.

"We're going to take a DNA test to verify it, but he and Zara are fairly certain he is."

Lily looked over to Chris. "Did they really leave?"

Chris shook his head. "No, we thought it best if Noah was out of the way when all this was going down, so he's over at my house with Hunny and Zara. I'm going to see if he wants to stay with me for the rest of his Christmas vacation so we can get to know each other better."

"But what do you think?" Ian asked Chris. "Is the DNA test just a formality?"

Marie shook her head. "I can't believe I'm the only one who noticed the resemblance."

Danielle looked to Marie and smiled. "If I remember correctly, you thought Noah looked familiar, but you didn't say who he looked like."

"Who are you talking to?" Lily asked. "Eva or Marie?"

"Marie," Danielle explained. "She noticed Noah looked familiar when he arrived."

Walt grabbed Danielle and pulled her off the arm of the sofa onto his lap and hugged her. "It terrifies me to imagine what could have happened." Danielle turned around in his lap, now sitting sideways, and hugged him.

Lily, who sat between Walt and Ian on the sofa, chuckled. "Looks like you're both serious about this officially dating thing."

"Pretty much." Danielle laughed, hugging Walt again.

Eva, who hovered in the corner on an imaginary chair, smiled at the couple. "They do look right together," she mused. "The Universe does know what it's doing."

"One good thing came out of this," Walt said, his arms still around Danielle as she rested her head against his shoulder. "Danielle and I get the house to ourselves through the New Year now that Simon and Loyd are locked up, and Chris has invited Noah to stay with him."

Chris raised his glass in salute to Walt. "It's the least I can do for you guys basically saving my life. And I also appreciate you kicking those two SOBs on their butts."

Walt nodded at Chris. "Like I said, my pleasure."

Lily stood up and grabbed Ian's hand, pulling him to his feet. "We need to get back home. We have a Christmas Eve party to host, and people are going to start showing up in about an hour."

Danielle whispered something into Walt's ear. He nodded. She jumped to her feet, and just as Ian and Lily started for the door, she yelled, "Wait! I have something I need to tell you all."

They all turned to face Danielle and Walt.

"Walt and I have decided we aren't going to start dating," Danielle said.

Heather frowned and looked to Walt, who remained sitting on the sofa. "So what was that all about?"

"What do you mean you're not going to date? You two are obviously crazy about each other," Lily said.

Chris sat back in his chair and glanced from Danielle to Walt. "I think what Danielle is trying to say, they aren't going to date because they're already married."

Both Danielle and Walt looked to Chris in surprise. "How did you know?" Danielle asked.

Danielle then looked to Marie, who shook her head. "Don't look at me. I didn't tell anyone."

"Married? You're married?" Lily asked.

Danielle nodded and held up her right hand with the gold ring. She slipped the ring off her right hand and put it on her left.

"You didn't tell me!" Lily cried.

"I'm sorry, Lily."

Lily didn't get angry; instead, she ran over to Danielle and threw her arms around her, giving her a tight hug. She then hugged Walt.

"But you can't tell anyone yet," Danielle said.

"You want to keep it a secret?" Lily frowned.

"I think I understand," Ian said. "People are just getting used to the idea of Walt and Danielle, and considering the reality they believe is not the reality that is, I don't blame them for rolling this out slowly."

"We weren't going to say anything to anyone for a while," Danielle explained. "But I just didn't want to keep it from you anymore. All of you have always been there for me—for Walt. You're our closest friends."

Lily narrowed her eyes and studied Danielle. "Just how long have you two been married?"

Danielle flashed a guilty smile at Lily. "Almost seven months."

"Seven months!" they all shouted.

Danielle shrugged.

"What are you going to do?" Lily asked. "Just start telling people one day you're married?"

"We're going to have a wedding," Walt said. "Here, in Marlow House, like you and Ian."

"When?" Lily asked.

Danielle looked down at her hand and slipped the ring off her left hand and placed it back on her right one. "We figured we would date for a few months and then announce our engagement."

"Valentine's Day," Lily said.

Danielle frowned at Lily. "Valentine's Day what?"

"Shoot for a Valentine's Day wedding. It's not like you'll need a long engagement, which would seem silly since you're living under the same roof anyway."

Danielle looked to Walt and cringed. "That's less than two months away, do you think it's too soon?"

He smiled and shook his head. "I think a Valentine's Day wedding would be perfect. Considering all that's happened since Clint's accident, I have a feeling people might be able to understand a whirlwind engagement."

"A wedding!" Lily squealed.

"You have to keep it to yourself for now," Danielle reminded her. "Of course, I want you to be my maid of honor."

"Yes! I will be honored!" Lily hugged Danielle again.

When the hug ended, Danielle looked at Heather and asked, "I'd love for you to be one of my bridesmaids, Heather."

"Me?" Heather frowned, pointing to herself.

"Of course. I consider you one of my closest friends."

Heather grinned. "Gee, thanks, Danielle. I would love to be in your wedding."

Ian glanced at his watch. "Congratulations, you two, but Lily and I should probably get going. Before we tackle a Valentine's Day wedding, let's take care of Christmas."

Ten minutes later, Walt and Danielle stood at the front doorway of Marlow House, saying goodbye to their friends—whom they would be seeing within an hour across the street at the open house. Chris was the last to say goodbye.

"Thanks again. I'm so sorry I put you through this," Chris told Danielle. He looked to Walt and said, "And you too. I know you must have been worried about Danielle."

"Chris, I understand the desire to have a connection with family, even family members that you're estranged from," Danielle said.

"And now you've found your brother," Walt reminded him.

Chris smiled. "He found me."

"I do want to ask you something before you leave," Walt said.

"What?"

"Would you be my best man?" Walt asked.

Startled, Chris stared at Walt. "Me? I'd think you would have asked Ian."

Walt shook his head. "Of all my male friends—the ones alive today—you're the one I've known the longest."

"You met Ian before you met me," Chris reminded him.

"But he hadn't met me."

Chris smiled. "You're serious, aren't you?"

Walt nodded.

Chris's smile broadened and he held out his hand. "I would be honored."

Danielle stood by quietly and watched as the two men shook hands.

"THAT WAS SWEET OF YOU," Danielle told Walt after they closed the front door. They were the only ones left in Marlow House, aside from Max. Even Marie and Eva had left—with Eva going to Chris's house, and Marie following Lily and Ian across the street for the party.

"He just seemed like the right choice." Walt draped one arm over Danielle's shoulder, and together they turned from the now closed front door.

"And to think you used to have issues with Chris. I always knew you liked him."

Walt chuckled as they continued down the hall. "Now that we're married, Chris doesn't seem to annoy me like he used to."

They paused a moment at the open door leading to the downstairs bedroom. "At least we don't have to clean out the rooms Loyd and Simon used. The chief's men took all their stuff," Danielle said. "And I imagine Noah will stop by here later to get the rest of his things if he takes Chris's offer to stay with him."

"He'd better take Chris's offer, or Chris can forget being my best man."

Danielle laughed. "Let's go upstairs and get ready for the party."

When they reached the staircase, they paused a moment and looked up toward the second floor.

"I think Simon lied to me," Walt said.

Danielle glanced at Walt. "Well, he tried to murder me. But what do you mean he lied to you?"

"He told me *It's a Wonderful Life* was one of his favorite movies. I don't think that's true."

"Uh, yeah. I have to agree. Simon seems more like a *Krampus* sort of guy."

"What's *Krampus?*"

"It's a Christmas horror movie."

"A Christmas horror movie? That doesn't seem very Christmassy," Walt noted.

"Neither is almost getting poisoned on Christmas Eve."

Walt nodded. "True."

They started up the stairs.

"It's kind of nice being in the house—just you and me," Danielle mused. "It feels like our home—not your house or mine, but both of ours."

"I agree." He looked at her inquisitively. "You aren't considering closing the B and B, are you?"

Danielle looked up to Walt and shrugged. "I still enjoy it—but if it was something you wanted me to do, I wouldn't be opposed to seriously considering your wishes."

Walt laughed and kissed Danielle's nose.

"What?" She frowned. "You didn't think I would take your feelings into consideration?"

Walt chuckled and shook his head. "No, it isn't that. Rather the opposite. Where I came from—"

"You came from here," Danielle reminded him.

Walt grinned. "I'm referencing time not place. Where I came from, a wife didn't consider her husband's wishes—she simply acquiesced."

Danielle arched her brows. "Really now, did Angela simply go along with all your demands?"

"Angela? Oh no." Walt chuckled. "But then, Angela plotted to kill me."

"Yeah, well, if you thought you were always going to get your way because you're a man, I might have to kill you myself."

Walt patted her backside good-naturedly. "I suppose for my own safety it's a good thing I would rather be married to a woman who doesn't expect me to do her thinking for her."

"Plus it would be boring. But seriously, I wouldn't be opposed to closing the B and B if you hate it."

"I don't hate it," Walt said. "I've actually enjoyed meeting many of the guests—some, like Chris's uncles, I could have done without. But what about you? Are you finding it isn't what you want to do anymore? You mentioned how you enjoyed having the house to ourselves."

"I still enjoy the business. And I do enjoy having the house to ourselves. One doesn't discount the other. In fact, running Marlow House as a bed and breakfast, it doesn't just afford me the opportunity to meet new people, it makes me appreciate my home even more when I don't have to share it with strangers."

"And then there is the baking without guests staying here," Walt reminded her. "It would be a lose-lose situation. I would either gain a ridiculous amount of weight—or if you decided to hang up your apron, I'd be deprived. After going almost a hundred years without chocolate cake—and having tasted your chocolate cake—I'm not ready to give that up."

FORTY

M arie found Danielle sitting at her dressing table, applying her makeup. She had changed into a festive red dress, and around her neck she wore the Missing Thorndike, its diamonds and emeralds transforming the simple dress into an elegant Christmas ensemble.

"You look gorgeous," Marie gushed.

Danielle turned from the mirror and smiled at the ghost. "I thought you were across the street already."

"I was. And then I popped over to check on Adam, and he's running late. I came back here and found Walt at the kitchen table, so I figured it was safe to pop up here."

Danielle grinned. "Safe?"

Marie smiled. "You are practically a newlywed, dear, and the way that man looks at you, I don't think it would be wise to just barge in. It could be rather embarrassing."

Danielle chuckled and turned back to the mirror and applied some lipstick.

"I didn't know you were going to wear the Missing Thorndike tonight," Marie said as she took a seat on the foot of Danielle's bed.

Danielle shrugged. "I just thought it would look good with this dress."

"It does."

"I hope Eva doesn't mind."

"I'm sure she won't. It's a shame to keep something that lovely locked away. Plus, if Eva wanted to, she could conjure up her own version of the necklace."

"I just don't have the heart to sell it. And I figure Walt's a pretty safe guy to be around when wearing expensive jewelry. Plus, it'll just be friends tonight, and I didn't broadcast I was wearing it."

"You look very festive, and Walt's rather dashing tonight too. I didn't have a chance to tell him yet. He seemed rather engrossed in whatever he was writing, so I didn't disturb him. I just came up here."

"Ahh...I bet it's that note he wanted to put in the Christmas card he got for Ian."

Marie arched her brows. "Walt got Ian his own Christmas card?"

Danielle recapped her lipstick, set it on the vanity, and turned to face Marie. "It's more of a thank-you note. If it wasn't for Ian, Walt would never have met his agent—and then the publisher. While many authors successfully self-publish these days, Walt really doesn't have the skill sets to do all that's required of an author who's not using a traditional publisher. Walt's still figuring out the computer."

"I have to give him credit for that. That whole internet thing is beyond me."

Danielle stood. "You ready to go?"

"OH MY GOSH, she's wearing the necklace!" Kelly whispered to Joe. The two stood by the dining room table in Lily and Ian's house, sampling some of the appetizers.

Holding a small poinsettia-patterned paper plate in one hand, Joe was just adding a meatball to the plate when Kelly's comment had him looking toward the entry hall. Danielle and Walt had just arrived.

"Definitely a couple," Joe muttered under his breath, noting the possessive way Walt held one hand against the flat of Danielle's back.

"I have to admit they do look good together," Kelly said begrudgingly. "I still can't believe they showed up, considering what went down today."

"We're here, aren't we?" Joe asked.

Kelly glanced up at Joe. "True. And I'm sorry for being so grouchy when you told me you had to go into the office this morning. I had no idea what was happening. I can't even imagine how Danielle and Chris pulled it off—convincing those two monsters they were dying."

"I can't get over how Heather's cat just happened to take that moment to run through the office. I wasn't sure how they were going to make Chris's uncles believe they drank the wine. Up until that point, those two were watching them like hawks." Instead of adding the meatball to his plate, he popped it into his mouth and then speared another one.

TWENTY MINUTES later Kelly threw her arms around Danielle and said, "I'm so happy you're okay!"

Startled by Kelly's show of affection, Danielle reluctantly returned the hug. Walt had already left her side and was over talking to Ian, giving him the card and note he had penned.

"You and me both," Danielle said with a smile when the brief hug ended.

"Joe was telling me one of your other guests is Chris's biological brother?"

Danielle glanced briefly at Joe, who stood quietly at Kelly's side. "Yes, they believe so. But they're having a DNA test to make sure."

"One thing I don't understand, was there another couple staying at Marlow House?" Kelly asked.

Danielle shook her head. "You mean besides Chris's uncles and brother?"

"Yes. I thought Lily said you had a newlywed couple staying with you."

"Oh, that…We had a newlywed couple make a reservation for Christmas, but they cancelled at the last moment," Danielle lied.

Kelly frowned. "Funny, I must have misunderstood her. I thought they had arrived."

Danielle smiled sweetly and shook her head. "No. Just Noah and those homicidal maniacs."

Kelly shivered. "So freaking creepy to think what they were planning!"

"One thing that was peculiar," Joe said. "Those two insisted

Noah was staying at Marlow House with his wife. Of course, they admitted they never saw a wife. Not sure why they got that idea."

"I've no idea," Danielle said with a shrug.

Danielle was still chatting with Kelly and Joe when Brian Henderson arrived. She spied him from across the room talking with Lily.

"Brian showed up," Danielle said. "I wasn't sure he would."

"He doesn't really have family to spend Christmas with," Joe told her.

"If you two will excuse me, I have something to say to Mr. Henderson."

"I wonder why she called him Mr. Henderson?" Kelly asked Joe after Danielle walked away. Her eyes still on Danielle, she watched as she approached Brian, and to her surprise, she witnessed Danielle slug Brian's arm, and then Brian broke into laughter.

"REALLY? *She was kind of a pain in the ass?*" Danielle said.

"You are." Brian continued to laugh.

"And it's not like it's going to mess up your Christmas," Danielle went on.

No longer laughing, Brian grinned. "And it didn't mess up my Christmas. See? You're still alive."

Danielle grinned and shook her head. "You are such a rat sometimes."

"I knew you were probably listening in."

Danielle let out a deep sigh. "I really can't believe we're all standing here—that it's Christmas Eve and…"

"And you could be dead right now?" Brian asked, his tone now serious.

Danielle nodded. "Thanks for being there today. It made it less stressful knowing you and Joe were upstairs watching."

"It was pretty chilling, actually. I know I've had issues with Chris in the past, but after watching his uncles plot to murder him—listening to what that one said to him when he thought Chris was dying—it made my stomach turn. I've never witnessed such evil before."

"I have to agree with you." Danielle glanced around. "Any idea when the chief is going to be here? He's still coming, isn't he?"

"Yes. He was still on the phone when I left the office, talking to the authorities in California. From what I overheard, I think California's going to get a shot at them first."

"What do you mean?"

Brian nodded at something behind Danielle. She turned around to see who he was nodding at. It was the chief. He had just arrived, and with him were Evan and Eddie Jr. The boys dashed off to the table to get some food, while the chief headed in Danielle's direction.

DANIELLE AND WALT retreated to Ian's office with the chief for some privacy.

"Chris should be here pretty soon. He took Noah over to Marlow House to get his things," the chief explained when they were alone.

"Brian said something about California getting a shot at the uncles first. What did he mean?" Danielle asked.

"We had to massage the facts," the chief explained. "We can't really tell them Zara's ghost helped us foil the murder plot."

"Yeah, well, I know all about massaging facts," Danielle grumbled.

"So the revised version—Before Zara's disappearance, she told Noah she thought Chris Glandon was his brother, yet she didn't know where he was now. Noah is officially telling the police he had no idea she had contacted the uncles, which is why their name never came up when they were investigating her disappearance. He's claiming he decided to come here for Christmas to follow the trail Zara had been investigating before her disappearance."

"What trail?" Walt asked.

"One of the things she learned was that a Chris Glandon had stayed at Marlow House. Noah is saying he decided to start his search at Marlow House—and by pure coincidence he found the Glandon uncles were also guests. He's saying that's why he was eavesdropping on the uncles, to learn more about his brother, but instead he overheard a plot to kill Chris and Danielle. At least, that's the new version," the chief explained.

"What does that have to do with California getting the uncles first?" Walt asked.

"The storage unit where they found Zara's body, it was rented by a man who worked for the uncles. He was their gardener. He died not long after Zara went missing. It looks like he might have helped the uncles move the body, and then they decided he was a liability, so they got rid of him."

"We heard Brian telling Loyd and Simon that," Danielle said. "But I hope they have more than that to nail Zara's murder on them."

"They do. They have Zara's Volkswagen. It was parked in their garage."

"They didn't get rid of her car?" Danielle asked.

The chief shook his head. "Nope. It looks like they didn't believe there was anyone who would connect the missing woman to them. They figured they could keep her body indefinitely in the freezer, and as long as the storage rent was paid, there wouldn't be a problem. They just never figured on a rat chewing through the cord and the body thawing out."

"What about the storage unit?" Danielle asked. "If the guy who rented it died, wouldn't his family go into it and find the body?"

"Apparently, there was just a sister, and she didn't think he had the storage unit anymore," MacDonald explained.

BRIAN STOOD BY THE FIREPLACE, cocktail in hand, surveying the room. He estimated there were about twenty or so guests. Understandably the conversation on most lips was about what had gone on that day. The only two who were undoubtedly thinking of Santa Claus and not attempted murder were Evan and Eddie Jr. The pair sat across the room by the Christmas tree, sneaking Sadie bits of cheese.

Needing to use the restroom, Brian set his now empty glass on a table and headed for the hallway. Once there, he couldn't recall which room was the bathroom. He pushed open the first door. It was the master bedroom.

He was about to close the door when he realized he had inadvertently sent a gust of air into the room, causing a piece of paper to float from the table next to the doorway onto the floor. He paused a moment and picked it up, intending to return it to the table. In

253

doing so, he glanced over it. It was a handwritten letter to Ian—signed by Walt.

Letter in hand, Brian stood there a moment, thinking of that other letter—written by that other Walt—and how the handwriting had eerily resembled the note written by whoever had foiled the robbery attempt at Marlow house a year and a half ago—almost a year before Clint Marlow ever came to town.

Brian set the paper back on the table and glanced around. He could hear the voices and music coming from down the hallway, but he was alone. On impulse, he removed his cellphone from his pocket and snapped a picture of the handwriting before closing the door and resuming his search for the bathroom.

THE GHOST WHO WAS SAYS I DO

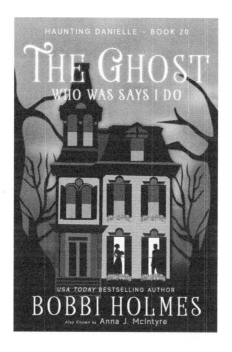

RETURN TO MARLOW HOUSE IN
THE GHOST WHO WAS SAYS I DO
HAUNTING DANIELLE, BOOK 20

A Valentine's Day Wedding at Marlow House?

Love is in the air—along with secrets—some are deadlier than others.

Will secrets from Clint Marlow's past come back to haunt Walt and Danielle?

NON-FICTION BY

BOBBI ANN JOHNSON HOLMES

Havasu Palms, a Hostile Takeover
Where the Road Ends, Recipes & Remembrances
Motherhood, a book of poetry
The Story of the Christmas Village

BOOKS BY ANNA J. MCINTYRE

COULSON FAMILY SAGA

Coulson's Wife

Coulson's Crucible

Coulson's Lessons

Coulson's Secret

Coulson's Reckoning

UNLOCKED 🔒 HEARTS

Sundered Hearts

After Sundown

While Snowbound

Sugar Rush

Made in the USA
Las Vegas, NV
16 December 2022

62895065R00156